DEMENTED

JOE CLARK

Paperback: 978-1-73329-440-9
Ebook: 978-1-73329-442-3

Cover: Debbie O'Byrne

This book is dedicated to my friend and fellow author, Serenity Rose, who encouraged and advised me throughout the writing of this novel.

1

They gathered at the same table in the Il Mediterreano on Connecticut Avenue in D.C. every Friday night. They called themselves The Gal Friday Group. Most of them had mid-level jobs as administrative assistants, accountants, or lawyers. Cindy Foster had been promoted to manager of the Tax Services department at the D.C. office of America First Financial Services recently, but the group decided she could stay because she was one of the founding members. Ellen Magee was a partner in a law firm, but it was a small one, so that didn't count. There were twelve women in the group, but there were always a few no-shows.

Six women were seated at the table next to the restaurant's main aisle the first Friday in May 2009. Cindy sat facing the door, Ellen across from her.

The restaurant was full that night. Having a conversation with anyone more than a couple of feet away was difficult. The Gal Friday Group had split in two. Cindy was engaged in a discussion about balancing home and career with June Wilson, an accountant from payroll, and Ashley Maddox, an executive assistant.

Ellen Magee was a woman's lawyer focusing on divorce cases, discrimination suits, domestic violence, and sexual harassment cases. Anne Michaels, to her left, was another lawyer who was cutting her teeth on women's issues. Betty Saunders, on her right, was a public affairs specialist.

Cindy suddenly jerked her head up, her eyes wide in disbelief. She stared toward the entrance, transfixed.

Ellen turned to look. Two men had entered the restaurant and were walking toward their table. Their expensive suits and flashy ties were overkill for the Mediterreano. The man in front was middle-aged, medium height, balding, and bespectacled. The second was a six-foot-tall, 220-pound athlete. He had sharp, Teutonic features with blond hair and blue eyes. His gaze was fixed on Cindy as he made his way into the restaurant.

Blue Eyes touched his companion on the shoulder and directed him to a small table off to the left. He took a seat that gave him a direct line of sight to Cindy.

They ordered and fell into conversation. The short guy was animated. The taller guy seemed bored. He would occasionally look over at Cindy.

She picked at her food and tried to follow the conversation at her table, but the man's attention bothered her. She did her best to hide her discomfort. When she made eye contact with Ellen, she could tell she wasn't succeeding.

Ellen was struggling to stay engaged with her conversation. She would look at Cindy and then over at the intruders. She would go back to the conversation briefly, and then return to Cindy. Her gaze darted between her distressed friend and the men at the other table.

Shortly after eight, Cindy called for her check. Almost immediately, Blue Eyes tapped his companion on the arm and pointed to Cindy. Baldy turned to look at her, pursed his lips, and nodded. The two men rose and ambled across the room toward the Gal Friday Group.

Ellen threw her napkin down on the table and pushed her chair back. There was fire in her eyes.

Cindy shook her head and mouthed, *No*.

Ellen froze. With a slight nod of her head, she signaled, *What gives?*

Cindy grimaced in response. She recognized the men. Blue Eyes was Adan Jackson, a senior account manager at AFFS. This would have to be handled diplomatically.

Ellen relaxed a little and waited. Her hands rested on the edge of the table, ready to push off and spring into action at the slightest hint of trouble. She tracked the approaching men with a fierce stare.

An elderly man sitting behind Cindy had pushed back from his table so that his chair was almost touching Cindy's. He was reading the *Washington Post*. He paused to look at Adan and his companion as they walked in his direction. The glance was so subtle that Cindy missed it, and Adan ignored it.

The account manager halted next to Cindy. He looked down with a faint smile. "Cindy, this is Ron Goldsmith, CFO of HamNX. Ron, this is Cindy Foster, the manager of our Tax Services section. She is going to be handling your account."

"It is a pleasure to meet you, Ms. Foster." Goldsmith extended his hand. "I look forward to working with you."

Cindy shook his fleshy, sweaty hand. His limp grip offended her, but she smiled. "We spoke on the phone on Monday. It's a pleasure to meet you in person."

Goldsmith surveyed the table and saw five unfriendly faces. He turned back to Cindy. "I apologize. I didn't mean to interrupt the proceedings. I just wanted to say hello. Maybe we can get together for lunch next time I'm in town."

"I would like that," Cindy said. Her smile seemed genuine.

He turned and walked back to his seat. Adan paused to wink at Cindy before following his client back to their table.

She paid for her meal and went to the ladies' room.

When she came out, Adan was waiting for her. "Didn't you use to be Cindy Smith?"

She glared but said nothing.

He squinted and bit his lip. "Ah'm trying to remember where we first met."

"At my wedding reception," Cindy snapped. "You showed up without an invitation."

Adan screwed up his face in a doubtful expression. "No." He shook his head. "Ah'm sure you are the Cindy Smith I dated in college."

"You have me confused with somebody else."

He grinned. "You were a year behind me at Georgetown. You were the last good girl Ah dated."

The way he said "good girl" made her stomach churn. She fought to stay in control, but when she looked into his face—and she could not help looking—she saw that sadistic grin and those predatory eyes. She could feel him on top of her. The metallic smell of testosterone made her itch all over. A scream tried to force its way out.

Cindy choked it back and pushed past him. She charged through the restaurant, past the patrons enjoying an evening out. Cindy caught Ellen's worried expression out of the corner of her eye but kept going. She did not stop until she reached the ticket kiosks on the second level of the Metro station. Tears streamed down her cheeks. She leaned against one of the boxy machines for some time, sobbing and fighting for control.

2

Cindy squirmed. She couldn't sit still. The voice in her head screamed, *Go home. Now.* She ignored it and turned left off of I-97 onto Race Track Road. A half-mile later, an almost imperceptible bend in the road put her on 11th Street in Bowie. As she continued down the two-lane country road past farms and recently built housing developments, she grew more and more convinced that she had taken a wrong turn.

The road ended abruptly at an intersection. A railroad overpass to her right led to what looked like a shopping area. On her left, a street led south to a housing development. Across the intersection, Cindy saw some old stores, probably constructed before WWII. According to her GPS, she had reached her destination.

She closed her eyes and took a deep breath. When she opened them, she scanned the buildings from left to right. A leprechaun painted on a large, plate-glass window caught her attention. It identified an ancient building almost hidden by the overpass as the Old Bowie Town Grille.

Cindy rolled toward the restaurant. An SUV, a couple of trucks, and a sporty Lexus sat in a parking lot nestled between the Grille and the overpass. She studied them as she pulled into the lot.

There was no sign of her contact, but she didn't know what to expect. The woman was supposed to be waiting for her in the parking lot. She considered going back home and calling Ellen. Or calling Ellen and complaining that her detective was a no-show. She settled on the latter and pulled into a parking space at the rear of the lot. She turned her car off and surveyed the parking lot one last time.

Shit! Did I come to the wrong place? Or did that stupid detective blow me off?

She was still sitting in her car, wavering between going back home and calling Ellen when the sound of a car door opening and shutting caught her attention. She looked in her rearview mirror. A woman had emerged from the Lexus and was heading toward Cindy's Fusion. She was slender, with black hair and Mediterranean features. Not someone who could help with the problem.

Cindy got out of her car and walked across the lot.

The woman extended her hand. "Cindy Foster? I'm Nickey Arnold."

Cindy shook hands but said nothing.

Nickey smiled. "Why don't we go inside where we can talk?"

She led the way past the counter and cash register that served as a gateway between the front entrance and the modest dining area. The restaurant had just opened for the day's business. The lunch crowd had not shown up yet. Nickey found a corner table, where she and Cindy were unlikely to be disturbed. The meeting with the PI had been arranged by Ellen Magee to get Cindy some help after the run-in with Adan Jackson at the Gal Friday get-together a week earlier.

Cindy studied the menu avoiding eye contact. When the waitress came to their table, she ordered the salmon.

Nickey ordered a Chicken Caesar salad. She turned to her companion and broke the awkward silence. "Are you okay? Ellen said the incident at the restaurant was pretty serious."

Cindy brushed her hair back and licked her lips. "It was upsetting, but I'm okay." Her voice was barely audible.

"Can you tell me a little about yourself? You work for America First. How long have you been there?"

Cindy'sgaze focused on her folded hands resting on the table. She cleared her throat. "Almost ten years."

"Was that your first job?"

"Yes. I went to work there right after graduation." The words came out in a slow monotone.

"You're married and living in Bowie?"

"Yes."

"How long have you been married?"

Cindy looked up at Nickey and grinned slightly. "We celebrate our first anniversary next month."

Nickey smiled. "How is married life?"

"Great. Are you married?"

"No." Nickey sighed. "I don't think that is ever going to happen."

"Why not?"

Nickey screwed up her face and shook her head. "I'm not ready to settle down." She smiled enigmatically. "Marriage isn't for everyone."

Cindy's eyebrows shot up.

Nickey pressed on. "Your husband is Eric? How did you meet him?"

"We met at work. He is the manager of the office computer system." Cindy smiled. Her eyes looked off to the right. "He's a hands-on kind of guy who will come around to check on complaints and answer questions."

"So, one thing led to another, and the two of you got married?"

"Actually, he's shy," Cindy replied. "He wouldn't ask me out. A mutual friend set us up on a double date. She and her husband took us to see *Cats* at the Lazy Susan Dinner Theater." Cindy was becoming visibly more comfortable and animated.

"When was that?"

"September 10, 2006."

"You waited a while to get married," Nickey observed.

"We lived together for over a year." Cindy studied her hands. She seemed to be telling her story to the table. "We talked a lot about where we wanted to be in five or ten years. We both wanted a family and a home." She paused to look up at Nickey. "One night, I decided that I wanted to have children, and soon. Eric said if we were going to bring children into the world, we had to be committed to raising them. That was the end of October 2007. A week later, he proposed, and I said yes."

When their food arrived, they paused to sample the dishes.

Nickey asked, "How's the salmon?"

"Pretty good. Very tender, but they might have overdone the lemon. How's your salad?"

"It'll keep me alive." Nickey grinned mischievously. "Chicken salad is not an Irish dish, but it's an excellent food choice."

Cindy's eyebrows arched. "Do you like Irish food?"

Nickey rolled her eyes. "I'm Greek. I love Greek food. But when I was in the Marines, I learned to get by with whatever slop they put in front of me."

Cindy laughed.

"Can you tell me a little bit about this guy at work?" Nickey asked. She lifted a piece of chicken on her fork. "What's he doing to bother you?"

Cindy's smile vanished. "He manages to walk past me once or twice a day and make eye contact."

Nickey took a sip of her wine. "That's it? He doesn't say anything or touch you?"

"No. I am pretty sure that he is trying to see how far he can go without getting into trouble."

"Have you talked to anybody besides Ellen about him?"

"A couple of my friends." Cindy shrugged. "They haven't noticed anything."

"And his supervisor?" Nickey prompted.

"I can't go to him. Adan's a senior account manager, and I don't have anything concrete." Cindy lowered her eyes and bit her lip. "But he's making me uncomfortable."

"That should be enough to go to management these days."

Cindy shook her head vigorously. Her voice was choked. "It isn't. I talked to Ellen. He can go anywhere, any time he wants, and claim he was just doing his job."

Nickey nodded. She asked in a soft voice, "How long has this been going on?"

"I don't know. Six months." Tears glistened in Cindy's eyes.

"Why did you wait so long to do something about it?"

"I expected him to stop," Cindy snapped. "The way he came on to me at the restaurant was too much. Ellen said you could take care of it."

Nickey was impassive. "To the best of your knowledge, when did it start?"

"Early last year."

Nickey put her elbows on the table and clasped her hands with her thumbs touching her lips for a few seconds. Then she asked, "Was there some sort of trigger event that you can identify? Were the two of you in a flirty conversation or something?"

Cindy's jaw tightened. She rolled her eyes and shook her head. "We bumped into each other at a holiday party at the end of 2007." She shrugged. "But it was nothing. We were just at the same table at the same time getting food. I was there with Eric."

"This guy thought it was something. Why was he there in the first place?"

"It was a company party. We both work for America First. We work in different departments, so our paths don't cross."

But you have been running into each other regularly since that encounter?"

Cindy nodded.

Nickey eyed her suspiciously. "Is there anything else?"

"He crashed my wedding reception."

"Does Ellen know about that?"

Cindy shook her head. Nickey's eyes narrowed. Her head tilted back. "And you just forgot to mention it to her because…?"

"I pushed it out of my mind. I didn't want a scene in front of all those people," Cindy said in a panicked voice. "Eric doesn't know anything about what's going on, and I want to keep it that way."

Nickey sipped her wine as she studied Cindy. "My fee is two hundred dollars per hour with an upfront retainer of two thousand dollars. If it looks like I am going to need more than fifty hours, we can talk about a deal."

Cindy's lip quivered. "Can you get him off of my back?"

"There are no guarantees in a situation like this."

"So, I just hand you a bunch of money and hope that you do something about that piece of crap?"

Nickey glared at her. When she spoke, her voice was flat, harsh. "Your best bet is to find another job."

"I am not going to let him run my life," Cindy shot back. "I just made manager, and I intend to keep moving up the ladder."

Nickey leaned forward, staring directly into Cindy's eyes. "Then you had better be prepared to fight."

3

Nickey left the meeting with one thought: *That woman is hiding something.*

She spent the next few days pulling together info on Adan Jackson and Cindy Smith Foster: public records, newspaper mentions, web citations. Neither of them had a high profile. According to one website, Jackson had been arrested for assault back in the early nineties. She would have to get a contact to look up the police records for confirmation.

Sergeant Jack Edwards. Nickey smiled and licked her lips.

On the surface, both Cindy and Adan led normal, Gen-X lives. Adan had a brief bio on the America First website. He grew up in Meridian, Mississippi, and attended public schools. After high school, he participated in a seminar for future business leaders at Oxford and then toured Europe. He graduated from Georgetown cum laude in 1996 and completed his MBA in 2000.

Adan joined AFFS in the summer of 1996. He had worked on a dozen major projects. In 2008, he was promoted to senior account manager. That meant he was on his way to becoming a partner in the firm.

Nickey began her research with Georgetown yearbooks from '93 through '96. Photos showed Adan developing and maturing. He played football and wrestled. He was active in the drama and history clubs. At least for the first two years. He wasn't in any clubs in his junior year. He didn't play football in the fall of 1994, and he didn't wrestle that year. He was back playing football and wrestling in his senior year. He rejoined the drama club but seemed to stay in the background.

She hired a detective working out of Meridian to provide a detailed profile of Adan and learned that the Jackson family had a long history in Meridian. The city grew out of a railroad station where the Southern Railway connected to the Mobile and Ohio Railroad. As the city grew, the Jacksons built an empire based on land, banking, and railroads. Adan's great-grandfather founded Jackson and Sons Financial Services during the Roaring Twenties. The firm weathered the stock market crash and the Great Depression and entered a new era of prosperity with the outbreak of World War II.

Adan Jackson's father, George, was born in 1946. He joined the Air Force in 1968 after earning a degree in accounting. He served two tours in Vietnam. In 1972, he married his college sweetheart, Camille Witherspoon.

A year later, George Jackson resigned from active duty and joined the family business as a vice president. Adan was born that August. George and Camille had four other children: Helen (1975), Beau (1978), Mary (1980), and Andy (Andrea, 1987).

George's brother, William, took over as president of Jackson and Sons when the father retired in 1990. George decided to move on. He was able to get a position with the Brookings Institute in Washington, D.C., starting in 1991. The family relocated to D.C. at the end of the school year.

George Jackson bought a large house on one-and-a-half acres of woodland overlooking the Chesapeake Bay. It had its own private dock, tennis courts, and a swimming pool. He also bought a condo near the Brookings Institute offices in Dupont Circle. Camille managed the home in Annapolis and raised the family. She was actively involved with charities and politics. George divided his time between the house in Annapolis and the condo in D.C., where he could focus on his work.

The children followed a simple pattern. They went to local high schools, where they did well academically and athletically. They were friendly and well-liked. After high school, they went on to expensive, private colleges, where they gravitated toward business and finance.

Andy was the exception to everything. Her arrival was a surprise. After high school, she went to Notre Dame of Maryland University in Baltimore, where she majored in education. She was getting ready to graduate in May 2009. Nickey arranged to meet with her before graduation.

Adan had done nothing in Meridian to get arrested or kicked out of school. He was a leader and well-liked. He played sports and got good grades. In his senior year, Adan won a state wrestling title. He was a better than average football player but not good enough to get a scholarship.

His family background and his degree from Georgetown put him on a fast track up the corporate ladder. He moved in heady circles, but his life was otherwise unremarkable.

Cindy Smith came from the other side of the proverbial tracks. Their home was only a few miles from the Jacksons' estate, but it might as well have been in another country. The Jacksons were in the upper one percent; the Smiths were in the middle of the pack. They still believed that America was the land of opportunity. They were certain their hard work would pay off one day.

She grew up in a modest, ranch-style single-family structure in the Eastport suburb of Annapolis. Her father, Ed Smith, worked in the accounting department at Aeronautical Radio. Her mother, Marie, worked as an administrative assistant with the Annapolis Property Management Company. Her older brother, Ed, was a chief petty officer. Her younger brother, John, was an electrician's mate, petty officer first class.

Cindy graduated from Annapolis High with a 4.0 GPA. She applied for and won scholarships. The gap between what those scholarships offered and the actual cost of attending college for four years was disheartening. She applied for a Pell Grant and loans then made up the difference by working part-time. Cindy started at Prince George's Community College in January 1995. She transferred to Bowie State University at the beginning of her junior year. AFFS offered her a job after graduation, but her degree from Bowie State didn't get her any special consideration. She landed in the Tax department and started working her way up. She was promoted to manager after nine years with the firm.

* * *

Thursday was Nickey's day off. Her schedule was empty except for a meeting with Adan's sister, Andy, in the afternoon. But she couldn't get Cindy Foster's case out of her head. It was all too neat. No missteps.

Except that Adan seemed to be stalking Cindy. That could be put down to an overactive imagination if Adan hadn't crashed Cindy's wedding reception.

Adan's interest in Cindy made no sense. She was average at best. Five-foot six, slightly built. Light brown hair, hazel eyes, plain face. Makeup could help, but she didn't do anything to make herself more attractive. Tall, good-looking Adan shouldn't have any trouble finding women to date. So, why was he going after Cindy?

They were about the same age, and their careers centered around money and finance. But they came from different worlds. They just happened to have ended up in the same office building working for the same company. They had little day-to-day contact at work. They never met socially.

Nickey changed into her workout clothes, grabbed her bike, and pedaled to the Planet Fitness five miles away. Her mind ran through Cindy's story over and over again. There was a casual, meaningless encounter at a food table during a company holiday party. Then, he made time every day to run into her at work. He crashed her wedding reception. He accosted her in a restaurant. That bothered her so much, she hired a private eye to get him off her back.

She worked through a brisk, twenty-minute circuit training routine. Then twenty minutes back to her condo and a shower.

A question jumped to the front of the line during Nickey's ride back from the gym. Cindy started college at PGCC in January 1995, the second half of the school year. A year and a half after she graduated from high school. What was she doing for eighteen months?

That question led Nickey to an odd coincidence. Adan apparently took a semester off at the beginning of his junior year of college. He started back to school in January of 1995. Perhaps the mysterious assault charge was responsible for the gap. She would have to talk to Jack about that.

The detective became intrigued by the fact that these two people who had nothing in common both sat out the fall semester of 1994 when they should have been in school.

Nickey threw together a Greek salad: lettuce, chicken, tomatoes, cucumber, olives, and onion sprinkled with feta cheese and topped with olive oil. She poured a glass of lush Agiorgitiko wine, then sat and pondered the problem while she enjoyed her lunch. Only one explanation made sense—one disturbing explanation.

She called her client.

Cindy answered on the second ring. "Ms. Arnold. What can I do for you?"

"I wanted to thank you for your prompt payment of my retainer."

"No problem."

"I have been doing some digging into your background," Nickey said casually

"Why are you checking into my background?"

"That's what I do." She took a sip of wine. "Something puzzles me."

Her client growled, "Forget it."

"I have to consider the possibility that you and Jackson met before the holiday party," Nickey explained.

"We didn't," Cindy snapped. "You can drop that part of your investigation."

The detective sipped her wine. "Did you know that the two of you started college at the same time?"

There was an extended pause, a definite break in the rhythm of the exchange. "No, I didn't realize that," Cindy answered calmly. "Did he go to PGCC as well?"

Almost spilled the beans, didn't you? "No," Nickey admitted. "He went to Georgetown."

"So, I would have no way of knowing when he started college."

"True." Another sip of wine. "What I wanted to ask you about was why you didn't start college right after high school."

Another thoughtful pause. "I needed money. I worked at Walmart." Her voice was controlled but with a hint of bitterness. "I continued working there until I graduated from Bowie."

"You carried a heavy load and got good grades."

"Yes. A lot of people do that," Cindy snarled. Pure venom this time. "If there is nothing else, I have to get back to work." Her tone was dismissive.

"Nothing else," Nickey purred. "Thank you for clearing that up."

Nickey sat back and closed her eyes. *Plausible. Mostly true. But you're awfully touchy. What did you leave out?*

4

Nickey could not risk being late for her meeting with Andy Jackson. Arranging it had been a challenge. Andy had not bothered to return her first three calls. When she did answer, she said, "I don't know why you keep calling this number, but I wish you would stop."

"It's about your brother, Adan," Nickey explained.

"What about him?"

"I need your perspective for an article in an industry newsletter."

After a long pause, Andy asked, "What kind of article?"

"He is being featured in our annual survey of rising young financial executives."

"What do you want from me?"

"How do you feel about your brother? Can you describe him in three words?"

"Smart, funny, caring, hardworking." Andy paused and laughed. "I guess that's more than three words."

"That's great," Nickey gushed. "That's exactly what I'm looking for. I need to talk to you because I can't get that kind of assessment from anybody else."

"I don't know." Andy sounded suspicious. "I don't see how that's important."

"It makes him human," Nickey assured her. "Look. Can we just meet and talk for a few minutes?"

"I'm swamped. I'm finishing up exams, and then I have to get ready for graduation."

"I will keep it short. You have my word," Nickey promised. "I won't put you on the spot. This is a positive article. Your input is really important."

"I guess. But not this week."

"Next week?"

"My last exam is on Tuesday," Andy explained. "I am taking Wednesday off to catch up on my sleep."

"Could we do it Thursday, around eleven?"

"It would have to be later. Four would be a good time for me," Andy countered.

"All right. I can switch my other appointments around. Do you want to meet in front of the student union?"

Andy paused before answering. "What is your name? Who do you work for?"

"My name is Vanessa Rizzo. I am a staff writer for Insider News."

Andy paused again. She blew out a breath of air. "Okay. I'll see you on Thursday."

"In front of the student union building?" Nickey pressed.

"Yeah. Doyle Hall."

"I'll see you Thursday at four," Nickey said. "I will be wearing a green blouse and gray slacks."

* * *

The trip from Nickey's condo to the campus used to be straightforward. Get on 95 north from the Baltimore Beltway to Charles Street, which took you past Johns Hopkins and Loyola straight to Notre Dame. Urban renewal, new construction, and new traffic patterns eliminated the direct route. The drive gave Nickey time to get into the role of Vanessa Rizzo.

She stood outside Doyle Hall on the Notre Dame campus for about ten minutes.

Fair-skinned, auburn-haired Andy showed up in a bright red tee and white shorts. She walked up and extended her hand. "Ms. Rizzo? I'm Andy Jackson."

The detective took her hand. "I'm pleased to meet you. Call me Vanessa."

Andy stood for a moment, taking stock of her contact. "Could you tell me again who you work for and what you want to talk about?"

Nickey handed her a plain business card. "I work for Insider News. It's a trade journal. I'm doing an article on rising young stars in the world of finance. Adan is one of the people we want to highlight."

"I've never heard of it."

"I'm not surprised. Not many people have heard of us. And quite frankly, most people would find our stuff boring. But some important people pay attention to what we have to say. Getting a mention in an article like this is a big plus for a young executive."

Andy squinted and curled her lip for a second. "Why don't you talk to my parents?"

"I am trying to set up an interview. I was hoping I could get your take on your brother before you graduate and disappear."

Andy pursed her lips and exhaled through her nose. "All right. Let's go inside and find a seat." She led the way up the stone stairs and through the front door. They crossed a large, open area to stairs that led to a mezzanine, which housed a cafeteria and small, semiprivate alcoves. Each of the cubbyholes had a small square table with four metal chairs. Andy picked out an empty table and took a seat. She watched Nickey remove a small writing pad from her purse and get settled. "What are you looking for?"

"Human interest stuff. Something that makes Adan come alive as a person." Nickey paused. "His bio on the America First website is boring. He was a standout in high school and graduated cum laude from Georgetown. He has done a good job on a number of projects." She opened her mouth as if to vomit. Andy chuckled. "When I look in the Georgetown yearbooks, I find a good-looking, well-rounded young man, an honor student, and an athlete. His extracurricular activities included the drama club and the history club." She shrugged. "None of that distinguishes him from thousands of other promising young executives."

Andy tilted her head and looked off toward the ceiling. When she returned to meet Nickey's gaze, she said, "Adan was fourteen when I was born. He went on a year-long European trip right after high school. The following year, he entered Georgetown. I was nine when he started working for America First. I don't know what I can tell you."

"Did he live on campus?"

"Most of the time."

"Was there a period of time when he lived at home?" Nickey asked hopefully.

Andy started to say something, then paused. "We live near D.C. Georgetown is an easy commute. Adan would come home on weekends, and sometimes he stayed for a couple of days."

"What about summer vacations?"

She hesitated again. "I told you I was young at the time. I think he either traveled or worked over the summers. Why are you so interested?"

"I was just trying to figure out if you two spent any time together."

"Before we moved up here. He was in high school, and I was his kid sister."

"So, you two aren't close?"

"Oh. We're very close. We just haven't spent a lot of time together."

"What are your earliest memories?"

Andy grinned. "He could be a good friend. He liked to tell me stories."

"Anything else?"

"Mom says he changed my diapers and gave me bottles when I was a baby."

"Sounds like he has the making of a good father," Nickey observed. "Do you have any Adan stories from your teen years?"

Andy perked up. "Our drama club put on *Romeo and Juliet* in my senior year. I was Juliet. Adan spent a lot of time at the house, helping me practice."

"Was he any good?"

Andy chuckled. "He was great. He knew the entire play almost by heart. He could do all the parts."

Nickey smiled thoughtfully. "Does he have a favorite play?"

Andy tilted her head and pursed her lips. "I think it would be *Hamlet*."

"Why is that?"

"He said Hamlet is Shakespeare's most relevant character. Adan thinks of him as a misunderstood genius. A man who is too big for the world around him so he can never fit in."

"Isn't that an unusual interpretation?"

"I suppose. I'm not an expert."

Nickey made some notes. She turned back to a page with questions and ran her finger down the list. Halfway down, she paused and looked up at Andy, squinted, and puffed out her lips. She shook her head and went back to the list. "How about after he started working for America First? Did he move out right away?"

Andy looked up toward the ceiling for a second. She nodded. "I am not sure why, but Adan moved out right after graduation. I guess he had gotten used to living in D.C. Maybe living at home was too boring."

"Are you planning on moving back home after graduation?"

Andy laughed. "I have a job lined up at Roland Park Middle School. I'm going to stay up here in Baltimore and work on my masters."

"Is it just living at home, or are there other issues?"

"You said you wouldn't put me on the spot," Andy protested. "I just want to be with people my own age. I feel comfortable up here in Baltimore."

"Okay. I was out of line," Nickey apologized. "Just one more thing. Do you know how Adan picked his condo?"

"He wanted to be downtown but not near Dad in Dupont Circle, so he moved to Woodmont." Andy paused and bit her lip as she looked up.

"I guess you haven't seen much of him since he moved out."

"He used to spend time at home on weekends and holidays. But he was busy working on his MBA."

"Did he ever talk about anyone he was dating or bring a girl home to meet the family?"

Andy eyed her suspiciously and shook her head. "I don't think there has been anybody special in Adan's life. He's too busy. I guess he takes after Dad."

Nickey scribbled some notes. She looked up at Andy and screwed up her face then looked back down at her notes. Her finger ran over her list of questions. She shook her head. She looked up with her lips pressed together as if she had a question but wasn't sure she should ask it.

"Was there something else?" Andy said with a bit of an edge to her voice.

"Nooo." Nickey drew the word out.

"If you want to ask about the rape, go ahead," Andy snapped.

"I wasn't going to." Nickey smiled reassuringly. "We don't have to mention it in our story."

"Whatever you have heard is wrong," Andy retorted. "Adan had nothing to do with it. He just went into the room to break it up when he heard that woman screaming."

Nickey took her time. She said softly, "Can you tell me what really happened?"

"It was a frat party. One of Adan's friends showed up with a date. Later on, the two of them went upstairs. People do that, you know."

Nickey nodded. "Then what happened?"

"Adan noticed they were gone a long time and got worried. He went upstairs to check and heard the woman screaming. He chased his buddy out and helped her get dressed. She later claimed it was a gang rape."

Andy paused for a breath. Nickey closed her eyes and shuddered.

Andy's expression hardened. "The other guy confessed and went to jail." She leaned across the table and stared into Nickey's eyes. "Adan wanted to fight the charges, but our lawyer said he could get serious time if the jury believed the woman. So, we worked out a deal with the DA and the woman. Adan had to go to jail for a couple of months. But the charge was bogus. Adan wouldn't do anything like that."

Nickey sat wide-eyed, unable to come up with a response.

Andy stood. "Believe whatever you want. What I told you is the truth."

She stormed out of the building.

5

By the time Nickey reached her car, she had decided that a chat with Sergeant Jack Edwards was in order. She sat behind the steering wheel and debated her options. Catching him at home seemed like the best plan. But he could be at his apartment in D.C. or at his girlfriend's house in Virginia. Nickey bet on sex.

The drive to the MacMahon residence in Centreville, Virginia, took over two hours at that time of day. The sun had already set by the time she parked her Lexus in front of the large, old house on Eagle Tavern Lane.

Eve answered the door, wearing a denim shirt, khaki slacks, and sneakers. "Nickey. This is unexpected."

The PI beamed. "Hi, sweetie. Can I come in?"

Eve stepped back and held the door open.

Her visitor walked to the center of the room and turned around. "How are you doing?"

"What's on your mind, Nickey?"

"We haven't talked in a while, and I've been thinking about you."

"I'll bet. Can I get you something?"

"I could use a glass of wine, but coffee will work if it's not too much trouble."

"Have a seat. I'll be right back." Eve pointed to a large, overstuffed couch that looked like it had been around forever. Probably early twentieth century, with a stiff, sturdy cover designed to survive a large brood of active kids. It was dark brown with a forest motif that hid dirt well. She disappeared through a doorway that led to a hall. When she returned, she had a tray with grapes, provolone cheese, salami slices, and two glasses of sauvignon blanc. She set the food on the oval, glass-topped coffee table in front of her visitor and pulled over a hassock for her own seat.

Nickey raised her glass. "To best friends."

Eve touched glasses but said nothing. She took a sip of wine. "What brings you all the way out here?"

"I've been following your blog."

"Thank you." *Get to the point, Nickey.*

"And you're doing all right financially?"

Eve rolled her eyes. "Mom has a big house. She lets us stay here rent-free. Joe is doing his share with the kids' expenses. So, I'm fine."

"And Jack?"

Eve frowned. "What about Jack?"

"I heard he's staying with you."

"I have no idea where you got that."

"He isn't staying with you?"

"No." Eve pressed her lips into an angry line and shook her head. "He is not living here with me."

"But he stays here sometimes?" Nickey pressed.

"Off and on. What's on your mind?"

"Is he here now?"

"No."

The next question was tricky under the circumstances. Nickey made a cracker sandwich with the provolone and salami and took her time eating it. She washed the last bite down with wine. "Are you expecting him?"

"I don't know." Eve made no attempt to hide her irritation. "If you want to talk to him, give him a call."

"I need some information," the detective explained.

"I am not going to be your go-between with Jack."

"You owe me a favor," Nickey insisted.

"For seducing my husband or for pushing me into prostitution?"

"You went along with that because you knew it was the only way you could get your story," Nickey chided. "I looked out for you because I cared about you. I didn't charge you for all the fact-checking I did."

Eve's head drooped. She shook her head slowly, eyes closed, mouth compressed in a tight line. *OK, we did it to ourselves. You just played your part. You fucked Joe because that's what he wanted.* She straightened to confront the detective. "BFF is a stretch, but yes, you've always had my back. No, you never asked to be paid for investigating those prostitute stories that went into my book."

The detective stood and walked over to the fireplace. She picked up a picture. "Six of you. When was this taken?"

"1987. Ted was home on leave after graduation from West Point."

"You look like Becky in this picture. How old were you?"

"Fourteen. I was getting ready to start high school."

"This looks like a miniature version of Bill. How old was he? Ten? Twelve?"

"Twelve. He's two years younger than me. We were like the second set of kids."

Nickey turned to look at her friend. She raised her eyebrows. "You're younger, but there doesn't seem to be a break."

"Liz is something of an oddball in our family. Ted, Mary, and Sue are all success stories. I'm a struggling writer. Bill is a public defender." Eve shrugged. "Major Elizabeth MacMahon is a fighter pilot. She goes her own way. She shows up at family gatherings but keeps to herself."

Nickey returned the picture to its place on the mantel. She strolled back to the coffee table and picked up her wine. Raising the glass half-way, she stood with one hand on her hip. Her attention focused on the woman sitting on the hassock with her red hair, ivory skin, and unwavering emerald eyes. "I have a new client. She needs some help."

Eve pursed her lips as she considered whether or not to get involved. She took a deep breath and slowly exhaled. "What kind of help?"

"A guy at her office is stalking her."

"What do you expect Jack to do?"

"I just want somebody to look into police records from about fifteen years ago."

"What's going on, Nickey?"

"I think the two of them have a history, but I can't prove it." The detective returned to the MacMahon family photos on the mantel. As she browsed, she said, "My client claims that she had a brief encounter with a male coworker at a holiday party two years ago, and now he is making his presence known every day at the office. It's intimidating, but she hasn't been able to put a stop to it. A couple of weeks ago, a mutual friend referred her to me."

"And?"

Nickey whirled to face Eve. "I need to know what I'm getting myself into. When I confront this guy, I need to know whether he just misinterpreted a casual encounter at a party or whether he is carrying a grudge from years ago."

"Or whether he's a serial killer toying with her before he finishes her off?"

"That is the worst of the three possibilities." Nickey's voice was suddenly cold and hard.

Eve said softly, "What's her name?"

"Cindy Foster, but it would have been Smith back then."

"And his name?"

"Adan Jackson."

"I'll talk to Jack tonight and give you a call tomorrow."

"Thanks."

6

Eve was putting the finishing touches on a blog post about sexual harassment in the workplace when the snake charmer ringtone interrupted. "Hi, Nickey, I was just about to call you."

Nickey skipped the preliminaries. "What's going on?"

Eve chuckled. "As soon as I mentioned Adan Jackson last night, Jack went off and called a buddy. When he came back, he said Ed Twomey would give me the story, but I have to interview him at his house."

"Did Jack tell you what happened?"

"No. He just said something needed to be done, but it was out of his hands."

"Done about what?"

Eve sketched a dark figure with a dagger on her pad. "Whatever is going on between Jackson and Cindy Foster, I suppose."

Nickey said nothing for several seconds. She exhaled noisily. "Does this guy Twomey know anything about Adan Jackson?" She added, "Who is he anyway?"

"He's a retired police detective. Jack used to work with him."

"Does he know anything about Adan?"

"Jack didn't say. But if I read him correctly, they both know what's going on."

"Call him and ask. I don't want to waste time on a dead end."

"I can't do that. Jack set me up with an interview." She sighed. "I have to play it straight."

Nickey's voice softened. "What do you have in mind?"

"I'll tell him I'm working on an article about sexual assault."

"It was rape," Nickey countered. "He raped her."

"Are you sure? Is he listed in the National Sex Offender Registry?"

"No," Nickey admitted.

"We'll have to let Detective Twomey tell it his way."

"Adan did it," Nickey snarled. "He got away with it somehow."

"Can we at least wait until we find out what Twomey has to say before we start leveling charges?"

"All right. Where does he live?"

* * *

The Twomeys lived in Chevy Chase, an upscale but densely populated neighborhood that spread across northwest D.C. and into Maryland. Their house was a modest colonial with stone facing. The overhanging roof that covered the front porch was supported by three massive, white columns. A decorative stone walkway led from the street to the porch and then around the left side of the house to the fenced-in backyard. Azalea bushes and tulips grew along the fence on the right side of the house. A trellis running from ground to roof supported a magnificent rose bush that protected the porch.

A tall, thin woman with smooth, cocoa skin, high cheekbones, almond-shaped eyes, and short, cropped white hair answered the door.

"What can I do for you?" she asked in a husky, cultured voice.

"I'm Eve MacMahon, Jack Edwards's friend. This is Nickey Arnold. I called you a little earlier about an article I am working on. We would like to speak to Detective Twomey."

The woman smiled pleasantly. "I'm Nor. Jack said we should expect a visit. Please, come in. Ed is out back."

Nor led her guests through the house. When they reached the porch, she called, "Ed, you have company."

The backyard was small. A toolshed took up one corner. Ed had managed to create a garden along the fence surrounding the yard. He was growing tomatoes, squash, beans, carrots, peas, and radishes. He even had a dozen tall cornstalks at the back. The grassy area in the middle was dominated by a large, round table with an umbrella for shade. There were six chairs at the table.

Ed rose from his gardening and turned to face his company. He was tall and youthful except for a crown of white hair. He pulled a rag from the back pocket of his coveralls and wiped his hands as he crossed the yard with long, gliding strides. "I apologize," he said as he extended his hand. "Y'all caught me in the middle of something."

Eve shook his hand. His grip was polite but firm. "I'm Eve MacMahon." She gestured toward the detective. "This is my associate, Nickey Arnold."

Nor said, "They are here to talk to you about sexual assault."

"Have a seat." Ed indicated the lawn chairs. "Nor, can you get us some tea?"

When they were settled, Eve said, "I am a freelance writer. I focus on the challenges that women face in the workplace. Jack told me a little about you, Detective, and I thought a man's point-of-view might make a nice change of pace."

"Ed," he corrected. "Just call me Ed. I'm not sure what I can tell you. I worked homicide for most of my forty years on the force."

Eve nodded. She rested her arms on the table and folded her hands. "A lot of women are killed as a result of domestic violence. Do you know anything about that?"

"The domestic violence was over and done by the time I got to the scene," Ed said wryly. "But you're right. There is a connection."

"How does that happen?"

"I'm not rightly sure. Lots of couples have argued and fought for years without killing each other. All I can tell you is that I'd get a call. I'd go out to the scene, and a woman would be lyin' there dead. It didn't make any sense. And after you got the explanation, it still didn't make any sense. Why kill her and ruin your life? Why not just walk away?"

Nor served the tea. Ed took a big drink from his glass. "Is that what you really wanted to talk about?"

Nickey cleared her throat. "There may be a problem, Ed."

"What's that?"

"We have a friend who feels threatened by a man in her office. All he has to do is be in the same corridor with her, and she gets anxious. She thinks he knows how she feels and makes a point of reminding her that he's around."

Ed rubbed his chin. "So, he's hurt her befo', and she's afraid he's gonna do it again."

Nickey nodded. "That's what it looks like."

"Looks like?"

"She claims she only recently met the man," Nickey explained.

"But you think she's lyin'."

Nickey studied Ed while she considered her response. "Do you know a man named Adan Jackson?"

He nodded. "I do," he said. "I most certainly do."

"Can you tell us about him?" Eve asked.

Ed stroked his chin. "He and a couple of other boys raped a woman named Cindy Smith ten or fifteen years ago."

Nor interjected, "It was sixteen years ago, Ed. October 1993."

Ed turned to Nor and grimaced. He turned back to Nickey. "I suppose your friend is named Cindy Smith."

Nickey shook her head. "Foster. She's married now, but her maiden name is Smith."

"If it's the same Cindy Smith," Ed said, "she has good reason to be afraid."

"How come he isn't a registered sex offender?"

"Beat the rap."

"How?"

"First off, one of them, Troy Mondale, pled guilty. Didn't even put up a fight. Then the Jackson boys' lawyer got her videos entered into evidence."

"The Jackson boys?" Nickey interjected.

Ed frowned. "Adan and his brother, Beau." He paused and sipped his tea. "The DA saw his case goin' down the tubes. He claimed Mondale was the ringleader and let the Jacksons off with a misdemeanor assault charge."

Nickey's jaw tightened. She fixed an angry stare on Ed.

Nor watched her with a concerned expression. "What are you thinking, baby?"

"I've got to stop him," Nickey said.

"How you gonna do that?" Ed challenged.

"The way I always do it," Nickey said dismissively. "I'll find something that scares him more than jail and threaten to ruin his ass if he doesn't back off."

"Are you sure?" Nor asked.

"His kind always has a closet full of skeletons," Nickey said. "I'll find one."

"You best be careful," Ed warned. "He's dangerous."

Nickey glared at him. Her lip curled up into a sneer. "So am I." She nodded. "So am I."

"What happened, Ed?" Eve asked.

"It wasn't my case. It was sexual assault. Like I said, I was in homicide," Ed began. "I interviewed Mondale once. I didn't talk to the others. But I read the report and heard some stories." He took a sip of tea. "The woman was makin' porn movies. She was a big deal with a website. Went by the name Delilah." He shook his head. "They musta seen her stuff and got the idea it'd be fun to get her in a room and take turns with her."

He took a sip of tea. "When the DA started puttin' his case together, he decided it was Mondale's idea."

Ed looked at Eve with a sad expression and shook his head. "I talked to Mondale. Nice kid. I can't believe he would come up with something like that. I told the DA it was entrapment." He paused for another sip of tea. His jaw tightened. He looked at Eve and then at Nickey. "But you know, the DA had to put somebody behind bars. Mondale had already confessed, and the Jackson boys looked like they'd get off one way or another." Ed looked down at the ground and then up at his guests. "So, he did what he had to do."

"Do you know what was on the videos?" Eve asked.

"Never seen 'em," Ed growled. "Didn't need to and didn't want to. Some said they would make you sick."

"Do you know if they are still around?" Nickey asked.

"Nope. Never had anything to do with 'em. Sergeant Bennett was in charge of the investigation. She might know."

The conversation died. Eve looked around. Ed. Nor. Nickey. They were all slumped in their chairs. She stood. "I guess we had better be going." She took Ed's hand. "I want to thank you so much for your help."

Nor stood and hugged her. "It was so nice meeting you."

Eve turned to Nickey, who was staring vacantly into space. "Come on."

Nickey came out of her daze. She stood and smiled at the Twomeys. "Thank you so much for your help."

Nor led them back through the house. When they reached the front entrance, she gave Eve another hug. "You and Jack should come over for dinner."

Eve said, "I would like that. I'll have to talk to Jack. But I can't make any promises. He stays busy."

The older woman smiled and nodded. "I know. I hadn't seen or heard anything since the divorce. It was such a surprise when he called the other night."

Eve smiled. It was a faint, sad smile. "He isn't over the divorce. He's still in love with Virginia."

"She's a lovely woman," Nor acknowledged. "But it won't work. She's pushy. Making her way up the corporate ladder. I wouldn't be surprised to find out she's running Bank of America one of these days. She's not a cop's wife."

"I don't think I am either," Eve scoffed.

Nor grinned. She almost laughed. "You're over here doing police work. You fit right in."

Eve hugged her. "I'll talk to Jack."

Nickey and Eve walked back to their cars and drove off.

7

Nickey arrived at Ellen Magee's condo on Connecticut Avenue at 10:37 on Saturday morning. She knew the exact time because she had to sign in at the front desk before she could take the elevator up to the fifth floor.

Nickey followed Ellen into the converted one-bedroom apartment. A short hallway led from the entrance past a kitchenette on the right to the living room. A breakfast counter separated the two rooms. A hall on the left led to the bedroom and bathroom. The dining area was off to the right of the living room. A picture window at the far end of the apartment looked out onto Connecticut Avenue.

As they passed the counter, Cindy called out curtly, "How are you coming with Adan Jackson?"

The detective looked in her direction. Cindy sat on a barstool next to the counter. She had turned to face the hallway. There were two coffee cups, along with two breakfast plates and a half-eaten Danish on the counter. Nickey pointed to a couch along one wall in the living room and said, "Why don't we sit over there by the coffee table?"

Cindy frowned. "I want to know if you have made any progress."

"I have." Nickey held up a manila envelope and nodded toward the couch. "Let's go over there so I can show you what I've got. There are some things we need to discuss." She walked to the dining room table and dragged a chair over to the coffee table. "Ellen, could you and Cindy sit on the couch?"

Ellen shrugged and started toward the couch. Her friend watched the action as if it was a sideshow. Ellen waved and said, "Come on, Cindy."

The response was an angry stare. Cindy's jaw was clenched tight. Her lips pressed into a line. She did not budge from her seat at the end of the counter.

Nickey stood, hands on her hips, glaring at her client. When she got tired of waiting, she reached into her envelope and pulled out a piece of paper. "This is a cashier's check for a thousand dollars. I am making you a one-time offer that I have never made to anyone before."

She paused and waited for a reaction. Cindy held her ground. Nickey placed the check near the Danish on the counter. "It's a generous partial refund of your retainer. If I walk out that door, you are on your own. I will forget about you, Adan Jackson, and your problems."

"What's going on, Nickey?" Ellen demanded.

"I am not going to continue working on this case if your friend isn't going to cooperate."

Ellen turned to the young woman sitting in stoic silence at the counter.

Cindy roused herself to object, "I have cooperated. I told her everything."

"We have some things to discuss," Nickey said. "Either the two of you get over here so we can get down to business, or I'm leaving."

Ellen glared at Cindy. "You owe me," she snarled. "I set this up because you said you needed help. Now get over here."

Cindy slid to the floor and walked grudgingly to the couch. Ellen walked around the coffee table and took a seat next to Cindy.

When they were settled, the detective began. "I believe that I have pieced the picture together. I am ready to start the next phase."

"How many phases are there?" Cindy asked sarcastically.

"That depends on the outcome of this meeting." Nickey flashed a patronizing smile.

Ellen frowned. "Will you please tell me what is going on, Nickey?"

"I need Cindy to be completely open and honest with me. I can't continue on this case if she doesn't trust me."

Cindy insisted angrily, "I told her everything. I told her exactly what I told you."

Ellen looked at Nickey. "What's the problem?"

"Cindy, did you have any kind of a relationship with Adan before you bumped into him at that holiday party?"

"No. I told you before, and I am telling you now. I never saw him before that night. He may have been checking me out, but the first time I met him was at the Christmas party."

Ellen bit her lip as she watched her friend fidget. That exchange seemed to make her uncomfortable.

Nickey asked, "After high school, you worked at Walmart for eighteen months before starting at PGCC. Is that correct?"

"Yes. I told you that."

Nickey pulled a sheet of paper from her envelope: a copy of a page of headshots from a yearbook. She had circled the photo of a student named Cindy Smith. Nickey said, "Freshman class at Georgetown, 1993-1994 school year. Is that you?" Cindy blanched but said nothing. Nickey pulled another sheet of headshots from the envelope. She had circled the picture of a young man. "Sophomore class, 1993-1994." She said as she pointed to the headshot. "That's Adan Jackson in his second year at Georgetown. Did you know each other?"

Cindy stared in silent horror. She was on the verge of tears. Her lower lip trembled. She raised her hands to ward off the attack.

Nickey continued. "While you are considering your answer, there are a few other things you should know. Adan Jackson was arrested for assault in the fall of 1993. My contact with the D.C. police wouldn't give me any information. He sent me to Detective Ed Twomey, who retired from the force a few years ago. When I asked Ed if he knew Adan Jackson, he said, and I quote, 'I do. I most certainly do.'"

Cindy stood abruptly and pushed past Ellen. She stormed over to the window that looked out onto Connecticut Avenue. Her head was down, her shoulders hunched, and her fists clenched in tight balls.

Ellen walked over and put an arm around her friend. "What happened?"

Cindy was sobbing, but she managed, "He raped me. I couldn't keep going, so I dropped out. I spent six months in therapy before I was ready to go back and try again. My therapist and I agreed that I should start over with a clean slate. I buried that part of my life. I never mentioned Georgetown again."

Ellen looked over at Nickey. "Is that all?"

Nickey wanted to pull out the rest of the story, but she didn't want to fight with Ellen. She shook her head sadly. "No. There is one more nasty issue that needs to be dealt with, and Cindy is probably going to need your help."

Ellen led Cindy back to the couch, then went to the kitchenette to get a bottle of wine and some glasses. "Cheap stuff. Just perfect for situations like this."

Nickey sipped from her glass and studied Cindy. "Detective Twomey mentioned some videos."

Cindy snapped to attention. "What did he say?"

"The Jackson brothers were able to beat the rape charges because their lawyer got your videos entered into evidence."

Ellen gasped. "Jackson *brothers*? Adan wasn't alone?"

Cindy started sobbing again.

"Adan, his brother, and another guy named Troy Mondale. I am going to guess that at least one of the videos depicted a gang rape."

Ellen tried to comfort Cindy with a hug. She shook her head in disbelief as she struggled to cope with the implications of Nickey's revelations.

"I needed money," Cindy explained. Her voice was muffled because her head was buried in Ellen's chest. "We couldn't afford Georgetown, but I figured

I needed that degree to get a good job. I had a small scholarship. I was working at Walmart. There were just so many extras that had to be paid for." She looked up at Nickey. Her eyes were red, and tears stained her cheeks. "A friend put me in touch with the producer. After I made a couple of videos, he asked me about doing a gang rape. It was two thousand dollars. That was four times what I had been getting, so I agreed."

Cindy pushed Ellen away and rose to loom over Nickey. She said fiercely, "You can't tell anybody about those videos. I don't know what Eric would do if he found out. I would probably lose my job if AFFS got wind of them."

"They can't fire you for that," Ellen objected.

"They won't have to. You have no idea what life on campus was like after word got out."

"It's not whether but when," Nickey said softly. "Adan is just waiting for the right moment to start leaking them."

Cindy shook her head. "He doesn't have them. They're gone."

"You may be right," the detective countered. "But I wouldn't bet on it. Take a moment to do a search on Linda Lovelace when you get the chance. Her breakout movie, *Deep Throat,* is available for free on YouTube. It's been off the market for thirty years." She walked over to the breakfast counter and picked up the cashier's check. "Do you want this?"

"No," Ellen blurted out. She stood and stepped around the coffee table. "Do what you can to get Adan off her back. Cindy and I will start getting ready for the fallout from the videos."

Nickey came over to give her a hug. “I’m sorry, but that stuff had to come out.”

Ellen squeezed her. “I know. Go get Adan, but be careful.”

8

Adan Jackson went days without sleeping. Not all the time, but often enough to make it a normal part of his life. Sometimes it seemed like a superpower that enabled him to conquer tough challenges. He absorbed information and ideas effortlessly. The words to express his own thoughts poured out like water in a rainstorm. Then came the days when getting out of bed was a struggle. Days he spent brooding over his life and the way people treated him.

When Adan did make it to work on those days, he was virtually useless. He might review and comment on a few reports. But he wasn't productive. Office rules prevented him from taking a drink or smoking a joint. So, Adan watched a movie or listened to an audiobook he had downloaded to his phone. Anything to keep him going until the end of the day. On unbearable days, he walked over to the Gold's Gym a few blocks away and worked out.

He kept a supply of marijuana at home to help him through rough periods.

In his youth, as he liked to think of the years before he turned thirty, Adan could take advantage of the sleepless nights to complete challenging assignments. He could master a subject or write a paper in days instead of weeks when his mind would not let his body rest.

Those times were behind him. He had a staff to handle research and reports. Adan Jackson was paid to generate business. That was it. Nothing more and nothing less.

He reserved a small, underutilized conference room for a weekly Thursday staff meeting. Those meetings bored him. They were a waste of time, so he routinely canceled them. When Adan needed to discuss something with some of his staff, he would hold an impromptu meeting in his office. He instructed his secretary to release the conference room reservation to anyone who asked. No one ever asked. Adan generally took Thursday afternoon off because the scheduled meeting had been canceled. Sometimes he walked. Sometimes he sat in a bar and observed. Often, he managed to find a woman who was free for an afternoon of sex.

When Adan first graduated from college, he threw himself into his work on sleepless nights. He earned an MBA from Georgetown University. That got old. He developed a pot habit. A joint or two would help him relax and get him through a long night. He watched TV or jumped into social media and vented his opinions on whatever topic was trending. But he soon tired of trading virtual blows with idiots.

Adan didn't like lying around his apartment in a stupor. He got in his car and went out looking for action. He searched out dives instead of upscale venues like the Marquee Bar at the Omni Shoreham hotel.

One place that got his attention was the Tahiti, a gentlemen's club or, more plainly, a dive that featured women prancing around naked and men who threw money at them.

He quickly realized that he stood out in these bars. He was a strikingly handsome man wearing tailor-made suits. His remedy was to build a new wardrobe for these outings by shopping online at Macy's and Penney's. Those outlets didn't sell riffraff clothes, but they didn't cater to high-end executives either. He added a black wig with spiky, disheveled hair, thick, black eyelashes, and thick glasses with clunky black rims.

The disguise, along with the new wardrobe, shielded Adan from the people he encountered on his outings. Greg Jantzen was the exception. He spotted Adan as a wealthy executive slumming for a change of scenery. A man who would make an easy mark. The two men met on a warm winter night in February.

Adan wandered northeast instead of going south to DuPont Circle. He ended up in Shepherd Park on the border between D.C. and Maryland. The Boundary Line Bar caught his attention, and he decided to check it out. Adan, aka Peter Baeker, took a seat at a table against the wall, where he was able to observe most of the activity in the bar.

Shortly after his beer was served, a burly, blond man walked up to the table, beer in hand. "Would ya mind if I joined ya?" he asked. "I don't like to drink alone."

The man was a giant. Taller than Adan by a few inches and perhaps fifty pounds heavier. But he seemed pleasant, and he had a winning smile. Adan nodded and indicated a seat on the other side of the table.

The man chuckled as he sat down. He reached across the table to shake hands. "Greg."

Adan shook his hand. "Peter."

They watched the basketball game in progress on the TV over the bar in silence. At the halftime break, Greg said, "What brings you here tonight?"

"Ah felt cooped up." Adan eyed him suspiciously. "Ah needed a change of scenery."

"I do that every night."

Adan turned back to the TV and finished his beer. When he saw the waitress looking his way, he raised his hand, index finger extended.

"So, you have a job?" Greg asked.

Adan squinted at the man. He took his time considering his answer. "For the time being."

"If yer bringin' work home with ya," Greg laughed, "yer in good shape."

The waitress showed up with Adan's beer. He put a ten on her tray and waved her off. After taking a swig of his beer, he explained, "Ah'm a tax consultant. Ah'm busy preparing and filing taxes at this time of year."

Greg arched his eyebrows. He nodded in approval. "Do you need some help with your taxes?"

"I'm a full-time, part-time contractor. I've been doin' my own taxes for years."

Adan considered that answer while he sipped his beer. "Home repairs?"

"I'm a handyman. I'm a licensed plumber and electrician, but I can fix anything."

"How is business?"

"Booming."

The men went back to watching the game. Occasionally, one or the other would comment on a play or a call by the refs. The Wizards star Gilbert Arenas was no match for the Cavs star LeBron James. He was the hottest player in the league.

Greg asked, "You play much basketball?"

"No. A pickup game or two. Ah played football."

"Yer pretty small for that game, if ya don't mind my sayin' so."

"Ah was big enough for college."

"Where'd ya go to school?"

Adan scowled at the man sitting across from him. "Trust me. You've never heard of it or me."

Greg grinned broadly. "What position did ya play?"

"Tackle, end, linebacker. Wherever they needed me."

The Wizards were clearly out of it with five minutes to go in the game. Adan stood and started to walk away. He stopped and extended his hand. "Nice talking to you, Greg. Ah've got to get back and put in a couple of more hours before Ah go to bed."

Greg shook his hand. "Likewise, Peter."

The big man watched his new friend walk out of the door before he rose and went to the bar to pay his tab. He strolled out to the parking lot and watched "Peter" get into his car. As the man drove off, Greg took note of the make and model of the car. He also got the license number. He was sure he would be seeing more of "Peter" in the near future.

9

Troy Mondale began his prison term in City Lockup in Washington, D.C., in November 1993. He had been charged with the rape of a classmate, Cindy Smith. He confessed to his part in the crime and entered a guilty plea. The judge handed down a sentence of fifteen years in the Maryland State Penitentiary. By the end of 2004, Troy had earned enough points to merit a transfer out of secure lockup in the pen. He moved to the half-way house in March of 2005 after securing employment with Tri-State Construction, Inc.

He earned a reputation as a hard worker and a leader during his six months on the work-release program. His sentence was reduced because of good behavior. He got out in September 2005, and Tri-State hired him full-time. He went to work on a construction project in southwest D.C., near the Potomac River waterfront. The job paid ten dollars an hour. That was enough for a modest apartment and food. Troy's boss, Chris Holcombe, loaned him money to buy the clothes he needed.

His room took a third of his monthly pay, but it was furnished. It came with a king-size bed, a chest of drawers, and a closet, TV, and Wi-Fi. The kitchenette had a microwave and a refrigerator.

He got along fine on two inexpensive meals each day. Troy was as close to heaven as he ever hoped to get. And he had money left over. He was able to pay back the loan from his boss in a matter of months.

Freedom was a strange, uncomfortable feeling for Troy. He was okay on the job. But at night, he found himself in an alien world. He could do whatever he wanted, but it felt like people were watching him. They were waiting to see how the ex-con would screw up. He created Tom Jones, an alter ego with a reputable past, as a cover. Most of Jones's clothes came from the Salvation Army because that was what Troy could afford. A wool skull cap and a navy pea coat came first because they were common in the wharf area where Troy lived and worked. He added military-style boots, jeans, and a blue denim shirt.

Troy began spending nights in local bars, watching and listening. He practiced using a deeper voice and added words like "aye" and "mate" or "matey" to his vocabulary. After a while, these mannerisms became second nature when he donned his Tom Jones costume.

He had avoided fights in prison, and he continued the practice after he was released. Tom Jones got into a few scuffles. They weren't much, but they did establish his reputation.

Jones told people that he had been in the Navy for twelve years. He let it be known that he had boxed during his time in the service. Troy developed a prosthetic to make it look as if Jones had a boxer's pug nose.

He tried changing his eye color with a pair of brown-tinted contacts, but brown eyes and red hair didn't look right. He stumbled across the phenomenon of heterochromia—mismatched eyes, for example, one brown eye and one blue. Tom Jones developed heterochromia. His left eye was brown, while his right eye was blue. He developed a scar on his right cheek and figured out how to put a removable gold cap on his upper right incisor.

Over time, Troy grew comfortable enough as a free man that he did not need Tom Jones, but he liked the persona. So, he went out as the thuggish, ex-Navy boxer from time to time, just for the hell of it.

Troy was popular despite his own feelings of discomfort and inadequacy. He worked hard. Sitting around killing time set him on edge. He was smart. Troy had been a pretty good jailhouse lawyer. His buddies at the construction site came to rely on his legal advice. They also depended on him for tips on taxes and finances.

He discovered that Mr. Holcombe hated keeping the books because he could not figure them out. An accountant was hired, but Holcombe had to provide all the information. Troy offered to help. His boss told him he was crazy. There was no way the books were going to be turned over to an ex-con.

By the middle of 2007, almost two years after Troy had gotten out of prison, he had a solid reputation. He was respected and well-liked. Holcombe softened his position. Troy could look over his shoulder and provide pointers. When Holcombe got very busy outside the office, he asked Troy to go ahead and take care of the books until he could check them. Little by little, Troy worked his way into the role of bookkeeper. That led to a raise. He was making $12.50 an hour by the end of the year.

He splurged on Black Friday and bought a Kindle. It provided access to a treasure trove of books, magazines, and newspapers. Troy quickly discovered the wonders of the internet through his new tablet and the free Wi-Fi that came with his room. He looked up his own name and found that he had made the Justice Department's National Sex Offender Registry. Troy knew he was on the list, but he was shocked to see his picture pop up on the screen, along with other information, including where he lived and where he worked.

Troy had no access to computers, let alone the internet, while he was in the penitentiary. The idea of getting online to search for information about anything and everything did not come naturally to him when he first got out. He caught up rapidly when his Kindle made him aware of the power of the internet. Finding himself online made him wonder about the others.

A search for Adan Jackson led to a biographical entry on the website of a company called America First Financial Services. Adan was now working in America First's D.C. offices. The third member of the rape gang, Beau Jackson, was working in the New York offices of the same company. Troy found over one hundred listings for Cindy Smith using WhitePages.com. He couldn't figure out which one was the Cindy Smith.

He wanted to know more about their lives. It angered him that they had achieved success and prosperity while he battled for survival in prison. He was forced to make do with a low-end job while they held positions he couldn't even apply for. Adan's smug self-importance infuriated him. Cindy irked him. True, she was the victim. But she had actively promoted gang rape through her videos and her website. Cindy was an abettor, a co-conspirator, whether anybody else agreed with him or not.

The problem ate at him when he wasn't on the job. He schemed. As he studied America First, he began to believe that he might have a chance to bring the Jacksons down. He thought he might be able to hack into the corporate computer system and find a way to attack Adan and Beau. It would be a big job with enormous risks.

Troy didn't see that he had anything to lose. He was no longer locked up, monitored by guards 24/7. But he was still a prisoner. He would never be really free.

It took until July for Troy to get hired onto the crew that cleaned the AFFS offices in downtown D.C. He gave his name as Tom Jones and dressed appropriately. By late July, Troy had been able to use a manager's improperly handled passcode to gain entry to the AFFS computer network. He set up a fake account that gave him access to Adan Jackson's financial and personnel records.

Troy began collecting information that he planned to use to send Adan Jackson to jail. He worked slowly and carefully. There was no deadline, and he did not want to get caught doing something illegal.

* * *

In August, the misfortune of friends dragged Troy in a different direction. He had become a jailhouse lawyer all over again at the Tri-State Construction yard. Troy was the go-to resource for legal help. Of all the cases he helped with, Eddy Wilson's turned out to be the most important. It was a game-changer that opened the door to Troy's future.

Eddy, a former marine, was charged with assault and battery because of an altercation in a bar. Witnesses claimed he had tried to avoid the fight, but the other guy wouldn't stop. Eddy threw a punch that landed the man in the hospital. The prosecutor seemed to believe that the ex-Marine should go to jail because he was so big and so well trained that the fight was unfair. "Lopsided" was the word he used.

He didn't have any family in the area, so he called Troy to come down and bail him out. The next day they went to the Legal Aid Society in D.C., where they met with an attorney named Marie Moretti. She worked things out with the prosecutor. Wilson's charges were reduced to a misdemeanor. He was required to pay a fine and attend anger management classes.

Marie was smitten. Troy was intelligent and good-looking. He was also willing to go out of his way to help a friend. They continued talking after Eddy left for home. At some point, the issue of the rape that sent Troy to prison came up. He told her what happened.

She shook her head. "You seem like a good person. How could you have done that to a woman?"

Troy's gaze dropped down. "I was stupid," he explained. His voice was flat. "I was fed a lie, and I bought into it without thinking."

"You just sat here and walked me through it without a flicker of remorse or any other emotion." Marie stood and leaned over the ex-con. Her eyes bored into him. She unleashed a torrent of words that ripped open a wound all the way down to his soul. "You raped a woman then held her down so your buddies could rape her." Fury contorted her face. "And that doesn't bother you. What is wrong with you?"

He continued to focus on his hands. Prison had taught him to avoid direct eye contact. "It bothers me immensely," Troy said, but he didn't sound bothered. He had trained himself not to react to that kind of attack. "The only way I can get through the day is to push it out of my mind. I can't change what happened. I have to move on. That means acting as if nothing happened."

"How convenient," Marie snarled. The sneer was still frozen on her face. She sat down and worked to bring her rage under control.

He heaved a sigh. "You asked me a question, and I answered it to the best of my ability. I can't allow myself to feel. I would lose my grip on sanity." Troy stood. "You don't need anything from me." He nodded toward her computer. "You have access to all the records."

He walked toward the exit, certain he would never again talk to Marie Moretti. Troy paused at the door and turned back.

"I'm sorry. I can't change what I did or who I am just to make you happy." And with that, he walked out of her life.

10

Less than two weeks later, Chris Holcombe called Troy to his office at the construction site. When he arrived, he found Marie waiting.

Holcombe nodded toward her. "The lawyer says she needs to talk to you."

Troy lifted his hands, inviting her to speak.

Marie cleared her throat. "I am trying to work a plea deal for a client. He's not cooperating."

He shrugged.

"I can get him three to five, but he has to cooperate."

Troy raised his eyebrows and shrugged. Marie said, "He wants to talk to you. He says you are the only one he trusts."

"What's his name?"

"Jesús Rodrigo."

Troy pursed his lips and nodded. "Boss, I should go talk to Jesús. Can I have the rest of the day off?"

Neither Marie nor Troy had much to say on the way to the jail. Troy was led into a small conference room. Jesús Rodrigo sat handcuffed to the table that took up most of the room. He was pissed, but he softened when he looked up and saw his friend coming through the door.

Troy sat in the chair across the table from him. "What's up, bro?"

The man held up his cuffed hands and shook his head.

"They're sayin' you cut him up pretty bad," Troy observed.

"It was self-defense."

"You stabbed him thirteen or fourteen times?"

"He was tryin' t' stomp me."

"But when you cut him up that bad and come away with just a black eye and a busted lip, it looks like you meant to kill him."

The prisoner's lip curled. He looked toward the door and shook his head.

"The charge is murder two. You are looking at five years minimum."

"I ain't never been in trouble before."

"No fights? No drunk and disorderly?"

Jesús shot a savage look at Troy and turned back to the door.

Troy waited until he had the man's attention again. "They've got a dead body and a knife. His blood and your fingerprints are on the weapon." Troy leaned close to his friend. "They want you off the streets."

"I ain't doin' no time," Jesús said fiercely.

Troy grimaced. He sat back and folded his hands on the table. His voice was calm. "Your case looks like a slam dunk. Five years minimum."

Jesús stared directly into Troy's eyes, his face taut with determination. "I ain't gonna do no time."

Troy studied the ceiling. "I see." He returned his focus to his friend, who was still staring a hole through him. "What about Elvera?"

"What about her?" Jesús sneered. "They're tellin' me to forget her. She's gonna dump me. As soon as I'm sent away, she'll find somebody else."

"Yeah. I guess that's likely to happen." A smile played across Troy's face. "But you can find somebody else too."

"How?" Jesús demanded. "I'm gonna be in jail."

"Not forever."

The prisoner clenched his fists and scowled.

"You ever graduate from high school?"

"Naw, man. I had to support my family."

"Okay. This is an opportunity. Get your GED." Troy was upbeat. He was met with a sullen glare. He continued, "You're a plumber's helper, right?"

Jesús nodded.

"Okay, you need to get your license so you can be a real plumber."

"How? How am I gonna do that?"

"You get your GED. Then you get yourself a technical degree. Then you get into an apprenticeship program."

"All of that while I'm in jail." Jesús scoffed.

"You can do it if you put your mind to it," Troy urged. "You have to take responsibility for fixing this problem, Jesús. I'll help you any way I can, but you have to be the man."

The prisoner sneered. He shook his head.

"It's the only way. Rotting in jail is worse than dying. You have to have a plan for success when you get out, or you are going to end up back in there."

"I don't have to rot in jail."

Troy's eyebrows arched. "They aren't going to let you kill yourself," he warned. "That would look bad on their record." He leaned forward. His head and shoulders extended past his folded hands. He growled in a low voice, "And if you do succeed, it will kill your momma." He pulled back. His brow crinkled with concern. "What about your sister, Jeannie? And Alex? Do you want Alex to kill himself?"

Jesús's eyes widened. His mouth opened, but no words came out.

Troy proclaimed with absolute certainty, "That is what's going to happen if you don't sign this plea deal and do your time like a man."

* * *

Marie walked two steps behind Troy as they left the police station. His pace was brisk, but he stared down at the ground. His shoulders slumped as if the battle with Jesús Rodrigo had drained every ounce of his strength.

"Just drop me at the construction site," Troy mumbled as they climbed into her car.

Marie pulled into the traffic before asking, "Can I buy you dinner?"

Troy shook his head. "*No.*"

Marie did not catch the response. She didn't need to. He didn't seem to be in a social mood.

11

Over the next couple of months, Marie found excuses to meet with Troy. She would call him or stop by to discuss some case. She discovered that he never ate lunch but could be persuaded to have dinner with her. His father had died when he was a teen. His mother was a program manager at Goddard. She had worked and earned a degree while taking care of Troy and his sister after her husband passed away. His sister and her husband were rocks in his life. She taught high school math and science. He taught engineering at American University. Their support got him through prison, but he didn't see much of them. They were busy, and he had to get his life straightened out.

Troy had entered Georgetown to study law but switched to business in his sophomore year. Ironically, that was how he became friends with Adan Jackson and Cindy Smith. He ended up getting a degree in business management from the University of Maryland University College while in prison. He went on to complete a correspondence course in law. When Marie offered to help him get his license to practice law, Troy declined.

"Construction is a good occupation," he observed. "It's honest work. When you finish a job, you've made something people can use."

On a Saturday evening in late October, Marie drove to Troy's apartment and parked her car. They walked to a restaurant a few blocks away for dinner. The sidewalks were crowded with couples and groups enjoying a night on the town. National and international news was uniformly bad, so people talked about other things. Marie chattered about fashion and plays.

Troy was quiet. He knew how boring his work was to outsiders. Besides, he didn't like to discuss the people he worked with. Marie had some choice words for politicians and judges, but she wouldn't talk shop with Troy. Dinner wasn't much because neither of them was a big eater.

On the walk back to his apartment, Marie asked if he knew how to dance.

Troy squinted at her suspiciously and rocked his head thoughtfully. "I used to before I went to prison."

"There's a charity ball next Saturday evening. I am expected to show up."

His lips curled into a cockeyed smile. A silly grin spread across her face. "What does that have to do with me dancing?"

"I would like you to be my date."

He shook his head. "That would be awkward."

A poker-faced stare replaced her smile. She focused intense black eyes on him. "You didn't tell me that you were the leader of the gang."

The fury on his face sent a shiver of terror through Marie's body. "That isn't what happened," he roared. He stepped in front of her, his face inches from hers, blood vessels bulging. "I was not the leader. I was the fall guy."

She held her ground. "Court records identify you as the leader."

"That's a lie," he bellowed. "Adan Jackson set the whole thing up. He was obsessed with her porn videos."

"He got off."

"Because of the videos," the ex-con raged. "Once they were in evidence, he could claim he believed the sex was consensual. She knew what would happen if she had to take the stand," he seethed. His lip curled into a sneer. "Nobody wanted that trial."

People on the sidewalk were looking away and rushing past them. One man paused as if he was about to step in and break up the argument.

Troy took a deep breath and backed away. "I was already in jail. It was easy to pin it all on me." He stared savagely into her eyes for a full second. Then he snarled, "Fuck it."

He turned and started walking away. His body was rigid, his fists clenched.

"I know," Marie called. "I figured it out. I just needed to hear you say it."

Troy turned back to face her. The hurt and anger were palpable. "Why the fuck would you do something like that to me?"

She walked up to him and took his hands. "Now, I want to know: Are you the same man who raped that woman?"

"A dozen years in prison forced me to change," he croaked. "But I'm still Troy Mondale."

She shook her head and smiled hopefully. "I don't know any other man who could have talked to Jesús Rodrigo the way you did," Marie said in a firm voice. Her eyes focused on him in a stare that cut right through to his soul. "I don't know many men who would have even tried."

She ran her hand across his cheek and into his hair. "The Troy Mondale I know wouldn't attack a woman. He couldn't. That's not who he is."

"That's not a popular opinion."

"Eddy Wilson turned to you for help. Jesús Rodrigo demanded to talk to you. People know you're one of the good guys."

Troy took a deep breath and exhaled. He nodded. "Thanks. I appreciate that."

"So, you will accompany me to the dance?"

He grinned sardonically and pushed her hand away. "Let me think about it." Troy closed his eyes and shook his head as he turned to continue his walk.

"I need an answer now."

Troy stopped with his back to her. He stared into the distance as he ran a hand through his hair. When he turned to face her, his face was devoid of emotion, his voice flat. "All right."

* * *

After the dance, Troy accompanied Marie back to her place. She held his hand and led him to the apartment. He could feel a slight tug as she overcame his hesitation. The room was large and open. He felt cold and unwelcome as he stood just inside the threshold, looking around. A dining room was off to his left. A hallway on his right. A gray ceiling-to-floor blackout blind had been drawn across a window on the other side of the room. A large, expensive-looking oriental rug covered the floor.

She led him across the rug with its cascade of flowers and birds. A few steps from the hallway, she spun abruptly and crashed into him. Her arms wrapped around his waist. He hesitated. His hands slid down the silky red dress that fit her body like a second skin. She looked into his eyes and waited for his first kiss. Her mouth opened, inviting him in. When their tongues touched, an electric shock ran through his body.

She kicked off her shoes as she nuzzled his ear. "Can you help me out of this dress?"

A hot fire ignited in Troy's gut. It flared up his chest and engulfed his arms. He felt weak and shaky.

"Please," she urged.

He pinched the zipper and tugged. It slid down the curve of her back and halfway down her butt. Marie reached back and pushed his hand. Her skin was soft and warm. He let his hand slide up her back, feeling her ribs with his fingertips. When he reached her shoulder, he pushed tentatively against her dress. She slid one arm free. He crossed to the other shoulder and pushed slightly on the dress. Her other arm pulled free.

Marie shimmied the dress to the floor and stepped back. Her bra and thong didn't hide much. She let him take in the scenery while she unbuttoned his shirt and pushed it to the floor. She took his hand and dragged him into her bedroom.

Caresses and kisses led to peeling away what was left of their clothes. He was tentative at first. She coaxed him past the initial doubts. Troy experienced the naked passion of a lover for the first time in almost twenty years. She drew him into her bed and held him close as he probed. The dance of love built to fiery explosions, followed by blissful sleep.

They did not leave her bed until noon the next day.

Marie threw on a pink cotton robe and tied the sash at her waist, creating a plunging neckline that exposed her boobs. She started the coffee and eggs and cut up a grapefruit while Troy dressed.

When he stepped into the kitchenette, he said, "Wow."

She turned and smiled. Her cheeks reddened. "Ready for breakfast? I'm making an omelet."

"I'm ready for whatever you're serving."

Marie looked down at the skillet. She was smiling, but her cheeks were bright red. She poured two cups of coffee and put one on the table for Troy. Back at the stove, she turned the omelet before serving the grapefruit. When breakfast had been served and she had gotten settled, she sipped her coffee while she studied the man sitting across from her. "Are you really going to stay in construction?"

"I don't see why not. I'm happy with the situation."

"But you're wasting your talent."

"At least I'm not sitting in prison wasting my life."

She straightened and stared at him with intimidating intensity. She took a bite of her omelet and sipped her coffee. "You have talents that not many people possess. You are not putting them to good use in your present situation."

Troy put his elbow on the table and buried his face in his hand. He massaged his forehead, put the other elbow on the table, and clasped his hands. Returning her gaze, he said, "Desk jockeys don't understand construction. It's challenging." He took a bite of egg and chewed. "I can move up into management. I might even get a chance to build a skyscraper. I won't get opportunities like that as a lawyer."

"You could have your own law practice. Be your own boss. It would take some time and hard work, but I don't think it would be any harder than breaking into management at Tri-State."

He put a section of grapefruit in his mouth and crushed it. The cold, acidic juices filled his mouth with a refreshing sensation. "Why are you so determined to turn me into a lawyer?"

"You started out in law. Switched to business. Earned a business management degree and went back to law. What is it about law?"

His gaze drifted down to her chest. A devilish grin spread across her face. He sipped his coffee and watched her with unabashed pleasure, knowing there was nothing but her under that robe. He chuckled. "I think it's the challenge of putting the facts together and finding a winning argument."

Marie stretched her arms back, widening the plunging neckline and exposing more skin. "I like fighting the assholes who want to put guys like Eddy Wilson in jail. I love it when I can kick their butts."

He nodded and smiled appreciatively. "Superhero syndrome."

She pouted. "Is that a bad thing?"

"Not when you're fighting for my buddies and me."

Troy stood and walked around to where she sat. For a brief moment, he stood towering over her while she looked up expectantly. He grabbed one side of her robe and pulled. She came to her feet. The robe fell to the ground. She threw her arms around his neck and pulled him in for a long hungry kiss.

She stepped back. "No fair."

"What?"

"You're still dressed."

It took him fifteen seconds to shed his clothes.

As he pulled her in for another kiss, her hand slid across his rock-hard erection. "What's this?"

He scooped her up—one arm around her back the other under her butt—and headed down the hall to the bed.

Her legs wrapped around his waist. She giggled. "My breakfast."

Troy set her on the bed. She lay back and spread her legs while he climbed on top. They screwed long and hard before collapsing, huffing and puffing, on the bed. His head lay on her chest.

Marie stared at the ceiling, absently stroking his cheek. "I read somewhere that that was as good as a five-mile run." A few minutes later, she said, "I could get you some clients like Eddy and Jesús, except they would be paying clients."

Troy kissed her on the cheek. "I don't want to be a lawyer."

"I know, but there are lots of people out there who need someone to talk to. Someone with firsthand knowledge who can explain the system and give them advice."

"How many? How much would I charge? How would I find them?"

"If only we knew somebody who had a degree in business."

He pinched her butt. She jumped.

"Well," she said, "you got the degree. Did you learn anything?"

"Yes,"

"Prove it."

12

Troy's life was suddenly a mess. He had been working an obscure construction job while digging into the secrets of his archenemy, Adan Jackson. Marie Moretti came along and offered him a better deal. He wanted her, but he wasn't ready to give up on his mission.

He lived for months in a twilight zone. With Marie, he was working to make the world a better place. Without her, he was an ogre plotting the destruction of the handsome prince and the beautiful princess.

During those months, the couple's business plan developed into a business. Building a reputation and a clientele pushed them to their limits. Marie worked two jobs, one to provide steady income and one to create the future. Troy worked three. He stayed on the cleaning crew that gave him access to the America First computer system.

By April 2008, Mondale Legal Consulting Services was pulling in enough income to justify renting an office. Marie found a small one in a high-rise near George Washington University. Troy left his job at Tri-State and his room in Southwest D.C. He subleased an apartment on Connecticut Avenue in Adams Morgan, a trendy part of town popular with young professionals. His new place put him in easy walking distance of Mondale Consulting's office, Marie Moretti, and America First.

Troy and Marie spent more time together. They hung out in her condo or in his apartment on most weekends. The sex was good, and they enjoyed each other's company. But she clung to her independence, and he kept his secrets.

He was not going to let her know that he was hacking into a corporate computer system to get dirt on Adan Jackson. He did not want to tell her that he planned to destroy the man, no matter what the cost. Better to let Marie go on believing that he had emerged from prison ready to lead a noble life. Troy kept the truth, and Tom Jones, locked away in his apartment. When the two were together, he was the man she loved and who loved her.

Mondale Consulting provided unexpected opportunities. It had enough business to be self-supporting but not enough to keep him fully occupied. Much of the work was scheduled outside of regular business hours. He was teaching a seminar on prison systems one night a week at GWU. He could do his research and work on his writing anywhere as long as he had access to Wi-Fi. Troy could not have imagined such an arrangement when he left prison.

He upgraded to an iPad Pro. A table at a restaurant in Cap Gallery became his de facto place of business. Somedays, he didn't even bother showing up at the real office. Marie let it slide as long as the work was getting done.

* * *

One Friday evening, Troy took a walk along Connecticut Avenue. He happened upon the Il Mediterreano, a few blocks north of his apartment, and decided to give it a try. As he walked into the dining area searching for a table, he noticed a woman with light brown hair who brought back memories. She was engaged in a lively conversation with a group of women. When she turned her head so he could see her face, he froze.

It was Cindy Smith. Their eyes locked briefly before she went back to her friends as if nothing had happened. He realized she had not recognized him and continued past her to an empty table.

Troy came back a week later. He took a seat at a table in a corner where he could survey the room while he ate and perused a newspaper. Cindy was sitting with the same group of women. A man sitting alone on the other side of the dining area caught Troy's attention. He was going through a newspaper, but he would occasionally glance over at Cindy's group. Troy got a strange sensation in the pit of his stomach. He couldn't be sure, but he had a feeling Adan Jackson was stalking Cindy Smith.

He got together with Marie the following morning and stayed with her until Sunday afternoon. That was their usual arrangement. She had work to do, and he needed some alone time. After he left her place, he went back to his apartment and put on Tom Jones.

Cindy and the mystery man occupied Troy's thoughts as he trekked over to his job on the cleaning crew. The man was big. His hair was wrong, but even seated, he looked big enough to be Adan. On the other hand, Troy had no idea what his old college chum looked like these days.

That night, Troy found Adan's office and sat at his desk. It was so neat that Troy wondered if Adan did any work there. The only picture on the desk was a family photo that showed Adan and Beau as teenagers. There were no pictures of women.

Troy decided he would have to stake out America First and wait for Adan to show up. He got to the mall before seven on Monday morning. He found a seat where he could observe people taking the elevator up to the America First offices. Cindy showed up a short time later and took the elevator to the sixth floor. That was a shock. She was working in the same office as the man who led the gang rape. *Does she know he works there?*

Adan arrived just before ten and went straight to the seventh floor. Troy recognized him immediately. He had matured and put on some weight, but he was still trim and athletic. His blond hair was still cut short.

Adan went out for lunch at noon. He left shortly after four in the afternoon. Cindy skipped lunch and stayed until five.

Troy watched the elevator every day that week. Cindy had a fixed schedule. Adan's arrivals and departures varied from day to day.

Over that week, Troy developed a new character so he could get close to Cindy and her group: an old man with long, unkempt gray hair, a beard, and a mustache. The next time Troy went to the Il Mediterreano, he wore the costume. Cindy paid no attention to him as he moved to a table directly behind her and took a seat. Troy ate his dinner and read his newspaper.

He listened. It was difficult at dinner time, but he had gotten pretty good at picking up the threads of a conversation while he was in prison. The women were talking about their jobs and their families.

That September, Troy took advantage of an opportunity to purchase his own condo. It was in Adams Morgan, a few blocks from the apartment. He was still close to Marie, the office, and America First.

A couple of months later, a slender brunette with rosy cheeks and bright, penetrating brown eyes walked up to the elevator while Troy was waiting for a ride. He recognized her as part of Cindy's group and looked away in panic. But she positioned herself directly in front of him and smiled brightly. "Hi. I'm Ellen."

He forced a smile and extended his hand. "Troy."

"I used to see you at the restaurant."

He stared at her in mute horror. He thought of himself as invisible.

Ellen continued, "The Il Mediterreano right down the street. A group of us get together there every Friday night."

"Oh!" Troy fumbled for words. "Yes. It's a nice place."

"But you haven't been there in a while."

He frowned. "No. The project I'm working on keeps me busy. I eat in and work most nights."

They chatted. She was a lawyer. He told her that he was in business development.

Ellen handed him a business card as he was getting off on the third floor. "If you need a lawyer, give me a call."

He paused to observe the elevator's progress. It stopped on the fifth floor.

Troy shuffled back to his condo. He walked over to the window without bothering to turn on the lights. He stood watching the traffic on the street below. It had not occurred to him that anyone noticed him. Ellen not only took notice; she had cataloged him. His old man costume seemed to have fooled her. At least she acted as if she hadn't realized he had sat with his chair pushed close to Cindy on a few Friday nights.

13

Things were not going the way Troy had hoped. He was struggling. Mondale Consulting was no longer an exciting new challenge. He still made a good impression both in group presentations and one-on-one meetings. His students in the GWU course were enthusiastic.

Troy's obsession with Adan and Cindy was the problem. It was taking over his life. Getting the goods on Adan had become his top priority, but he wasn't finding anything. That depressed him. He sat for hours, listlessly staring at his tablet. He took long walks. He killed time scanning through papers and magazines.

Marie made her move on a snowy Sunday evening in December. The weekend had been great. The weather outside was abominable, and yet Troy was getting ready to take off.

She asked, "Where are you going?".

"Back to my place."

"Why don't you stay here with me?"

He scowled at her. "I've got something to do."

"What is that?" Her voice was quiet but firm.

"It's a special project."

She tilted her head. “A secret project?” He didn’t answer. She walked over to him, reached up, brushed her hand across his cheek, and let it rest on his neck. “You can’t keep secrets from me, Troy Mondale. Don’t try.”

“It’s just something I have to take care of.”

“If you think you are going to bring down Adan Jackson, forget it.”

His head jerked back.

“Hacking is a federal crime. That means the federal prison system instead of the state pen.”

“What are you talking about?”

“The only way you can get evidence of Jackson’s financial misconduct is to hack into America First’s computer system. That is a federal crime.”

He gently pushed her hand away and started toward the door.

“I am your lawyer,” she called after him. “Much more importantly, I love you. I will never betray you. But,” she warned, “I am not going to visit you in prison.”

He turned to face her. There was a fierce, angry look in his eyes. “You don’t know how much this hurts. You have no idea how this feels.”

“I wasn’t shafted, and I didn’t spend a dozen years behind bars,” Marie acknowledged. “But you are closer to me than anyone has ever been.” She raised her right hand to her chest. “I feel what you feel. I hate Adan Jackson. He disgusts me.”

“Do you really?” he sneered. “Do you feel a raging need to cut up his face?”

“I don’t care enough about him or his face to risk jail. I care about you.”

Troy stabbed his fingers into his chest. “He tried to destroy me.”

“He failed,” Marie retorted. “But you’re going to finish the job. The sad part is that he doesn’t care. You don’t matter to him.”

“He’s important to me,” Troy shot back. “I want him brought to justice.”

“Too late. He got away with it.” She stepped over to Troy and leaned in until her nose touched his. The fury in her eyes evoked terror. Troy gulped. “Get this through your thick skull. He is not important. He is, and always will be, a piece of shit.”

He pulled away and turned back to the door.

Marie closed her eyes and shook her head. “Do what you have to do.”

He walked out the door.

Before it slammed shut, she yelled, “I will not follow you to prison.”

He rested for a couple of hours and changed into Tom Jones before reporting to the cleaning job at Cap Gallery. It was an easy one. The work was much like what he had done in prison. Now he got paid to do it. The position gave Troy opportunities to collect information on Adan Jackson.

This night Troy snuck off to a computer terminal at around one in the morning. He intended to log in and pull up Adan’s records from the last week.

Instead, he sat and stared. He thought about Marie. He thought about what he was trying to do, and he realized it would never work. If anyone actually paid attention to what he was saying, they would figure out that he had collected the information illegally. He would be sent back to prison, and that would be the end of everything.

He got up, finished his shift, and went back to his condo.

Troy quit the cleaning job. Marie never brought the matter up again.

Mondale Legal Consulting Services prospered. Troy's reputation soared. Marie continued to work as a public defender because that was what she loved to do. Troy would occasionally don his old man costume and find a seat at Il Mediterreano, where he could listen in on Cindy and her friends.

14

Late on Monday morning, three days after the meeting with Detective Twomey, Eve was at her desk working on her blog. She was in a zone. The words flowed straight from her heart to the computer screen. Then her phone chimed.

She answered in a low, sultry voice, "Hi, baby, what's up?"

Sergeant Jack Edwards rumbled, "I need some help, Eve."

She sketched the stony face, broad forehead, intense black eyes, and pouting lips on the pad next to her laptop. "Oooh-kay."

"Ed and I have been talking about Cindy Foster's situation. He suggested that we make contact with Troy Mondale and get a read on his plans."

Eve rolled her eyes. "You want me to track him down and have a chat with him?"

"I thought you could do a story on his time in prison and what he's been doing since he got out."

Eve shuddered. "Another undercover assignment?"

"It's not like that," Jack sputtered. He paused then continued in his laid-back tone. "I just need to get a fix on him, and I don't want to send my detectives."

"Isn't that their job?"

"I have no reason to believe he is doing anything illegal. Cindy Foster hasn't filed a complaint. She hired a private detective to deal with Adan Jackson. She didn't mention Mondale."

"Then there's no reason to check up on him. Right?" Eve sketched herself pulling her hair out.

Jack continued to soothe her. "He's been out of prison for four years. No arrests, but I don't know what he has been up to."

"That shouldn't be hard to figure out."

"He worked for a construction company when he first got out. Now he has a consulting business."

"Consulting?"

"Mondale Legal Consulting Services."

"What's his angle?" she wondered out loud.

"Good question," Jack said. "I need someone to get me a good answer."

Eve rolled her eyes. She drew a meteor crashing down on her head. "Jack, I'm in the middle of a project. I don't want to take on another one."

"That thing about Obama's women?"

She curled her lip and shook her head. "Yes, I am writing about the women who are getting top posts in the Obama administration."

"This is a better story," Jack urged. "Besides, you don't have a deadline. I need answers now."

Eve scowled as she penned a large, thick question mark on her pad. "Who's going to buy this story?"

"That's your department. You're the writer."

"How about a hint. Where do I start looking?"

"I would like you to do this on your own," Jack answered. "This isn't police work. All I want is your take on him. As a favor to a friend."

She clamped her lips together and looked up at the ceiling. She began to count. At three, she coaxed, "Well, could you at least tell me what you know? As a favor to a friend."

"He worked for Tri-State Construction when he got out. He no longer works there, but he left on good terms. I can't get anything more without a warrant."

"So, he left to start his consulting business," she suggested.

"Probably."

"Is that all you wanted?" She asked, sounding miffed.

Jack chuckled. "I love you."

She drew a heart around his face and asked wistfully, "See you tonight?"

"Probably," he said and hung up.

Eve sat for a full minute, elbow on her desk, chin on her hand as she rehashed the conversation. Her attention drifted to the tiny room that served as her office. *The Wonderful World of Disney* was on display all around her. It had been her room as a child. Now it was her place of business as an adult, a published author, and the mother of two. So much for success.

She walked over to the window and looked out. The stand of trees where she played as a child was gone. A neighbor had moved into the house that replaced the trees. He had built a privacy fence around his yard. Her mother was putting in a flower bed and a vegetable plot. The backyard was still a playground for the time being. But her brother's children would be too big for the swings and the slide in a few years.

Eve turned back to the desk. Her gaze came to rest on her phone. She shook her head as a bitter smile crept across her face. "What the hell is this, Jack? You call me whenever you need a civilian to do your dirty work?"

The sound of her voice echoing in the stillness shocked her. The big old house felt like a mausoleum. Her children were in school. Her mom was in court with a client. She should be writing. *Would be* writing if Jack hadn't called to say he needed her help.

Eve could track down a Troy Mondale who was somewhere in D.C. doing something. But she needed to talk to somebody. She retrieved her phone and called Nickey as she paced back to the window.

The detective answered with, "Hi, sweetie. What's up?"

Eve sulked, "Jack just dumped an assignment in my lap. I could use some help."

"Sure. What do you need?" The woman was too damn cheerful.

Eve went back to her seat. She sketched a villain on her pad. "I have to find a guy named Troy Mondale and set up an interview."

"Detective Twomey's Troy Mondale?" Nickey whooped.

Eve sketched Twomey on her pad. "He and Jack talked this morning. They decided that somebody should check up on Mr. Mondale."

"Give me a few minutes. I'll call you back."

Eve went back to the piece she was working on. It was a blog post about Secretary of Homeland Security

Janet Napolitano. Nickey gave her just enough time to add a paragraph. "That was quick," Eve sighed.

"It was easy," Nickey said triumphantly. "Mr. Mondale is on the National Sex Offender Registry. He has a condo in the Kennedy-Warren building on Connecticut Avenue. He also has a website that lists the address of his consulting business. His office is in a high-rise near GWU."

"That's pretty swanky for a guy who just got out of prison," Eve observed.

"Very, very. Our boy must be doing okay. I'm sending you the information now."

Eve watched as the text message popped up. Nickey had included a cell phone number. "Got it. Thanks a lot."

"What's the real problem?" Nickey prodded.

Eve sighed. "It feels like he's using me."

"I don't think so," her friend countered. "Jack isn't the kind of guy who uses people."

"I know, but it still bothers me."

"Has anything changed?"

"He's stopped drinking." Eve laughed.

"You're the best thing that ever happened to him," Nickey assured her. "He's trying to make you part of his life."

"When it's convenient."

"He's a workaholic."

"He could do better than calling me with an assignment like I work for him." Eve pouted.

"You had a guy who doted on you," Nickey pointed out. "You dumped him."

"I didn't dump him."

"You put your career ahead of your marriage."

"I didn't dump him," Eve insisted.

"You went too far, and you knew what to expect."

Eve grimaced. Her assignment had been to get an inside look at the sex industry. She went all the way in and worked as an escort for a few weeks. Her marriage didn't survive. But she met Jack. Pluses and minuses. She wiped a tear from her cheek. "I suppose."

"I'm right, and you know it," Nickey said. "I've got to get back to work. Let me know how the interview turns out."

15

The phone number provided by Nickey was the logical place to start. Call the guy and set up the interview. Instead, Eve went downstairs for a cup of coffee. She returned with a glass of pinot noir. Her attention flitted from scene to scene on the wallpaper. *Question: Would you rather be Cinderella or Snow White?*

She sipped the wine. *Answer: Belle.*

Eve picked up her phone and called Troy Mondale. He sounded pleasant on the phone, but he was not interested in doing an interview. She did get him to agree to meet her at his office on Wednesday at 11:30.

Research and prep for the meeting interrupted her focus on the Obama women over the next day and a half. A newspaper story from December 1993 mentioned the rape. It said Mondale received a fifteen-year sentence for assaulting a woman at a party. Others involved in the incident had not been charged. The writer knew how to work around troublesome facts. Gang rape wasn't even suggested. The victim was not mentioned, and Georgetown got away scot-free.

Mondale's website listed Troy and a lawyer named Marie Moretti as principals in the company. It gave a brief biographical sketch of each. He graduated from Bowie HS before starting college at Georgetown. His college career was cut short in his sophomore year because he raped a classmate during a frat party. He spent the next twelve years in prison. He kept out of trouble and completed his college education while serving his sentence. After prison, he worked for a construction company, where he discovered that there was a need for someone with his background to help people understand prison. He and Marie, a public defender, met through their work for indigent offenders. They decided to start Mondale Legal Consulting Services to fill what they saw as an information void.

Eve brushed off the official bio. It was a marketing pitch to potential clients who found themselves in serious legal trouble. It gave her little insight into the man she was going to interview.

She entered the offices of Mondale Consulting at 11:33. Troy looked up from his work and stared in disbelief at the woman in the doorway. Shock gave way to a devilish grin.

"I know you," he crowed.

Eve answered his stare with a cold, hard gaze and then turned to survey the room. She had mastered the art of dealing with men like him. The sparsely furnished office had beige walls and gray industrial-grade carpeting. A couple of filing cabinets sat along the wall behind Mondale. A small table with a coffee maker and cups was stationed to the right of the door. To the left, a sofa and a magazine-covered coffee table. A conference table sat across from the couch. No bathroom; probably had to use the one in the hall.

She turned her attention to Mondale. A picture flashed into her consciousness. Eight men were sitting around a table in the Tahiti. One of them was a red-headed Irishman: tousled hair, sideburns flowing down to a short, well-manicured beard and mustache, brilliant blue eyes, and a roguish smile.

That man sat grinning at her from across the room. The beard and mustache were gone, but there was no mistaking the eyes. His forehead and shoulders were broad, but his body was lean. He must be one of those irritating people who never put on weight.

Eve shook her head. "No, we've never met." There was no hint of emotion in her voice.

He continued to study her from behind his desk. She wore a loose white blouse, black slacks, and loafers. The clothes didn't seem to matter. He ogled her unapologetically as if she was naked. There was no hint of shame. She could feel heat rising under her skin.

"I know," he cried exuberantly. "You're the dancer. I was at a friend's bachelor party. It was at the Tahiti. You came over to sit with us after your number."

Eve blushed.

Troy responded with a broad smile. "It was about a year ago, but you're not someone I would forget."

She conceded, "I worked there for a few weeks last year."

"You said you were a writer working on a story," Troy objected.

"I am."

"Writer by day. Stripper by night?" he taunted.

"I was researching a different story last year," Eve retorted.

He closed his eyes and put a finger across his lips. His eyes popped open. He wagged his finger at her. "Eve McMann. The story about prostitution. Is that the one?"

"Yes, I wrote that series."

"Ah. Great," Troy said. "This is good."

Her head jerked back. "It is?"

"I wasn't sure I wanted to give this interview. I'm leery of strangers. But you're not a stranger, and I like your writing."

Eve smiled appreciatively. "Thank you."

"What do you want to talk about?"

She pulled a chair over to his desk and took out her notepad. "Why don't we start with what you do here?"

"Not much. I talk to people. Most of them are facing jail for the first time," Troy explained. His eyes focused directly on hers, but his hands fidgeted. "We go over their legal situation. I try to help them understand the system." He paused to lean back in his chair. "The first meeting is dedicated to giving them an overview and some general advice. After that, we cover different aspects of prison life: facilities, staff, prison politics, behavioral norms." He stroked his chin. "I spend a lot of time on opportunities. My primary goal is to get them focused on coming out of prison ready to move back into civilian life."

"Your company is Mondale Legal Consulting Services. Are you a lawyer?"

Troy hesitated. "No."

Eve leaned forward and looked directly into his eyes. "Do you have any legal expertise?"

He winced. "Most of my knowledge comes from helping others with their legal problems. But I did complete a correspondence course in law while I was incarcerated." He smiled. "I also got to know real lawyers who were in prison with me. They taught me a lot." Troy paused for Eve to finish making notes and look up at him. "My partner is a lawyer. She has been practicing law for the last ten years. My mentor had his own private practice for twenty years before he became a full-time professor of law at George Washington University." He looked at Eve with extreme sadness and shook his head. "My background makes it difficult for me to get a license to practice law."

Her eyebrows arched.

Troy chuckled. "Com'on. You're not going to try to make me believe that you don't know about the rape, are you?"

"Of course, I'm aware of it," Eve retorted. "You mentioned it in your biography. I didn't realize it would still be a problem."

He laughed. It was a hollow, forced outburst. "I am a registered sex offender. That will always be a problem."

The response shocked her. It took her a minute to decide that Troy must be frustrated by the situation. "Can you tell me about the rape?"

"I was a sophomore at Georgetown. There was a freshman girl who had shown some strange sexual proclivities. A friend of mine knew her. He said she was looking for some excitement and would be up for a gang bang. I went along with it." Troy looked off into the distance. His face twisted in revulsion as if he was reliving the event. He shook his head. "But it was a sick game. My friend lured the bunch of us into a nightmare. He lied to me about her willingness. He convinced the girl that she was joining him for normal sack time." Troy was still staring off into the distance as if watching the events unfold. He shuddered. "I participated at first. When I realized what was really going on, I walked away." His voice cracked. He got up and paced in a circle with his hands locked against the back of his neck.

"Are you okay?" Eve asked.

Troy stopped pacing. "No." He turned to face Eve and shook his head. He continued his story in a choked voice. "When the police showed up a couple of days later, I admitted to everything." He returned to his seat but continued standing. He clamped large, powerful hands on the back of the chair to steady himself. "After I got a lawyer, I was offered an opportunity to withdraw my confession. That was a pointless gesture. I was guilty. They knew it, and I knew it. I wrote out an apology. The judge sentenced me to fifteen years, and off I went to prison."

"What happened when you got to prison?" Eve asked.

He ran his hands through his hair as he looked up at the ceiling. He sucked in a deep breath and let the air out in a long sigh. "Not today," he said in a husky voice. "Make another appointment, and we'll talk some more."

Eve paused on her way out the door. She asked casually, "Have you spoken to Cindy since you got out?"

Troy's jaw tightened. He studied her suspiciously. Finally, he said in a measured tone, "No. Nothing good could come from that. I will not be contacting her ever again."

16

When Ellen Magee called another meeting to talk about progress, Nickey saw an opportunity to tell her friend about Troy Mondale. She left early so she could have a few minutes alone with the lawyer to let her know that Cindy's third assailant was her neighbor. He had a condo two floors below her.

Cindy arrived ahead of the detective. She was entering the building with a bag of breakfast goodies from the Dunkin' Donuts a couple of blocks away when Nickey spotted her. By the time she signed in at the front desk, Cindy was halfway to the elevators. A man was approaching them on his way out of the building. He was looking down, as if deep in thought.

It was Mondale. Nickey recognized him from the picture on the sex offender registry. He wore a gray T-shirt and jeans. His shoes were inexpensive outdoor fare: soft black uppers and thick soles for comfortable walking. He crossed the corridor rapidly, even though he was not hurrying.

The detective discreetly watched to see what would happen when the two of them ran into each other.

Cindy strode across the atrium with single-minded determination. She did not seem to notice her old nemesis. Troy glanced sideways at her as she hurried by him on her way to the elevator.

A moment later, as Troy approached Nickey, he raised his head and briefly fixed his intense blue eyes on her. He passed without breaking stride. But she was sure he had registered her interest.

By the time she reached Ellen's condo, Nickey had decided against telling her friend about Troy. Best to let sleeping dogs lie. There was no need to make this case more complicated.

Inside the apartment, Cindy had settled at the end of the breakfast bar next to the wall. She had a cup of coffee and a plain doughnut. Her doughnut bobbed as she ranted about Adan's behavior. Cindy paused and nodded in Nickey's direction but continued listing Adan's daily assaults on her. When her wrath had run its course, she turned her attention to the detective. "Have you made any progress?"

Nickey was behind the counter, helping herself to a cup of coffee. She set the pot down and turned to her client. "A little. I have a contact who may know him."

"And…?"

Nickey scowled. "I'll get in touch with him to see if he can introduce me to Adan."

"How long will that take?" Cindy demanded.

"Not long. But I need leverage."

"Just tell him to back off or else," Cindy snapped.

The detective cocked her head. "Or else what?"

Cindy turned to Ellen for help. The lawyer blushed and choked on a bite of doughnut. She asked, "What are you looking for?"

Nickey's eyes opened wide in disbelief. She looked at her friend and then at her client. "Something to offset a collection of damning porn videos."

Ellen swallowed. "Can you be more specific?"

Nickey came around to the front of the breakfast bar and picked up a chocolate doughnut. She took a seat on the barstool at the end, opposite Cindy. Her gaze focused on her client. She finished a bite of her doughnut and turned toward Ellen. "Misconduct. Is he embezzling or overcharging clients?"

Ellen tapped her lips and scowled. "Why would he do that?"

Nickey smirked. "Adan Jackson comes from wealth. He believes he's entitled." She nodded toward Cindy. "And he led a gang rape on a fellow student."

Cindy snapped to attention. "Troy Mondale was the leader. He charged into the room and said, 'Let's go,' or something like that. Adan and Beau grabbed me and held me down. Troy pulled my pants down. Then he fucked me." Cindy's features twisted in fury. Her voice was rising. "He forced himself on me." She stepped toward Nickey with her teeth bared. "When he was finished, he said, 'You'll keep this to yourself if you know what's good for you.' Then he just walked out. Beau and Adan followed him."

Nickey recoiled. She slid from her stool and walked over to the window. *Walked out just like that? Bullshit. They all fucked you. It was a gang rape.*

She stood looking out onto the traffic below. She had blown that exchange, but at least she hadn't said anything about Mondale. They had no idea that he was being interviewed by her friend, Eve. That could not be shared right now. The focus had to be on Adan.

When Nickey had regained her composure, she turned back to look at her client. "How did you end up in that room?"

Cindy looked as if she had been slapped. Her mouth dropped open. She started to speak a couple of times but caught herself before any words came out. Finally, she said, "We were at a party in a frat house. We had been drinking, and Adan was getting frisky. He said he could get us a room upstairs where nobody would bother us." She shrugged and looked down at her coffee. "I liked him. He was hot."

Nickey walked back to the breakfast bar. She stopped in front of her client, who was staring down at the floor. The detective put a hand on her shoulder. Cindy raised her head. Her mouth clamped shut in grim determination. Her eyes burning with hurt and anger.

"Is it possible that Adan set the whole thing up?" Nickey asked.

The stricken woman shook her head but said nothing.

Ellen demanded, "Why the fuck are you defending him? He's going out of his way to make your life miserable."

Cindy ran her fingers through her hair. She looked down at Ellen's feet. Her jaw muscles twitched. Tears were glistening in her eyes when she looked up to face Ellen. "I don't know. It just seemed like Troy was running the whole thing."

"I guess it doesn't matter," Nickey intervened. "Here's the situation: Adan has leverage over you. He has or knows about the porn videos. You need leverage over him."

"What kind of leverage?" Cindy asked.

"Something that could get him fired and possibly send him to jail. Anything that will make him think long and hard before he brings up those videos."

"How do we get that?" Cindy whimpered. Her eyes were closed. She knew what the answer was going to be.

"Our best bet will be his financial records."

Ellen shook her head. "That's not a good idea."

"It's all we've got," Nickey countered.

"But Cindy could get fired."

"Or she can continue to live in fear and misery."

"I'll do it," Cindy snapped.

They munched and sipped while they tossed around ideas. Gradually a plan began to form.

Cindy took the lead. "They are preparing for an audit. They need help reviewing the records. I can get on the review team. That will give me an excuse to go over Adan's records."

"What if they assign you something else?" Ellen challenged.

Cindy rolled her eyes and shook her head while silently mouthing some response. "Just tell me what I'm supposed to look for," she huffed.

"Billing," Nickey said. "Is he charging time to clients or accounts that he is not servicing? Expenses. Is he padding his expenses?"

"How will she know if he's padding his expenses?" Ellen demanded.

"She'll have to bring the files back here so we can study them," Nickey said dismissively. Then she added, "But there will be patterns. He will either do things habitually or say he does them habitually. We'll start there."

Cindy grumbled, "I've reviewed my share of expense reports."

They went over what records they expected to find. Nickey got Cindy to tell them everything she could about Adan and his habits. Ellen scheduled a meeting in one week to review the situation. She did not want her friend to go too long without supervision.

17

Nickey Arnold joined the Marines because of a hundred-dollar bet. She had just graduated from high school. The tough, demanding, devil-dog culture suited her well. Her fellow Leathernecks trained to be the best and expected to be winners in every situation. Earning their approval was a major accomplishment.

She chose the military police on a whim. It took her two years to work her way into investigations. Nickey was a sergeant by the time she completed her four-year enlistment.

After the Marines, Nickey earned a degree in criminal justice from George Mason University. She worked part-time for a private investigator named Craig Foley to help pay her way through college. After graduation from GMU, Nickey entered the police academy. But she clashed with instructors and fellow students. When she got an offer to join Craig full time, she dropped out of the Academy to become a private investigator.

Nickey found her niche as a hired gun for attorneys in D.C. and Baltimore. She specialized in divorce cases. Her main job was to dig up dirt in support of a client's case. She was not above creating the dirt when necessary. In her view, the men were dirty. She was just letting them give her the proof. In Ellen Magee's words, Nickey was "taking care of the garbage."

She had collected information on well over a hundred men in her brief career as a private investigator. Her reports started with who the man was sleeping with, how much he was worth, and other divorce-related data. She also collected tidbits about interests, hobbies, quirks, friends, and acquaintances. When Nickey searched her database for Adan Jackson, she discovered he had been friendly with one of her targets from a divorce case a couple of years earlier.

The man was Jacob Andrej Kovacs. He had had a string of affairs that went on for pages and included men and minors. His wife sued for divorce because she had found a new lover who wasn't willing to share her. Jake was a shipping magnate, and a multimillionaire even after the divorce settlement.

"Hi, Jake, it's me, Nickey," she said when he answered his phone.

"Is it Nickey or Natalie?" Jake growled.

"Don't be like that," she purred. "You're better off without her. She was a lying, cheating bitch."

"Who took me for ten million."

"She was your wife for twenty years, Jake. She deserved something."

"What do you want?"

"Now we're talking." Nickey laughed. "I'm interested in meeting a friend of yours, Adan Jackson."

"I don't know him that well, and I like you too much to introduce you to him."

"Sounds like my kinda man."

"Seriously. This guy hurts people just for the fun of it. He's what you call a sadist."

"But you two are friends."

"His family has money. We've bumped into each other at social gatherings."

"You're sure?" Nickey sounded skeptical. "Didn't the two of you hire a dozen whores and have a contest to see who had the most stamina?"

"That's an exaggeration."

"So, you're more than just casual acquaintances."

"Which is why I could not in good conscience introduce you to him."

"I have to talk to him, Jake," Nickey insisted.

Jake sighed. "There's a get-together next week. He'll be there."

"Are you going?"

"I don't plan to go." He sounded weary.

"But you could go and take me," Nickey urged.

After a long pause, Jake conceded, "I suppose I could."

"Come on, Jake. I need to meet Adan Jackson." Silence. Nickey waited. Then she said, "Are you still there?"

"I'm thinking."

"Does that mean you'll take me to this get-together?"

He paused again before replying ominously, "There is one condition."

"What's that, Jake?"

"It's a rape club. You go as my date, and I get to rape you."

Nickey blew air out through her pursed lips. "How bad is that going to be?"

"Nothing you can't handle," Jake said quietly. "But you better put on a good show."

"Text me the details. I'll see you next week," Nickey said and hung up.

18

When Eve showed up for her second meeting with Troy, he had company. He got up from his seat at the small circular work table and gestured toward Eve. "Marie, this is Eve MacMahon."

Marie got up from her seat behind the desk.

Troy gestured in her direction. "Eve, this is my lawyer, Marie Moretti."

The woman had an olive complexion. Her straight, black hair was tapered along her neck. She was five and a half feet tall with the boxy frame of an athlete.

"It's a pleasure to meet you, Marie," Eve said as they shook hands.

"I hope you don't mind if Marie sits in on this discussion," Troy said.

"Not at all." *But why would you need a lawyer for this interview?*

He indicated a seat at the table. "Please."

Eve walked over and sat down. Marie returned to her work.

Troy sat and asked, "Where were we?"

"I believe you were going to tell me about your experiences in prison."

"Oh yeah. But could you tell me again why you want to write about this stuff and how you found me?"

"I don't recall how I came across your name. Someone told me a little about you. When I followed up, I decided your story was a good one."

"Someone?" Troy said skeptically.

Eve frowned. "People give me story ideas all the time. I jot them down. When I need something, I look through the ideas file for one that appeals to me."

"But you write down who gave you the idea, don't you?"

Her eyes narrowed. She pursed her lips. "I can't tell you who gave me the idea at the moment," she said slowly. "I didn't think that would be an issue."

Marie interjected, "Troy was a little taken back by your question about Cindy."

Eve shrugged. "What about it?"

"How did you know her name was Cindy, and why would you ask if I was trying to get in touch with her?"

Eve's head jerked back. "What is this about? Her name came up when I was doing my background research." She flipped through her notebook. When she found what she was looking for, she ran her finger down the page and stopped on a note. "You said that you wrote her an apology before you went to prison. I just wondered if you were trying to reach out to her now that you are out."

Troy looked over at Marie. She shrugged and tilted her head. "That's a bad idea, if you think about it." He heaved a sigh. "She was hurt physically and emotionally. I am always going to be the asshole who did it to her. Nothing I say is going to change that. It's best if I just stay out of her life."

Eve made a note on her pad. "Did you know her at the time of the rape?"

"I was in a couple of classes with her. I knew her well enough to say hi when we met in the corridor."

Eve scanned her notes again. "You were a sophomore, and she was a freshman?"

He nodded. "I switched majors after my freshman year and had to go back and take some core business courses."

Eve looked up at him without raising her head. Her lips were pressed together in a tight line as she considered her next question. "Did you know about her sexual proclivities?"

His jaw tightened. He glared at Eve.

She quickly retracted, "I'm sorry. I didn't mean to push. Why don't we move on to prison?"

He took a deep breath and relaxed. "You sound like a lawyer."

"I grew up with lawyers. Some of it rubbed off."

Marie asked, "Who?"

"My mother and father were lawyers. My brothers are lawyers, and my sister teaches law. Cases were often discussed at the dinner table."

"Do they practice in this area?" Marie asked.

"Ted is a JAG officer. Bill is a public defender in D.C."

"MacMahon? Bill MacMahon?" Marie shook her head. "I don't know him."

Eve gave her a quick smile. *You will by this time tomorrow, won't you?* She turned to Troy. "Can we talk about prison a little bit?"

"The answer to your earlier question is that a friend of mine came across some videos that she had made. He showed them to me."

Eve flipped through her notes. "This was the friend who talked you into joining him and then lured Cindy into the room?"

"Yes."

"There were two brothers, Adan and Beauregard Jackson."

"Adan was the guy pushing the idea," Troy said in a low, angry tone. "Beau was just a kid. He shouldn't have even been at the frat house that night."

"How did he get in?"

"He was with Adan, who generally got whatever he wanted. Besides, Beau was big for fifteen. He was as big as Adan. Six feet and one hundred and sixty pounds."

Eve looked at her notes. "You said that at some point you realized what was really going on and walked away."

Troy nodded. "She wasn't faking it. She was terrified." His nose scrunched up as if he had just caught a terrible stench. A shiver ran through his body. "It was sickening. I had to get out of the room."

Eve paused for him to calm down. "Then the police tracked you down? I guess she told them what happened."

Marie got up and walked out of the office without saying a word. Eve watched her leave. *Girlfriend. She can't handle this.*

Troy ignored Marie and went on with his story. "Beau followed me out of the room and pinned me against the wall. He told me to keep my mouth shut or else. I could hear Adan telling her to keep her mouth shut. I was too scared to do anything. I wasn't about to go up against a kid like Beau Jackson." He shook his head and sighed. "I went home, thinking it would all go away. A few days later, some cops showed up and told me I was in trouble so I had better cooperate. I told them everything."

Eve jotted some notes and looked up at Troy. "Then you got a court-appointed attorney, but he wasn't much help."

He stood and took a couple of steps toward the middle of the room. "His hands were tied. The DA had all the evidence he needed to put me away, and I wasn't going to fight it. The attorney said he could try to get my confession thrown out." He shook his head. "I couldn't see how that would help. It didn't look like I was going to be able to make bail." He shrugged. "My best option was to take an early plea deal."

She scribbled more notes. "So, you signed the deal, and they shipped you off to prison. Were you scared?"

Troy paced to the far end of the room with his head down. He turned back to Eve and shook off some thoughts. "It all happened so fast I didn't have time to think about it. I started getting scared when they chained me up and put me on the bus for the ride from city jail to the state pen."

A terrible feeling of helplessness swept over Eve. She sketched a picture of Troy behind bars. When she had regained some control, she asked in a husky voice, "Did you have any idea at all what you were getting into?"

"I shared a cell with an old-timer in the detention center. He had been in and out of prison half his life.

He was going back because of a parole violation. He did his best to educate me."

His phone rang.

Marie must have heard it because she stepped back inside.

Troy listened. He said a couple of times, "I'll be right over." He ended the conversation with a firm, "I'm leaving right now. I will be there in thirty minutes."

He hung up and turned to Eve. "I have to go. We can pick this up later." He looked over at Marie and asked, "Are you coming?"

She nodded. The two of them walked out without waiting for Eve to finish packing.

Eve walked around the sparsely furnished office. Two certificates hung on the wall behind Troy's desk. A bachelor's degree in business management from the University of Maryland University College and a law degree from the Hollywood School of Law. A photo showed an older woman in her fifties or sixties. She was with a man and a woman about Troy's age. Next to it was a picture of Marie and then a profile picture of a young Troy Mondale. *Mug shot.*

Eve felt tears welling up. She took her things and walked out of the door, shut it, and checked to make sure it was locked.

19

Ellen's follow-up meeting and progress check came on the last Saturday in May. It had been four weeks since the incident at the Il Mediterreano.

She opened the door and invited Nickey in as soon as she arrived. "Help yourself to the coffee. The Danish is in the living room."

Cindy sat in a chair at the far end of the coffee table with her arms folded across her chest. She stared unblinkingly at Nickey. Her eyes followed the detective as she poured herself a cup of coffee and came into the living room. Nickey ignored her.

A couple of piles of paper rested on the table between Cindy and the Danish. It looked like the two women were working on the contents of the documents. Nickey paused to glance at the top sheets. They appeared to be Adan Jackson's financial records.

Nickey put her coffee down and took a seat. She cut a piece off the Danish and returned Cindy's stare as she chewed on a bite of the breakfast cake.

Cindy said, "Have you made any progress? Did you get in touch with your contact?"

"I'm getting together with him tomorrow night."

"And?"

"We are going to a party. Adan will be there."

"And he will introduce you to Adan?"

"I expect to meet him. If it goes well, he should be interested in a follow-up meeting with me. But there is no guarantee."

Cindy grumbled, "You and your friend are at a party with Adan. Why can't you just go up and introduce yourself?"

"That's not the way I work," Nickey said. "I want him to come on to me."

"Am I paying for this?"

"Yes."

"Then you goddamn better say something to Adan."

"He has to make the first move."

Cindy's lips pressed together into a thin line. Her chin trembled. She looked as if she was ready to cry. "How much is this costing me?"

"I've burned through your retainer," Nickey said. "I can send you an invoice on Monday."

"What the hell have you been doing for the last month?"

"I had to dig up the story because you wouldn't tell me what was going on."

"I told you to drop it. That's not what I hired you for," Cindy snarled.

Nickey glared at Cindy. She was barely able to control her fury. "Why *did* you hire me?"

"Ellen said you could make Adan Jackson leave me alone."

Ellen's mouth dropped open in shock. "That's not what I said."

Nickey watched the lawyer out of the corner of her eye. The look of horror on her face was priceless. *But that's what you wanted her to think, isn't it?* Nickey returned her focus to her client. "Why don't *you* walk up to Mr. Jackson and tell him to buzz off?"

"He won't listen to me," Cindy retorted. Tears began to run down her cheeks. She wiped them with the heel of her hand.

"Tell him you are getting ready to file a sexual harassment complaint."

"He'd laugh." Cindy shook her head grimly. "He won't listen to me."

"He won't listen to anyone unless there are consequences," Nickey said in a low, angry voice. She leaned toward Cindy and half-whispered, "He's a psycho. He's dangerous."

Terror spread across Cindy's face. Nickey turned to Ellen as if she was ready to lay into her. She breathed out heavily and turned her attention back to Cindy. "I have my way of doing things. If you're not happy with my work, just say so. You pay me what you owe me, and I'll walk away."

Cindy sat staring, teary-eyed and trembling.

Nickey watched her for a minute before asking, "What do you want me to do?"

Cindy closed her eyes. She shook her head slowly from side to side and mouthed, *I don't know.*

Ellen interrupted the standoff. "What's your plan, Nickey?"

"I want to get him alone so I can discuss the situation with him."

"Any idea when that will happen?"

"It shouldn't take long once I get him to make the appointment."

Ellen looked over at her friend. "Cindy?"

Cindy nodded.

Nickey said, "If there's nothing else, I'll be on my way."

She stood and turned to the door.

Ellen interjected, "Cindy was able to get on the audit team. It's been tricky, but she has been able to look into Adan's records."

Nickey turned back. She looked down at the papers spread out on the coffee table. Her lips curled into a sneer. "Keep up the good work."

She turned away and walked out of the apartment.

20

Jake picked Nickey up at her condo a little after 7:30 on Sunday night. His text called the event a Saturnalia at the Waverly Mansion, with a large crowd, food, and plenty to drink. He suggested that she bring along an extra set of clothes. She packed her things in a bag marked with her name for the night, Cindy Caswell.

Once they were in the car and on their way, Nickey pressed for details. "I thought you said this was a rape club."

"It's a big party," Jake replied. "A lot will be going on. The rape club is a small part of it."

"Does it last for days, like the Roman Saturnalia?"

Jake stared straight ahead. "I can't say. I have never been the last one to leave." He grimaced and shook his head.

Nickey grinned. "What can you tell me?"

"It's an orgy with food, liquor, and sex."

"Why didn't you want to go?"

"I prefer a quiet evening with someone I like."

"What about the rape club?"

"They'll have a room with a guard at the door. I can get in. You can't unless I vouch for you."

"And once we're inside?"

"There will be a small group of couples. They take turns acting out rapes. Some of them do their thing and leave. Others get their kicks from watching the action."

"Which are you?"

"I did it once. My partner hasn't spoken to me since."

They rode in silence until they left Maryland and entered D.C.

"I've driven by the mansion several times," Nickey ventured. "There's not much to see except a wall."

Jake glanced over at his passenger. "The wall surrounds three acres of woodland. The house sits on a small hill, almost in the very center of the property. It has two stories above ground and one below. The upper level used to have eight bedrooms."

"*Used to* have?"

"Some of the rooms have been repurposed. All of them except the master bedroom will be open to the guests tonight."

"What's downstairs?"

"The grand ballroom. That's where the party takes place, except for activities that spill over into the den or move upstairs."

"No kitchen?"

"That will be off-limits. The dining room will be used for a smorgasbord."

"How many guests?"

"I don't know. Probably somewhere between one hundred and two hundred."

"Can they accommodate that many cars?"

"They manage. I plan to park along the driveway. You don't mind a little walk, do you?"

* * *

The Waverly mansion was a mixture of antique and modern. The original building was constructed of red brick in 1887. A major renovation in the 1930s added rooms on the second floor and expanded the spaces on the first floor. A second major renovation in the 1970s modernized the place. Additional minor improvements have been made from time to time.

Motion sensors at every entrance turned on lights when anyone or anything approached. Cameras automatically located and tracked objects the sensors detected. Computers identified whatever the cameras followed and sent alerts out to cell phones.

Lights came on as Jake and Nickey approached the steps leading to the main entrance. The computer identified him as a guest and her as an unknown female. The door opened as they crossed the landing. A tall, strawberry-blonde wearing a loose-fitting toga invited them into the party.

The couple paused just inside the foyer. An elegant stairwell directly across from them led to the second floor. The entrance to the grand ballroom was immediately to the right of the stairs. The guests that Nickey could see from her vantage point were mostly naked or wearing very little: shoes, a pair of pants, a thong, and perhaps a bra. A few were fully clothed.

A temporary cloakroom had been set up just inside the front door. Anything and everything could be deposited there for safekeeping. Barcodes were used to keep track of the guests' belongings. Each guest was marked with a matching barcode when they dropped off their stuff.

Nickey stood for a moment, surveying the scene before turning to Jake and saying, "Let's just leave everything here."

The grand ballroom didn't look ready for waltzing. A plush carpet covered the floor. Scenes depicted on the carpet seemed to have been lifted from the *Kama Sutra* or the erotic sculptures on temples in India dedicated to Kama and his consort, Rati, the goddess of love, lust, and pleasure. A few divans or couches had been randomly placed in the room. Most of the action was taking place on the floor. Couples, threesomes, and even foursomes gathered in little clumps to practice the rites of carnal knowledge. Some of the guests were sitting it out on the periphery. They were either resting up or simply there to watch.

Nickey found the spectacle depressing. It lacked the passion of lovers going at each other in the primal dance of intercourse. This was sex for the sake of sex. The participants went through their paces with mechanical efficiency. No wonder Jake preferred a quiet evening alone with a friend. She asked, "Is it always like this?"

"Only during the orgies. They make it a very nice place for a dance when they host a charity event."

The detective and her escort circled the room, searching for Adan. Most of the guests ignored them. A few said hello to Jake and gawked at Nickey as if they wondered how he had come up with such a hot, young thing.

At one point, a young couple accosted them. The woman, a statuesque brunette with a dark tan except for the outline of her bikini, threw her arms around Jake and kissed him. She stepped back and said, "I'm Jan. This is Joe. We've been looking for you."

Jake sputtered, "I'm sorry. I'm sure we've never met."

Jan blushed. "Of course not. We just showed up. A friend gave us tickets and dared us to spend the night. We decided to give it a try. Now that we're here, we don't know what to do."

"But you said you were looking for us," Nickey objected.

"We saw you wandering around the room like you were looking for something," Joe explained. "We thought you might be lost too."

Before either Jake or Nickey could say anything, Jan blurted, "We want to make love to you." She clamped a hand over her mouth and giggled. "I mean, we want to have sex with you."

Nickey surveyed the woman's husband. He was tall, lean, muscular, and tanned to a deep bronze. His cock was pointing straight up. She turned to Jake. He shrugged.

"That's what we're here for." He grinned, showing off a perfect set of white teeth that contrasted with dark skin, coal-black eyes, and a thick, black mane.

Nickey scowled at the young woman. "Are you sure you are going to be okay with this?"

Jan knelt on the carpet and pulled Nickey down beside her. She guided the detective onto her back and began kissing her. Joe knelt to eat Nickey's pussy. When he crawled on top of her and started humping, his wife pulled back. She watched in wide-eyed fascination.

After Joe came, he collapsed onto Nickey. Then he rolled off to the side.

Nickey breathed out a soft "Phew" and studied the ceiling as she caught her breath. She raised herself and grinned at Jake. Then she tugged on Jan's hand and nodded toward her escort and his erection. "Your turn."

The young beauty scooted over to Jake and pulled him to the floor. She mounted him cowgirl-style. Her mouth and eyes opened wide with pleasure as his engorged manhood slid into her. Joe looked on with a stunned expression. Jan rocked her hips, playing with the sensations. Her cheeks were flushed and her eyes wild with excitement. She came with a scream but kept riding until Jake came.

When it was over, she sat grinning down at him, her chest heaving.

Nickey stood and helped them to their feet. She smiled pleasantly at Jan. "We have to move on. We are trying to hook up with another couple. Enjoy the rest of your night."

Joe pulled his wife into his arms. They squeezed each other tightly.

Nickey grabbed Jake's elbow. "Where's Adan?"

"Let's go check the rape room."

They grabbed their clothes and climbed the steps to the second floor. A forty-something man with a stone-faced stare stood guarding the door to the second room on the left. He recognized Jake and told him that Adan and his date had entered the room ten or fifteen minutes earlier.

Jake turned to Nickey. "We have to get dressed. I didn't want them to be that far ahead of us."

* * *

The rape room was a large bedroom with no furniture. A gray six-by-nine carpet covered the center of the floor. The walls had been painted a shade of beige that almost matched the rug. When Nickey and Jake entered, eight couples stood in a circle around the carpet.

A man and a woman were on the mat, acting out their rape scene. The woman lay face down with a blond giant on her back. She was screaming in agony. He ignored her and continued thrusting. When he was finished, he put his hand in the middle of her back and pushed off as he stood. He kicked her in the groin and leaned toward her head.

In a voice loud enough for everyone to hear, he growled, "You worthless bitch."

The woman did not move for several seconds. A few people checked to see if she was okay. She pushed them away. She struggled to her feet, steadied herself, and started for the door. She stopped to glare at her partner.

She snarled indignantly, "You fucking bastard."

The man smiled broadly and laughed as she turned and left the room. Nickey decided he must be Adan Jackson, even though they had never been introduced.

Another couple stepped to the middle of the room and acted out their rape scenario. It was violent but not vicious. The woman screamed but did not sound like she was either frightened or in pain. When it was over, the man helped his partner to her feet.

Jake pushed Nickey to the center of the room and came at her. He charged like an enraged bear. Even in his sixties, he had the solid muscular body of a stevedore. She met him with a kick to the gut. He ignored it and kept coming. They wrestled. He forced her to the floor, but the wrestling continued. He pulled a switchblade from his back pocket and raked it across her cheek, leaving a bright red streak.

He held the knife to her throat and growled, "If you know what's good for you, you'll mind your manners."

Nickey's face twisted in a murderous rage as she struggled against her instinct to end the charade with a strike to Jake's trachea.

She relaxed and let her head fall back. An electrical outlet caught her attention. Her arms spread out, and her fingers dug into the carpet. She issued a stream of low, guttural sounds somewhere between a growl and a whimper as Jake's attack continued. He kept his knife pressed against her throat while he ripped away her panties, pulled his cock from his pants, and fucked her. When he had finished, he pushed himself to his feet and leaned over to spit in her face. He straightened and sneered hideously as he studied the bloody, disheveled mess before stalking out of the room.

Nickey was astonished by Jake's performance. It was rough but not as bad as it appeared. The onlookers clapped appreciatively. She pretended to be upset by what had just happened. On her way out of the room, she bumped into Adan and stumbled back. He reached out and caught her. His hand slid down to her butt and pulled her to his crotch. She smiled up at him.

He smiled down at her. "Great performance."

"Thank you."

He reached over with the forefinger of his free hand and swiped the red streak from her cheek. He put the finger in his mouth. "Jake has great taste in blood."

"I thought weapons weren't allowed."

"Real weapons aren't. Stage props—" His nose scrunched up. He winked. "Are you okay?"

"I will be."

"You certainly made it look real."

"I tried."

"How long have you been with Jake?"

Nickey shrugged. "We see each other off and on. It's nothing serious."

"What made you come tonight?"

"A whim," she said with a flick of her eyebrows. "Jake got an invitation and asked if I was interested in doing something different."

She could feel his cock swelling against her clit. He said, "Ah'm glad you came. You're the best thing I've seen all night."

Nickey pushed against his chest. "Thank you. I've really got to go pee."

He relaxed his grip. "What's your name?"

"Cindy."

"Cindy?" He squinted and tilted his head.

She added, "Caswell. What's yours?"

He released her. "Adan." She started for the door, but he grabbed her wrist. "Do you have a phone number?"

Nickey gave herself a moment to think about it before she rattled off, "202 555 1234."

He sent an air kiss and let her go. The detective rushed to the door. Jake was across the hall in the clutches of a middle-aged woman. Big tits, a great ass, and very amorous. He was smiling contentedly. A smattering of gray hair seemed to be the only hint that he was aging. When Jake looked over at Nickey and winked, she mouthed, *Are you busy?*

He grinned and lifted the broad's head for a passionate tongue-to-tongue kiss. Then he kissed her on the cheek and said, "Sorry. Duty calls. But let's get together later."

"Did he bite?" Jake asked as they hustled to the cloakroom for the rest of their stuff.

"Definitely."

The rape date was a success from the detective's perspective. Adan had shown an interest in her and taken her phone number. He was hooked.

Jake didn't seem happy about the whole thing. He passed on her invitation to come in for a drink. "I have to go someplace private and puke."

Nickey studied the man sitting next to her. He was ruggedly handsome in a sixtyish way - beefy but still firm and muscular, with dark, Mediterranean skin, black eyes, and a full head of black hair that was beginning to show signs of gray. She reached over and stroked his cheek. "Do whatever you have to. I owe you one."

He touched his forehead to hers. "I wish I felt better about it."

She kissed him. "If you ever get tired of sleeping alone in your million-dollar condo, come over to my place. I'll get enough ouzo to knock us both out and serve you a nice ten-course dinner."

"They don't have that many courses."

"I'm Greek."

A guffaw escaped. "You know, I think you are the only woman I could be truly happy with."

"You're delusional. No man could be happy with a woman like me. Are you going to come for dinner?"

"Ask me again after you are through with Adan," he said somberly.

She kissed him again and got out of the car. "I'll be in touch."

21

Ellen waited until Tuesday to call Nickey. "I'm doing what I promised," Nickey said. "Your friend is probably," she shook her head and corrected herself, "is, without a doubt, the worst client I have ever dealt with."

"I'm sorry. Cindy's trying, but she's under a lot of emotional stress."

"She had better get her attitude straightened out."

"I'll talk to her," Ellen promised. "But she is a kind, generous person and a good friend."

Nickey rolled her eyes. "She's treating me like an intruder, and that puts me in a difficult position." Her left hand reached across her chest and grasped her elbow. "I talked to her, and I agreed to this mission because you asked me to. I don't want it to destroy our friendship."

"Oh. God no," Ellen interjected anxiously.

"Cindy needs help."

"I know. That's why I sent her to you."

"Does she understand that?" Nickey glared at her screen saver and wished they were using Skype.

"She does. She's trying to do her part. She's gotten on the audit team and started digging into Adan's files."

"Has she figured out what she is going to do next time he corners her and starts dishing out verbal abuse?"

"He won't do that. And if he did, we could go to the police," Ellen shot back.

"Has she told you what he said to her in the restaurant?"

"No. I don't think it was what he said so much as the physical intimidation."

"He reminded her of the videos and the rape. Not explicitly. He said something like, 'Remember what a great time we had at Georgetown?'"

Ellen shuddered. "That wouldn't get much of a response from law enforcement unless we introduced the rape."

"What if his lawyers argued that she dated him while they were students at Georgetown, so introducing the rape would be prejudicial?"

Ellen didn't answer.

Nickey continued, "Adan is dangerous. Cindy had better start acting like she understands that."

"I know. I'll talk to her."

"I am ready to walk away," Nickey warned. "Somebody is going to get killed before this is over, and it's not going to be me."

"Don't do that. I'll talk to her."

Nickey stood and walked over to look out the window. She switched gears. "What has she dug up?" Her tone was businesslike.

"He travels a lot. He's out on travel about thirty percent of the time."

"That's the nature of the job," Nickey observed.

"He goes to California and New York regularly. We haven't had time to do a thorough check on his reports."

"His boss has. And accounting is keeping track of his travel expenses. They are all legitimate."

"He has a standing reservation for a conference room, but he never seems to use it for his meetings," Ellen said.

"Probably doesn't want to waste everybody's time on meaningless meetings."

"But he reports on the meeting every week," Ellen replied triumphantly.

"You've caught him fudging on an official report. So what? Is he holding the meeting someplace else?"

"We haven't been able to figure that out. But Cindy did hold her staff meeting in that room at the same time as Adan's supposed meeting."

Nickey nodded. "Good. She needs to keep that up. That might raise a red flag."

When Ellen began shuffling through papers, Nickey said, "Ellen, I have to get back to work. Can we continue this some other time?"

"Sure. I'm sorry about Cindy's behavior. I'll talk to her." Ellen hesitated. "Do you think she should get a gun?"

"No. She probably couldn't use it in an emergency, and if she tried, she would shoot the wrong person."

"Okay. I'll continue trying to make sense of what we've collected and get back to you. Have a great day."

"Thanks. You too," Nickey said and ended the call.

22

Adan called Cindy Caswell on the Friday after the orgy. He had tickets to a performance of *The Lion King* at the Kennedy Center on Saturday night. He wanted to know if he could pick her up at 5:30 for dinner. She said that sounded delightful, but they would have to meet somewhere because she had a late afternoon appointment. He suggested the Kennedy Center's Roof Terrace Restaurant. She said she would try to be there by six.

He was sitting next to the windows that looked out over the terrace onto the Potomac when she arrived. He stood and helped her with her chair. "Ah went ahead and ordered a merlot. Ah hope that's all right."

She smiled appreciatively. "That sounds nice."

Adan watched her scan the menu before asking, "What would you like to have for dinner?"

"The risotto sounds tempting, but I'm going to get the salmon. How about you?"

"Ah'm going to have to get the beef tenderloin."

She appraised him while the waiter was taking their orders. Tall, good-looking, rich, and charming.

After the waiter left, he smiled at her and laughed. "What?"

"I was just thinking how lucky I was to meet you."

He nodded. "Ah feel the same way about you." He sipped his wine. "What do you do exactly?"

Cindy flashed a quick smile. "I'm in personnel."

"Who do you work for?"

"I'm independent. I find people for one-of-a-kind jobs."

Adan was scrutinizing her. "Is that how Jake got to know you?"

She found his intense stare unnerving but kept her voice under control. "Yes, I did some work for him a few years ago."

"Ah'm surprised he never mentioned you."

"I'm surprised he even remembered me," she countered. "There are so many women in his life."

"Yes. He does like variety. But he usually stays away from those get-togethers."

Cindy grimaced. "I can see why. When he asked me, he said his life was getting boring, and he wanted to spice it up."

His eyes widened in surprise. "And you went along just like that?"

"I'm usually willing to try anything once." She pressed her lips together and shook her head. "How about you? I don't think you ever said what you do."

"I'm a venture capitalist. I help companies make a successful launch." He went on to talk about some of the successes. It seemed like he had played a vital role in every one of them. The dinner was pleasant despite the shop talk. Adan suggested they skip dessert and go somewhere after the show. He paid for the meal and got them down to the theater just in time to take their seats before the lights were turned down.

The Lion King was an uplifting entertainment experience. The music alone was enough to get a person revved up for a week. The stage performance was more challenging than an animated movie but worth the effort.

After the performance, Adan got a cab to take them to the Omni Shoreham. He put his arm around her, his hand resting on her hip as they walked to the car. The cabbie opened the door for them. Cindy stepped in and slid to the far side of the seat. Adan settled on his side.

"You seemed to enjoy the show," he observed.

"Yes, I loved the music."

"It's based on *Hamlet*."

"I wouldn't have guessed that. It doesn't seem very Shakespearean," she said.

"The young prince's father is killed by his uncle, and the prince escapes into exile. He hides, avoiding responsibility until one day he realizes he has to act. He returns to avenge his father's murder. The uncle is killed."

Cindy closed her eyes and pressed a finger against her lips. When she turned back to Adan, she said, "I guess I can see your point, but I'm not that familiar with the play."

"Read it in high school and forgot about it after the final exam." Adan laughed.

She grinned. "I read the CliffNotes, like everybody else."

"That's too bad. The play is terrific."

"It's depressing," she countered. "Hamlet is depressed. His girlfriend commits suicide. His mother marries the man who killed his father, and everybody ends up dead by the time the curtain falls."

"The deaths add drama and shorten the play," Adan explained. "A modern movie runs about two hours. *Hamlet*, as written by Shakespeare, would take about five hours. That is a long time for a show. Will throws in bawdy humor and violent deaths to spice things up and hold the audience's attention."

"It's still a downer," Cindy scoffed. "Hamlet is depressing. He is enough to ruin the play for me."

"He's stuck. He was raised to take over the throne. There is nothing left for him after his uncle murders his father."

"He's rich. He should be able to do anything he wants."

"A modern Hamlet would be able to find other outlets for his energy. He could build a new empire or buy a sports team or found a charity."

"Is that what you are doing?"

Adan eyed her suspiciously. "What do you mean?"

"You aren't from here. You have a southern accent. You're in exile. And you're a venture capitalist, which means you are building new empires."

Adan laughed. This Cindy was going to be fun. "Ah thought my accent was gone. Ah grew up in Mississippi. Finance has been the family business for over a century."

"What happened?"

"My father and my uncle were equals for twenty years while my grandfather ran the firm. When Grandpa retired, my uncle took over and reduced my father to just another partner. Pop couldn't accept that, so he found a position at the Brookings Institute and moved us up to D.C."

"No one was killed."

"Pop took it very hard. He might as well have been killed," Adan replied in undisguised anger.

"Are you going back?"

"Ah don't know. Pop still owns a piece of the firm. Ah could get that when he dies. But that isn't going to happen any time soon." He looked over at his companion and shrugged. "By the time it does, Ah'll have lived most of my life in D.C. My work and friends will be up here."

She closed her eyes and rested her head against the seat. "Is there an Ophelia in this story?"

Adan looked at her with a pained expression. He stopped breathing while he considered his answer. "There was a girl in college when Ah was a sophomore." He buried his forehead in his hands. "One night, a friend of mine raped her." His hands slid to the back of his head. His eyes were shut tight. "She left college. Just disappeared. It was like she had thrown herself into the Potomac and drowned."

They sat in silence the rest of the way to the hotel.

23

The ride from the John F. Kennedy Center for the Performing Arts to the Omni Shoreham takes about twenty minutes. Less if you are in a hurry. The driver figured his passengers were in no hurry. He took the scenic route through a wooded section of D.C. along the Rock Creek-Potomac Parkway. It was wasted on Adan and Nickey. They were caught in the grip of past horrors.

Nickey was shocked by the Shoreham as the cab rolled along Calvert Street toward the main entrance. The detective had driven past the place hundreds of times. It had always been a majestic D.C. landmark. This night it was a yellow brick fortress, eight stories high and three blocks long. She had never viewed it that way before. She had been inside on business at least a dozen times. Never before had she wondered how she would get back out once she was inside.

Adan helped her from the cab and offered his arm. They walked into the Marquee Lounge and found a table. He ordered scotch on the rocks. Nickey asked if they had ouzo. The waiter suggested Galliano. She nodded.

"Ouzo? So, you're Greek?"

"My grandparents came here from Greece."

"Where are you from?"

"I grew up in Annandale."

Adan grinned mischievously. When he turned on the charm, he came across as a fun-loving, twenty-something, college grad. "How did you end up being a one-woman executive search firm?"

"I made a bad choice. I got a pretty much worthless degree in psychology. My father used his connections at Mitre to get me a job in personnel." Nickey smirked. "I left there and went to work for a small recruiting firm. After a couple of years, I figured out that I could do just as well working for myself."

Adan shook his head. "Ah wouldn't have thought that was possible." He sat back to study his companion. "If Ah needed you to find someone for me, how would Ah get in touch with you?"

"You wouldn't. Normally, you would give your job description to human resources. If they had difficulty finding the right candidates, they might reach out to somebody who would recommend that they contact me."

"How do you stay in business?"

"Word of mouth. Repeat business. My clients like my services."

Adan smiled and shook his head.

Nickey asked, "Where do you work?"

He grimaced. That was a question he would rather not answer. "America First Financial Services in D.C."

"I've never worked with them."

"That's not surprising," Adan explained. "We don't do a lot of hiring from outside the company.

We bring in college grads from top business programs and develop them." He pointed to her glass. "You look like you could use another."

She picked it up and studied it. "Sure. Why not?"

"Ah have a room upstairs. Maybe we could go up there."

Nickey smiled. It was a queer smile, hinting of distrust. "I don't know. I really should be getting home."

Adan winked. "It's early." He sounded like the boss who wouldn't take no for an answer.

She scowled. "I do have to get home." She blew air out between her lips. "But I suppose I could come up for one drink."

"One drink." He stood and offered his hand. She took it, and they started the long walk to his room.

* * *

The Shoreham is a physically separate building from the Marquee lounge. The couple had to cross a driveway to reach the front entrance. The main lobby is a large, open area with an oak floor and high white ceilings supported by columns. Crystal chandeliers provide a warm, relaxed atmosphere. A forest-green carpet with an elaborate floral design and a brown border covers most of the floor. Open-air sitting rooms subdivide the lobby into comfortable spaces with well-made chairs, a couch, and a coffee table.

The lobby was crowded with patrons going about their lives as Adan and Nickey passed through on their way to the elevators.

His suite was on the eighth floor, some distance from the elevator. Soft lighting and a lavender carpet gave the hallway a dark, eerie feel. Nickey thought of

Anne Boleyn and the Tower of London as her mind churned through escape plans. She noted the door to a stairwell halfway between the elevator and his suite. If she had to make a run for it, she would use those stairs. He was a big, powerful, athletic man, but he wasn't built for running. He probably hadn't run a hundred yards since he got out of school. She was quick and agile, and she could go for miles. The key was to avoid getting trapped in a situation where his size and strength gave him an insurmountable advantage.

Nickey took one step into the living room of Adan's apartment and stopped. A bay window on the other side of the room looked out onto Calvert Street. A dining table with two chairs sat in front of the window. To her right, a couch rested against the wall. A cherrywood desk with a TV and office chair was across from it. A bed was visible through a door on her left.

Adan urged her into the room with a gentle push. She sashayed over to the dining table and set her purse down.

She slowly turned back from the window, taking in the room as she did so. The walls were painted gold. The furniture was covered with gold cloth, and gold-colored wall-to-wall carpet covered the floor.

Adan hung the Do Not Disturb sign on the outside door handle and turned his attention to his date.

She favored him with a wan smile. "Very nice place. I don't suppose you had much to say about the decor."

"No." He chuckled. "Ah have to live with what they provide. But Ah've grown used to it."

He cued up a playlist on the sound system. It started with an orchestral piece featuring themes from the opera *Carmen*. They stared awkwardly at each other until Nickey asked, "So, where's my drink?"

"Why don't you sit down and relax?" he suggested. "What would you like? Ah have wine, whiskey, and brandy but no Galliano."

"Wine sounds nice. White, if you have it?"

"I have chardonnay and merlot."

Nickey smiled. "I'll try the chardonnay."

He disappeared into the other room. She looked wistfully at the door to the corridor and rubbed her hands together. Her palms were moist. Her mouth dry. She slid her left hand to a slight bulge in her belt. A gentle push assured her that the knife was still there.

When Adan returned with the drinks, a look of irritation replaced his smile. She had not moved. He gave a slight shake of his head and held out her glass. She walked over to take it. They met in the center of the room.

"Why don't we go over and sit on the couch?" he suggested as he handed her the glass of chardonnay.

A smile played across her face. "I've done quite a bit of sitting today." She nodded toward a painting above the couch. It showed a toreador driving a sword into the neck of a bull in a crowded arena. "I'll bet that didn't come with the room."

He shook his head. "They had a still life, orchids in a vase. Ah replaced it. So far, they haven't complained."

"*Carmen*. A bullfighter finishing off his victim. Is that your style?"

"*Carmen* gets my juices flowing." He grinned, but it was sinister. The monster was beginning to emerge from behind the boyish facade.

"The music is exciting," she conceded. "But as I recall, her boyfriend kills her in the end."

"That's the kind of dramatic climax that keeps people coming back for more."

"Not in real life."

"Of course not," Adan scoffed. "You can't get away with murdering people in real life."

"How about rape? Can you get away with rape?"

"I wouldn't know," he snarled.

Nickey walked back to the dining table. She set her glass down and picked up her purse. "And we aren't going to try to find out tonight."

"What does that mean?" Adan demanded. He spread his feet into a fighting stance. He was getting ready to prevent her from reaching the door.

She looked directly into his eyes. "I am going downstairs and calling a cab."

She started to her right to go around him. He moved over to block her path.

"We're not finished," he said in a low, threatening voice.

Nickey veered to her left to get around him. He shuffled to his right and closed within inches. She stopped and looked up at him. "Keeping me here against my will is a serious crime. Don't try it."

"We're not finished," he repeated.

She brought her hands in front of her crotch, left hand clasping her right wrist. The purse dangled from her right hand. *Carmen* sent chills down her spine.

"You came up here of your own free will," Adan pointed out in a reasonable tone.

"To have a drink. I had a drink. Now I am leaving of my own free will."

"No. You're not," he corrected. "We came up for sex, and we are going to have a good fuck before you walk out of here."

"That sounds like kidnapping and rape, Adan," she warned. "You don't want to go there."

"When you walked from the bar with me and got on the elevator with me and came to my room with me, you gave implied consent."

"You asked me up here for a drink. Nothing was said about sex."

"We're adults. We both knew we were coming up here for sex."

"I told you that I want to leave, and we both know what that means," she countered.

"It's not that easy," he sneered. "You came up here with me, and you will leave here with me." He paused. "When Ah'm ready."

"Move," she ordered. "I'm tired of playing this game."

"You seemed to enjoy that little game the other night."

"Looks can be deceiving."

A malicious grin spread across his features. His predatory eyes focused on her chest. She backed away in a moment of panic. He stepped forward and grabbed the top of her dress. With one sharp pull, he ripped the front open all the way down to her belt. He wrapped a powerful arm around her waist and pulled her in. "Gotcha!"

Nickey squirmed, fighting to free herself, but her arms were pinned to her side. Adan grabbed the back of her head and pressed his mouth over hers. He forced his tongue inside in spite of her struggles. Her teeth clamped down on his tongue. The bite didn't cut all the way through, but the gouge was deep and bloody. His head snapped back. Her teeth scraped taste buds and skin from the surface of his tongue as he pulled free.

He screamed, "God damn —"

Her knee drove into his balls. His body folded forward. Nickey rammed her forehead into his nose. The big man dropped his bear hug and backed away. Her left uppercut snapped his head back. She clamped her hands on his rib cage and drove forward, knocking him flat on his back. The detective produced the switchblade from its hiding place. The blade leaped to the ready as soon as it cleared her belt. She stepped in close, placing her right foot inches from his crotch, daring him to make a move.

Adan looked at the blade and then at the woman standing over him. He stared in shock when he realized he had been set up. He raised his hands to ward off the attack. "Wait a minute. That's not necessary," he blustered. "Ah thought you liked this sort of stuff."

"Is that what you thought? What about the other women you've raped in this room?"

"What are you talking about?" he stammered.

"We both know what this is about," Nickey snarled. Her lip curled up in contempt. "This is how you get off."

"You can't prove that."

"I have been watching you for a while. I know all about you."

"What do you want?"

"You have been bothering a friend of mine. That is going to stop immediately."

He sat with a baffled look on his face as he ran through the possibilities. "Cindy?"

She ignored the response. "Or I go to the authorities with enough information to get you put away for a long, long time."

"Because of Cindy?" As soon as he said the name, the baffled expression dissolved into horror.

"And all the other women you have violated," she barked. "But you had better stay away from Cindy. Is that clear?"

He gulped. The look on his face was a mixture of fear and desire for this avenging angel. "You're not Cindy Caswell. Who the hell are you?"

The door to the hotel room crashed open. Someone had called hotel security. "Are you all right, Mr. Jackson?"

He looked up at his assailant. She was pointing at scratches his fingernails had left on her chest when he ripped her dress. "Yes," he said. A smirk flashed across his face. "It was a misunderstanding."

Nickey stepped over Adan's leg and retrieved her purse. "I was just leaving."

"Not until you give me some identification," the security guard growled.

She dropped the knife into her purse. "Sorry, I don't have any."

The guard reached for the purse.

Nickey pulled it away. "Not unless you have a warrant."

He looked as though he might make a grab for it. The detective's icy stare changed his mind. He settled for snapping a photo of her.

She pushed past him and strolled out of the room.

24

Sergeant Jack Edwards summoned Nickey Arnold to his office for questioning on Monday afternoon. He wanted the meeting because of a report about a scuffle at the Omni Shoreham involving Adan Jackson and a female guest. Jack and his squad had been able to identify Nickey as the guest using the hotel security guard's photograph. She was smart enough to agree to the meeting without discussion.

Jack's office was just large enough for his standard-issue, gray metal desk, three chairs for visitors, and a couple of filing cabinets. It did have a window. Nickey wondered if he ever looked at the contents of the file drawers. Everything had been digitized years ago. A USB stick could hold all of his case files with room to spare. He probably carried all the essential information in his head. But the two six-drawer cabinets sat against the wall, taking up space.

The sergeant was at his desk. Even seated, he was impressive: a big man with a massive torso, broad forehead, pouting lips, and intense, penetrating eyes. Just for an instant, Nickey entertained a vision of Jack with his arms wrapped around Eve, holding her naked body against his. She couldn't help herself.

Jack growled, "Wipe that smirk off your face. I want an explanation."

"Of course," Nickey purred. "What would you like me to explain?"

"Saturday night," he snapped.

"I was on a date. The guy turned violent when we got to his room. I defended myself."

"The guy was Adan Jackson. How did you end up in a hotel room with him?"

"We met at a party. He asked me to dinner and a show. After the show, we went to the Omni for a nightcap. He invited me up to his room for a drink."

"And you had no idea what he was up to until he attacked you in that room?"

"I thought he was going to show me his coin collection."

"Cut the crap," Jack barked. "Adan Jackson is the man who has been harassing your client. You went after him."

"Everything I told you is true except the part about the coin collection."

"You set him up."

"What's your point, Sergeant?"

"You had a knife, and you threatened him. That's assault with a deadly weapon."

"I carry a knife and a Beretta for self-defense. Both are legal."

"Assault is illegal."

"Self-defense isn't," Nickey snapped. "You saw the photograph, and you know he practically ripped my dress off." She stood and started unbuttoning her blouse. "I was defending myself. Do you want to see his claw marks?"

Jack waved his hand. "That won't be necessary." He walked over and shut the door to his office. "I want you to stay away from Jackson. Let the police handle this."

She shook her head. "You can't. You don't have any grounds."

He returned to his seat and tilted back. "He raped Cindy Foster."

She put her hands on his desk and leaned toward him. "He pled guilty to misdemeanor assault. That's water over the dam."

"What are you going to do about it?" he challenged.

The detective straightened. As she buttoned her blouse, she responded with a casual, "I've got him over a barrel. I plan to keep him there."

The sergeant screwed up his lips and shook his head. "That won't work. He can outwait you. He waited sixteen years before going back after Foster."

Nickey smiled demurely and suggested, "He does have a problem you might be interested in."

Jack raised his eyebrows but said nothing.

The detective continued, "I accused him of raping other women in that hotel room."

"And?"

"He didn't tell me I was wrong."

"So?"

"He lives in D.C. Why does he need a room at the Omni?"

"That's not much to go on."

Nickey shrugged, picked up her purse, and started for the door. She paused before stepping into the hallway and turned back to Jack. There was a twinkle in her eyes. Her voice was playful. "It's more than you had an hour ago."

25

Jack gave his visitor a few minutes to get out of the area then called Detectives Bill Andrews and Liz Smith into his office. She looked down the hall as if to make sure that Nickey was gone before going into the meeting. "That must have been an interesting conversation."

The sergeant growled, "We'll get to that. I want an update on Mondale and Jackson. Bill?"

"Mondale is staying out of trouble," the detective said. "He started a consulting business about a year ago. He talks to perps on their way to jail. Lawyers call him in for advice on sentencing, and he gives seminars on prison issues. He has two partners: a female public defender and a law professor from GWU."

"What about outside of work?"

"I haven't seen anything," Bill said, "but I haven't looked. You told us not to spend a lot of time on it."

Jack nodded. "We can't afford a big investigation. No crime has been reported, but the situation is heating up. I want to know if Mondale is a problem."

"What about Eve?" Liz suggested. "She could look into him."

Jack glared.

She smirked. "Oops. What does she think?"

"He's handling the situation. He told her about the rape and about going to jail. It upsets him, but he doesn't seem to be holding a grudge. He said it wouldn't do any good for him to contact Mrs. foster." Jack paused and looked over at the door. He stroked his chin. "Eve says the woman partner is Mondale's girlfriend."

The sergeant turned his attention to Liz. "What have you got on Adan Jackson?"

"His hours are flexible. He shows up late and works late. He travels frequently. A secretary I talked to couldn't tell me anything about the trips except that he meets with clients. He goes to New York a lot." Her lip curled into a sneer. "I'll bet it's to hook up with his brother."

Jack nodded.

Liz continued. "He goes out often. Sometimes he wears a disguise." She paused and put her index fingers in a steeple against her lips. "It's not much. He dresses down and puts on a wig and glasses. Then he'll go to a dive. I followed him to the Tahiti one night." She paused and looked at Jack with unexpected intensity. "Thursday, he went to the Boundary Line Bar in Shepherd Park. He watched a ball game and drank a couple of beers with a rough-looking character with prison tats. I looked him up when I got back to the office. He's an ex-con named Greg Jantzen, a violent repeat offender—multiple arrests for assault and robbery. Served five years for manslaughter."

"Why would Adan be talking to him?" Jack wondered.

"Not sure," Liz said. "They weren't talking business. Maybe he just needs some excitement."

The sergeant stood and walked over to the window. He ground one massive fist into his palm. Halfway across the room, he stopped abruptly and turned back to his detectives. "I want the two of you to find out what that bastard is up to." He walked back and stood over them. "Arnold thinks he may be raping women in his room at the Shoreham." The sergeant returned to his seat. "Liz, get a statement from her. Exactly what happened on her date with Jackson. She also said that he's leasing a suite at the Omni. Check that out." He drummed his fingers on his desk as he considered the situation. "I want twenty-four-hour surveillance on Jackson, and I want his phone lines tapped."

"What if he's not doing anything?" Bill objected.

"What do you mean?" Jack growled.

"He's a rich playboy. He meets a lot of women who are hoping to get lucky. He gets a big thrill out of chummin' around with a badass ex-con. That's not enough for a warrant."

Jack answered with a stony stare.

Bill stared back for a few seconds and then stood to leave. "Okay. We'll check him out."

Liz followed her partner out of the office.

26

Cindy was ordered up to Samar Agarwal's office shortly after ten on Friday. The summons sent her into nervous jitters. Her stomach knotted up. She went to the ladies' room and splashed cold water on her face to regain control. Agarwal was director of America First's Mid Atlantic operations. He did not speak to people at her level except for a friendly greeting at office functions. Unless there was a major screwup. She had last encountered the man at the company holiday party in 2007. That was also where she ran into Adan Jackson and discovered they were working for the same company in the same office building.

Her gut told her this meeting was going to be another disaster. Her stomach gurgled and shot bile up to her throat. Her ulcer was on fire. Agarwal almost certainly wanted to know why she had been checking into Adan Jackson's records.

America First leased most of the fifth floor and the entire sixth and seventh floors of the Cap Gallery building. Samar Agarwal's office took up the northwest corner of the seventh floor. His executive assistant occupied a spacious, well-furnished area just outside of the boss's office. She controlled one of the two doors to that office.

As Cindy approached her desk, the assistant looked up and said in a flat voice, "Go on in. Mr. Agarwal is expecting you."

The electronic lock buzzed just as Cindy reached the door. She opened it and stepped into the inner sanctum. The director was sitting behind his desk, arms folded across his chest. His body tilted back.

Adan Jackson sat facing him from across the desk.

They broke off their discussion and turned their attention to the new arrival as she walked into the room. A smirk flashed across Adan's face.

Agarwal smiled faintly and gestured to a chair next to Adan. "Please take a seat, Mrs. Foster."

His office was huge. Sparse furnishings made it seem cavernous. The dominant piece of furniture was a large, round conference table made from oak. *King Agarwal's Round Table* flashed through Cindy's mind.

Windows ran along the wall behind his desk and continued around the corner along the adjacent wall. A portrait of Gandhi hung in the center of the back wall. Nothing was out of place. Agarwal was a fastidious man. He had a single file open in front of him. His computer monitor sat off to his right, giving him an unobstructed view of the room.

Cindy pulled the chair toward the edge of the desk to give herself some separation from Adan. She nodded. "Mr. Agarwal. Mr. Jackson."

As she took her seat, she spotted his degree from Harvard and his MBA from the Sloane School of Management on the wall near the door.

"There is a small matter I am trying to sort out," Agarwal began. Cindy watched him intently and nodded. "Both you and Mr. Jackson reported using the small conference room in the east wing last Thursday. Either you squeezed both of your staff meetings in there at the same time, or one of you filed an erroneous report."

Cindy swallowed. "I have held my staff meeting in that room on Thursday afternoons a few times. No one else was using it."

"Mr. Jackson indicates that he has been using it every Thursday afternoon for some time."

Cindy looked down. The knot in her stomach made thinking difficult. She cleared her throat. "I don't know the answer. We have never encountered Mr. Jackson and his staff. Perhaps the meetings are at different times. Or maybe the days are just mixed up."

Agarwal turned to Adan for his response. The executive stared back, poker-faced. His arms folded across his chest. His legs stretched out, left ankle crossed over the right.

The director turned back to Cindy. "You are holding your staff meeting in that room on Thursday afternoons? So, several people are in attendance?"

"Yes, sir. Nine of us from one-thirty to two-thirty."

Agarwal turned back to his protégé. "Mr. Jackson?"

Adan sat up, pressed his lips together, and puffed air through his nose. "Mah meeting is from three to five. Unless we finish early. Ah go over accounts on a rotating basis with members of mah team. The makeup of the meeting changes from week to week."

"Your reports indicate that you have been meeting from one to four."

Adan's head jerked as if he had just been hit with an electric shock. He stared wide-eyed for a second and then shook his head, "Ah don't know how that happened." He squinted and pursed his lips while he worked it out. "Ah guess we met right after lunch for a while. People were showing up late. Ah think they needed some time to get their stuff together. Ah must have rescheduled the meeting time without telling Susan."

Agarwal scowled. "I hope you realize that honesty and accuracy are absolutely essential in our business, Mr. Jackson."

"Yes, sir. It won't happen again."

Agarwal's brow knitted into a frown. His lower lip pushed up against the upper. He tapped his fingers on his desk as he looked first at his senior manager and then at the newly minted manager. "Alright. Get this straightened out. If somebody outside this room starts looking into anomalies like that, we could be in trouble."

"Can I go back to work now?" Cindy asked as she stood to leave.

"Mrs. Foster," the director intoned, "it has come to my attention that you have been checking financial reports and payroll records."

She froze, then turned back to face Agarwal. She blinked. "Yes, sir. I volunteered to help with the preparations for our upcoming audit."

"It appears that you have focused on Mr. Jackson's records."

"That's possible, sir," she said diffidently.

"Have you found anything?"

"No, sir. At least I haven't seen anything so far."

"Do you expect to?"

"We were instructed to keep an open mind. It is better if we find problems before the auditors do."

Agarwal smiled. "That's true." The smile faded. His eyes narrowed. He studied Cindy with an intense, challenging stare. "I was told that you felt Mr. Jackson has been harassing you."

"That's not true," Cindy stammered. She caught herself and added, "I may have complained to some friends that I found it odd that he always seemed to be popping up wherever I was." She looked over at Adan then back at Agarwal. She shook her head. "But he has not harassed me."

"Good. I will not tolerate that sort of thing," Agarwal assured her. He waved her off. "Go on back to work." He turned to Adan. "Mr. Jackson, you need to watch your step. We cannot afford misconduct of any kind. Our clients need to be able to trust us with their money and their futures."

Adan responded with a vigorous, "Yes, sir." His Mississippi drawl deepened. "Ah had no intention of botherin' Mrs. Foster. She would just show up when Ah was on mah way to a meetin'. That's more like to happen now that she's managin' tax accounts for mah clients."

"Just be sure that you don't cross any lines," Agarwal warned. He made a fist with the knuckle of his right index finger, pointing at Adan. "Your father is a good friend. I wouldn't want to have to take any action that would jeopardize our friendship. But I put my responsibility to the company ahead of that friendship."

"Yes, sir."

"You can go back to work."

"Yes, sir."

27

The two men entered Robert's restaurant in the Omni Shoreham at 6:55. They could have been twins. Tall, blond, athletic, with rugged, sharp-featured faces. The one taking the lead was an inch or two shorter and bulkier. He had an air of impatience as if any delay would be an affront. The taller one was more laid-back and approachable. The maître d' had them seated at a table in a far corner. Initial small talk gave way to animated conversation.

The shorter man carried on about a recent to-do. "The bitch wanted me to take her to the room," he insisted angrily. "She planned the whole thing."

The taller man seemed baffled by that idea. "Why would she do that?"

"I think she was working for Cindy."

"Cindy? Smith? I told you to stay away from her, Adan," the taller man said sternly.

Adan whined, "I wasn't doing anything, Beau."

Beau's eyes opened wide in disbelief. "Nothing at all?"

"I just walked past her in the corridor."

That drew a scowl. "But you made sure she saw you, right?"

"That's okay, isn't it? There's no law against doing that."

Beau chewed a bite of salad and sipped his wine. "That may explain why she hired someone to send you a message."

Adan sulked. He sliced off a piece of steak with savage strokes and lifted the meat to his mouth but paused. Pointing his fork with the chunk of meat on its tongs at his brother, he proclaimed, "She had no right to do that to me."

"What were you thinking when you took that woman to your room?" Beau was the consummate counselor. He calmly took a bite of his steak and carefully chewed as he studied Adan. He took a sip of his wine and swallowed.

"She was just a crazy bitch who liked rough sex."

Beau looked down, shaking his head. He looked up at his brother with an ironic smile. "Sex? Is that what you call it when a woman knocks you on your ass and threatens you with a knife?"

Adan looked down at his plate and grumbled, "That was after we got in the room."

"Didn't you wonder why she was so easy?"

"No. She went along with Jake at the rape party." He stopped to go over in his mind what had happened. He looked his brother squarely in the eye and asserted, "There was no reason for her to have a problem with what we were doing."

Beau bit on his lower lip as he looked over the dining area. The room was full by this time. The last light of day was fading. Lamps gave the place a soft glow to go along with the soft music playing in the background. He looked back at his brother. "I suppose you're right." He looked down as he moved the food around on his plate. "What's next?"

"I have to send a message to Cindy to let her know that she can't get away with a stunt like that."

Beau snapped to attention. He sucked in a breath. *You idiot.* He let the air out slowly. "You need to be careful. You have a history with that woman. Threatening her could land you in court. You don't want that kind of trouble."

"I could send her an anonymous package with a copy of her porn videos as a warning."

"And she could go to the police or the FBI and tell them the whole story. You would be the prime suspect."

"I suppose you have a better plan," Adan sneered.

Beau took a bite of steak and chewed thoughtfully. "If Troy sent the videos, you would be safe on the sidelines."

"Why would he do something like that?"

"He wouldn't. But you could pin it on him. All you need is his address." Beau smiled at the beauty of his idea.

"He's in jail," Adan objected.

"He should be out by now."

"How are we going to find him, Mr. Genius?"

Beau stroked his chin as he considered the possibilities. "The National Sex Offender Registry. He had to register as soon as he got out of jail."

"Are you serious?"

"It's worth a try. I'll look into it."

28

Troy called Eve on Tuesday, the sixteenth of June, to say that he would be free at ten on Wednesday if she wanted to continue the interview.

A thrill ran down her spine, but she answered with forced calm. "I would like that. I have more questions."

"Great. I have to get to a meeting right now. See you in the morning." He hung up.

She leaned back in her chair and took a breath. After three weeks without a word, Troy had called her to continue their interview.

Eve had been working on the project sporadically. She had taken it on to satisfy Jack. Then she became interested in Troy and how he ended up in prison. Their last meeting had been cut short before he could go into his prison experience. The invitation to come back for another session could only mean that he was ready to talk about those dark years.

Her research after the last meeting had convinced her that the "punishment" part of *Crime and Punishment* was a huge story. The United States had the largest inmate population in the world. Two and a half million men were locked away in jails and prisons. The US also had the highest per-capita incarceration rate. Approximately one out of every one hundred males was either in prison or on parole. Almost half of them were African American.

Eve had written the first draft of a proposed article and sent out query letters. She wanted more from Troy on his time in prison, and now he was ready to give it to her.

Nickey wanted Eve to question him about another topic: his assessment of the man he had been friends with in college.

The two women had discussed the Cindy-Adan-Troy mess over lunch. Eve got a blow-by-blow description of her friend's night with Adan. The detective was upset with Cindy and Ellen, but she was worried about Adan. "I don't know if he has full-blown dissociative personality disorder, but he's close. At dinner, he was a charming gentleman. In the hotel room, he was a beast. A demented psychopath."

"Like Dr. Jekyll and Mr. Hyde?" Eve suggested.

* * *

When Eve arrived for the interview, Marie was working on a laptop at the small table. Troy was working at the desk. He suggested switching places with Marie so his chat with Eve would be more cordial.

Troy seemed upbeat. "Help yourself," he said, pointing to the coffee maker. "I apologize for not having anything to eat. We don't snack."

As soon as they were settled, Eve asked, "How did you make it through ten years?"

"It was twelve," Troy corrected. "I stuck to my plan."

"You had a plan?" Eve asked suspiciously. "How did you get that?"

"I fumbled around until I found things that worked. Prison is an alien world. Your first time in prison is the worst because you are starting from scratch. You watch what is going on around you. You listen to what people say. You keep trying things until you come up with a strategy."

Eve sipped her coffee. "What was yours?"

"Stay busy. I did my assigned work, and I volunteered for extra assignments. Most importantly, I finished my education. Those are the pillars that I emphasize for my clients."

"Sounds simple."

"It is, but you need some luck." He lowered his eyes and folded his hands on the table. His jaw was clamped shut. Painful thoughts churned through his mind. When he finally looked up, he said softly, "The way prisons function today, inmates have almost no chance of making it back to a normal life."

"People go to jail for committing crimes," Eve objected. "They create the problem, not the prison system."

Troy glared at her. "That type of thinking makes our system of punishment counterproductive. The idea of sending a person to prison to extract payback for a crime and discourage future criminal behavior is obsolete, outmoded. There is no evidence to support that approach."

"Don't you believe people should pay for their crimes?"

"I don't believe the concept makes any sense," Troy replied. "When you pay for something, you give up something of value in return for something you want. In that sense, the criminal gives up part of his life in return for redemption. If paying for a crime worked, someone like me would give up part of his life to serve a prison sentence. When that sentence was completed, he would be redeemed and could return to normal life." He shook his head. His lip curled up in disgust. "No one comes out ahead in our system of justice. Neither the victim nor society in general benefitted from the twelve years I spent in prison." He looked straight into her eyes and said in a low, angry voice, "I certainly did not get redemption in exchange for the price I paid."

Eve looked down at her notes and scribbled, *no one benefits—victim/society/prisoner*. She looked back at him and said softly, "That sucks."

Troy leaned back in his chair, took a deep breath, and let it out slowly. "Even worse, my imprisonment cost society a bundle. You paid about half a million dollars to keep me locked up in subhuman conditions for twelve years." He chuckled at the shocked expression on the reporter's face. "Was it worth it?"

"Not when you put it that way. But I bet you will never do anything like that again." She regretted the comment as soon as the words were out of her mouth.

"I would not have done it again, regardless. I wouldn't have done it in the first place if I had realized what I was getting into. I couldn't do that to my worst enemy, let alone a friend."

Eve looked up at the ceiling and uttered a soft, "Shit."

"You don't believe me?"

"I was raped by a friend. You just reminded me of him," she explained. "We had a blowup over it. Later, he apologized. He had come to understand what he had done. He was going to counseling."

"I'm sorry."

"Yeah. We all are." She sighed and flashed a wan smile. "So, what is your cure for the system?"

"We have to incentivize convicts to earn back their place in society and give them a chance to succeed."

"How?"

"Reward prisoners for doing what we want them to do. Give the ones who show that they are making an effort some benefits, like better quarters and less supervision. If they don't sustain the effort, send them back to the hellhole. Make education a real goal. Reward staff and inmates for success in raising the education and skill level of the individual prisoners. Emphasize family support."

Eve jotted some notes and looked back at Troy. "Aren't we doing those things already?"

"If we were, our prisons would be a lot less crowded. Seventy-five percent of the men who were released on the same day as me are back in prison already." He smiled. "I'm one of the small minority who has managed to stay out for at least five years." He added in a bitter tone, "But I am not home free. There is a target on my back."

"What is that supposed to mean?" she challenged. But she knew that Jack had sent her to spy on him because of what he had done sixteen years ago. She blushed.

A hint of recognition flashed across Troy's face. "I'm a convict, and I'm a violent sex offender. Those are labels I will carry with me the rest of my life. I cannot hold public office. I cannot even vote, although I am required to pay taxes. Many safety net programs and many jobs are off-limits to me because of my conviction. Those are punishments over and above the fifteen-year prison sentence that was imposed."

Eve pressed her lips into a grim line but said nothing. Her gaze met his. She didn't blink.

"I am automatically a suspect," he continued. "If there is a rape in Rock Creek Park and the police come across my name when they are looking for known rapists in the area, they will pay me a visit. They will demand to know what I was doing around the time the crime was committed."

Eve closed her eyes and shuddered. She took a moment to study her notes. "What do you think we should do about that?"

"That's a good question. We could set a schedule and benchmarks for restoring full citizenship to felons who have served their time. That would include protections against using his record as a justification for arbitrary search and seizure." Troy watched her scribble her notes. When she looked up, he said, "I think that will have to do it for today. I have appointments and a seminar to prepare for."

Eve reached over and squeezed his hand. "Thank you. I'll call you tomorrow to see if we can set up another interview. This is really getting interesting."

"Do that."

As she was packing to leave, she asked, "Could you answer a question about Adan Jackson?"

There was a long pause before he said, "That depends."

"I was just wondering what he was like in college."

Troy seethed. "Why?"

"Just curious," Eve demurred. "I didn't mean to upset you."

He bore into her with a hostile stare. Finally, he rumbled in a low, angry voice, "Adan was a born big shot. He walked into every situation as if he expected to be in charge. He was a brain and a big-time athlete. He was royalty. He got whatever he wanted." Troy looked away and shook his head. "Does that answer your question?"

"Yes," she said. "I'm sorry. I'm struggling to understand what happened."

Troy turned back to face her. "It was a senseless act of brutality."

He walked over and opened the door for his guest. "Call me tomorrow."

29

By Wednesday afternoon, Adan was in a funk so deep he was useless. He was still stewing over Agarwal's dressing down on Friday morning. Beau's attitude at dinner that night was insulting. In the end, his younger brother had come up with a good plan, but that didn't make up for his attitude. He had made it obvious that he thought he was having dinner with a fool.

Adan made an executive decision. He left work early, mailed the package to Cindy, and rushed home to play *Grand Theft Auto: The Lost and the Damned* for over an hour. When the game didn't work, Adan got up and poured himself a drink, scotch on the rocks. Then he retreated to his recliner and turned on *Rachmaninoff Playing Rachmaninoff.*

He pushed back in his recliner and took in the hot, bitter taste of the whiskey. Adan closed his eyes, shutting out the room's lavish furnishings and letting his world swell with the sounds of the piano while he savored alcohol-induced sensations.

He was perhaps halfway through the drink when it hit him. He should be talking to someone with a more down-to-earth attitude. Someone like Greg at the Boundary Line. Ten minutes later, Adan was on his way to Shepherd Park as Peter Baeker for a few beers with his buddy.

* * *

Greg turned so he could see who was entering the bar. Adan caught his eye and nodded. As soon as Adan was seated, the waitress, the short, dark-haired one who always took care of him, approached his table and asked, "The usual?"

Adan smiled slightly, nodded, and mouthed, *Yes*.

The waitress sashayed over to the bar to get his beer. Greg sauntered over to join his friend. On the TV over the bar, the Marlins were beating the Nats three-zip. At the end of the inning, as Washington headed out to take the field, Greg said, "You seem a little keyed up."

Adan turned slightly and raised an eyebrow. Greg nodded in the direction of his friend's hands. "You've been drummin' yer fingers and grousin' about the ump's calls."

Peter turned back to the TV. "Stressful day."

The leadoff batter for the Marlins hit a long foul ball. "Problems at work?" Greg asked without taking his attention from the game.

"Women."

"They're behind just about every problem in the universe," the big man observed. "What're they doin' this time?"

The batter reached first on a loopy pop up that dropped safely into right.

"One of the ladies at the office is complaining about sexual harassment."

"Ya mean actual harassment or overactive imagination?"

"A guy smiled at her a couple of times," Adan scoffed.

"We're livin' in tough times," Greg agreed. "Yer damned if ya do and yer damned if ya don't."

Adan finished his beer and held up an index finger. The waitress nodded and got him another one. He dropped a ten spot on her tray and watched her butt as she shimmied back to the bar.

"Is she makin' trouble for you?" Greg asked.

"Nah. It's a friend of mine."

"That's too bad," Greg said casually.

The Marlins' batter smashed a line drive into deep left field, putting runners on first and third.

Adan took a drink of beer and savored it. "Why is that?"

"Well, if it was you, I might be able to help."

Adan chuckled. "Put her in a pumpkin shell?"

Greg laughed. "That ain't what I had in mind."

A fly to right brought in the runner from third. The next batter went down swinging, and the batter after that lined out to short, ending the inning.

"What would you do if it was me?"

"I dunno. Maybe stop her on the street for a chat, or maybe bust up her car."

Adan's head jerked around. "If you accosted her on the street, she would report you to the police, and both of us would end up in trouble. That wouldn't work."

Greg nodded sagely. Adan took another drink of his beer. The Nats' leadoff batter hit a couple of foul balls but went down on a called strike.

Adan continued, "Why would she think that her car being vandalized had anything to do with the problems she's causing at work?"

"If she's smart enough to be working with you, she's smart enough to get the message."

The next Nats' batter hit a one-hopper down the third-base line. Cantu snagged it and threw him out at first. Zimmerman was up next. The count went to 3 and 2 before Zim hit a long fly to center for the third out.

Adan turned to Greg. "I don't see it. How would she make the connection?"

"What kind of car does your friend drive?"

"I don't know. I would have to check."

"Doesn't matter. I can get some guys to find a match for any car. They go by her house and make sure the car is seen while they smash her windows and slash her tires. Insurance covers the damage, but she reports it to the police. They investigate. They get a description of the car and ask her if she's having trouble with anybody. She mentions your friend. The police talk to him. He says he doesn't know anything about it and besides, his car was parked in front of his house at the time. End of story, except that she is convinced he really was responsible and he did it to teach her a lesson."

"Sounds like he could be in some serious trouble."

Greg shook his head and waved the idea off. "The police won't have anything. It'll blow over, but she'll remember."

The Nats' pitcher, Estrada, retired the Marlins in order. Adan watched the Nats get ready to take their turn at bat. "How much would an operation like that cost?"

Greg said nothing while the Marlins' pitcher, Johnson, put the Nats' batters down in order. He wanted his mark to stew. "I could get it done for a grand."

"A thousand bucks?" Adan was shocked.

"I'd need some help. We'd have to case the neighborhood and get the car. Then make the hit." The ex-con puckered out his lips and nodded. "A grand is cheap."

Estrada dismissed the Marlins' batters quickly. Adan called for another beer while the Marlins took the field, and the Nats came up to bat. Desmond got a single. Flores followed up with a solid double, and Desmond made it all the way home. One run for the Nats, but Flores was stranded on second.

"I'll talk to my friend," Adan said. "Supposing he is interested, how will we make the arrangements?"

Greg glared at him. "Be careful what you say. If your friend goes to the cops, we could all be in trouble. Especially you." Greg stared off into space and shook his head. He took a drink of his beer. "Maybe we should call this off. It's gettin' too complicated."

"It was your idea," Adan reminded him.

"I know. I was going to do it for you. But I don't know your friend. I don't think I can risk it."

Adan sat back and sipped his beer while he watched the Nats go down. The last batter took three called strikes. He didn't even take a swing.

Greg said, "Why don't you do your friend a favor? Get the bitch off his back but keep it between you and me."

Adan turned to face him. His lip curled up in disgust. "A thousand bucks is a big favor."

"Okay," Greg said. "I like you. Keep this between the two of us, and I'll figure out how to do the job for five hundred."

Adan folded his arms across his chest and looked away. When he turned back to Greg, he said grudgingly, "All right, five hundred. How do I make the arrangements?"

"Come back here with the cash, not a check. Small bills. In an envelope with the bitch's address and a description of her car and a description of your buddy's car." Greg thought for a moment. "Sit here. I'll bring a couple of beers. You hand me the envelope under the table, and I'll take care of the rest."

Adan stood. He seemed a little unsteady. He said, "Next week," and walked out of the bar.

30

The package arrived on Cindy's desk along with the rest of her morning mail. It was a plain manila envelope with bubble wrap to protect the contents during shipping. The words, "Eyes Only," had been scribbled in the lower left-hand corner. The return address was on Pennsylvania Avenue in D.C.

She knew something was wrong. It was a suspicious package that should be reported to security immediately. Instead, Cindy carefully slit the envelope along the top and peeked inside. A plastic DVD case peered back at her. She swallowed. Reaching in with two fingers, she delicately pulled the jewel case out onto her desk.

Someone had scrawled, "Play Me," on one face of the plastic case. A sticker on the front of the disc was visible through the plastic. It was the small icon that had graced her website in 1993. It announced: "Delilah Does It."

Cindy knew what was inside without opening it. She shoved the case back into its lair, dropped the package into a desk drawer, and slammed it shut. She raced to the ladies' room. Stepped into a stall. Locked the door and plopped down on the toilet. There she sat elbows on her knees and face buried in her hands. Her body shook uncontrollably.

When the initial panic had subsided, she began to work through the possibilities. *Nickey said Adan would probably threaten me with the videos. But he doesn't have them. The sworn statement I got from his lawyer before I signed the settlement agreement made sure of that. Besides, he would have dropped the disc on my desk to make sure I knew it was from him.*

She stood and walked over to the sinks where she washed her hands and splashed water on her face. *Not Adan's brother. He wouldn't have had a copy. Besides, he's covered by the affidavit.*

A scary thought hit her as she was drying her hands and face. *Troy. What happened to his copy? He went to prison in 1993, which means he's out. He could have sent that package.*

Back at her desk, Cindy sat down and smoothed her hair. She slid the desk drawer open very carefully as if a monster might jump out. The manila envelope was still there. She set it on the desk in front of her and stared at it. It had been sent from someplace on Pennsylvania Avenue.

An apartment or an office. I can check Adan's address, but it won't be on Pennsylvania Avenue. He'll have a place in Adams Morgan or Chevy Chase.

She looked around to make sure no one was watching, even though she had the tiny office all to herself. She took a deep breath before pulling up the employee list and typing "Adan Jackson" in the search bar. His photo popped up on the screen, along with publicly accessible contact information. His condo was in Adams Morgan on W Street.

Cindy switched to Google. The address on the envelope belonged to a large office complex called The Avenue. It was in Foggy Bottom, near George Washington University. She studied the map, looking for a clue. Nothing popped out at her. There was no connection. She could not imagine why anyone would have sent the ghoulish relic from her past. *Why would anyone even have a copy?*

She leaned back in her chair and stared at the screen. There was one person who might be able to help—the detective who had handled her complaint after the rape. Sergeant Lydia Bennett had given Cindy a card with the number for her direct line during the investigation. Bennett had been the one person who took Cindy's side throughout the nightmare. As the lead investigator on the case, she had been able to shield the coed from men like Detective Twomey.

Cindy kept contact information for both coworkers and friends on her cell phone. Most of it. But there was a small book in her purse that she had used before her cell phone took over. She held on to the relic in case something came up. Cindy retrieved the old address book and flipped through it. A dozen business cards that had been important to her at one time were stuffed into the book. Sergeant Bennett's card was in that collection.

A crisp, businesslike woman answered, "Captain Lydia Bennett. How can I help you?"

Cindy's heart sank. She needed several seconds to muster her courage. "Captain Bennett, this is Cindy

Smith. I don't know if you remember me. I was raped in 1993, and you investigated."

The voice softened. "Of course I remember you, Cindy. How are you?"

"I'm okay."

"You sound upset. What's the matter?"

"I think Troy is coming after me."

"Troy Mondale? What is he doing?" the detective demanded.

"I think he's out of jail and trying to scare me or something."

"Hold on." A minute later, Bennett came back on the line. "Yes. He's been out of prison for a while. What did he do?"

"I received a DVD in the mail today. There is no name on the envelope, but there's an address. I'm sure Troy sent it."

"What kind of DVD? What's on it?" Bennett sounded concerned.

"The videos." Cindy's voice cracked as she said the words.

"Are you sure?" Bennett pushed. "How would he get copies after all this time?"

"I don't know," Cindy fretted. "But *Deep Throat* is on YouTube, and that's older than Delilah's stuff."

"What's the address on the envelope?"

"2200 Pennsylvania Avenue."

"Give me a second." When Bennett returned, she confirmed Cindy's suspicion. "That's an office building near GWU. Troy Mondale is one of the tenants."

"He has an office?"

"His company is listed as Mondale Legal Consulting Services."

"Legal Consulting?" Cindy sneered. "That's rich."

Bennett chuckled and said, "I'll drop by and warn him to stay away from you."

31

Eve wasn't able to get together with Troy for another three days. He was working at the small table when she walked into the office. Marie was at the desk.

"Where do you want to go?" Troy asked.

"You're pushing an upbeat, positive attitude message at the same time you talk about how terrible life in prison is going to be. Can you explain that?"

"There are two reasons for the convict to have a positive attitude. The first is survival. Prison is a form of torture. Dehumanizing policies and practices are the norm. From top to bottom, hate and anger drive behaviors. Prisoners don't like themselves, and they quickly learn that those around them aren't any better. They become hyperalert and defensive. Any slight can trigger a brawl. Guards are often bottom feeders whose most important asset is the ability to cope with a bunch of big, dangerous scumbags. They quickly become enamored with their power over the inmates. Confrontations provide relief from the deadly monotony of prison life." Troy stood and walked away from the table while Eve made her notes. He turned back to face her with a big smile and tapped his heart three times. "A belief in your self-worth and a positive commitment to maintaining your humanity are the antidotes to those poisons. As long as you can hold on to your belief in your own self-worth and make yourself act like the person you want to be, you have a chance. You can be the kind of person who deserves a second chance at a normal life." He paused while Eve finished scribbling notes.

She looked up. "And the second reason?"

"If you want a good job after prison, you need to have knowledge and skills, just like everybody else."

"I see that you have a degree in Business Management from UMUC. What made you go that route?"

"Opportunity. We had access to the correspondence program from UMUC, and Business was my curriculum of choice."

"So, you walked into the education office and said, 'I want to get my diploma.'"

Troy returned to his seat. He grinned. "I was in there for six months before I found out the programs existed. My first lessons were hard ones administered by my fellow inmates." He exhaled noisily as he folded his hands behind his head and looked up at the ceiling. "Every time you enter a new facility, you go through in-processing, which starts with a strip search and a fresh set of clothes. Then you are grilled so the staff can figure out what to do with you. I was put in a cell with three other inmates and assigned to the crew that cleaned floors and toilets. Life is pretty simple there. My bunkmates filled me in on the rules of behavior."

Troy paused and chewed his lip until Eve looked up.

"After a few days, this guy named Mike came up to me in the yard and struck up a conversation. He wanted me to join a Bible study group. I wasn't interested in that crap. A week later, he tried again. I agreed because by that time I really needed to talk to somebody who seemed friendly. That was the smartest decision I made in a while. Those guys had developed a very positive approach to prison life based on their understanding of the New Testament. People like me who joined them suddenly had a solid group of friends and allies." He paused for a breath. "I was able to talk to them about the problems I was having with my cellmates. A few days later, I was moved into Mike's cell. As it turned out, he was a 'shot-caller,' a guy who has the pull to make things happen."

"What kind of problems?"

"I was a pathetic piece of shit. They used me because they could, and there was nothing I could do about it."

"Sexually?"

"That was part of it, but it was more than that."

"Were you raped?"

"I was smart enough not to resist."

"How many times?" she demanded angrily. She wanted to go after those assholes. At the same time, she knew there was nothing she could do. Tears welled up in her eyes.

He got up and walked away. He stood facing the wall with his hands clasped behind his back. A movement off to the side caught Eve's attention. Marie had gotten out of her chair. She looked like she wanted to do something but couldn't decide what. *She's going to put a stop to this.*

Troy broke the spell. "Mike was the one who turned me on to the real educational opportunities." The smooth, forceful rhythm of his voice calmed the atmosphere in the room. He drew her back into his narrative and gave her a chance to catch up. She began furiously scribbling notes as he continued. "The ones he knew about were high school level at best, but from there I was able to get a start on the college courses."

"So, the educational opportunities are there," she stammered.

"Some opportunities are provided. But..." He smiled broadly. "And there is always a 'but.'" He dropped his head and looked at the floor. His hands ran through his hair all the way back to his neck. He looked up at Eve. "The vast majority of the inmates have limited education. They read and write with difficulty, if at all. College-level courses make no sense for them." Troy sighed and shook his head. "The penal system is a one-size-fits-all operation. If most prisoners can't use college courses, they won't be offered." He brightened. "But they are available to inmates with enough gumption to go after them."

"It's not much different on the outside."

He nodded. "Students have to struggle to get admitted. They have to work their butts off to get through the coursework, and then they are stuck with a massive bill. But..." A sardonic smile crept across his features. "But they are not required to cope with the disentitlement, abuse, and daily emotional trauma that characterize life in prison." He rocked his head from side to side. "If college life was anything like prison life, the number of college graduates would drop dramatically." He turned and took a few steps then turned back. "And the suicide rate would go through the roof."

"How long did it take you to get your degree?"

"The first hurdle was finding the program and getting enrolled. That took a year or most of one. The second hurdle was getting the money to pay for school. That is another reason for low participation in courses that are not offered in-house. School costs money. Most prisoners don't have a lot of money, and prison rules prohibit inmates from earning meaningful incomes."

"But you have two degrees," Eve objected. "How did you pay for them?"

"Mostly my sister and her husband. My mother helped out after she got over the hurt and shame of having a son in prison for rape."

"That was very generous. It must have been difficult for them."

"I am sure it was. But my sister never said anything other than 'tell me what you need, and I'll get it.' As far as I know, her husband, Rick, backed her one hundred percent." Troy walked over and got himself a cup of coffee. He returned to the table and took a seat. "It was a loan. I would not take any money from any of them unless I signed an IOU. That was an important part of my rehabilitation. Now that I have some money coming in, I am repaying those loans. I'm just like every other college graduate in this country."

"Why did you switch from business to law?" Eve asked. "Did your prison experience push you in that direction?"

"In a way. Getting an advanced degree is much more difficult than getting an undergrad degree. Prison staff doesn't see any value in a Masters or a Ph.D., so they are unwilling to make any adjustments to accommodate the needs of grad students. I wanted to go for an MBA, but I switched to law because the correspondence courses were available."

"In other words, you just took the courses to have something to do?"

"Having a goal-oriented activity was important. It kept me focused and moving forward. The program is not recognized by the Bar Association. I can't take the bar exam and get a license to practice law." Troy's lip curled into a sneer. "It wasn't much of a course. The teachers were no help. I learned on my own by reading the materials and doing the assignments."

Marie interrupted, "Troy, it's about time for our next meeting. You need to wrap this up."

He nodded. Eve packed her things and stood. She squeezed Troy's hand. "Thank you for your time."

He said, "I think it's good for me to talk about this stuff."

The office door opened, and an imposing brunette wearing a navy-blue blazer entered the room. She looked around. Her eyes locked on Troy. "Mr. Mondale?"

He leaned back and folded his arms. He stared at the woman. His expression said he knew her and had no use for her.

She repeated, "Mr. Mondale?" When he didn't respond, she walked over and stared down at him. "Prison seems to have treated you well. You look healthy, and you've got your own business."

He raised his eyebrows and shrugged.

The intruder continued, "If you want to keep it that way, stay away from Cindy Smith."

Troy continued to watch her with a bemused smile.

"Do you understand me?" she demanded.

"Yes and no. I understand what you are saying, but I have no idea what you are talking about, Captain. It is Captain Bennett, isn't it?"

"So, you've been keeping track of me?"

"Not really. But I did hear that you had been promoted."

"Have you been tracking Cindy?"

"No. I did see her wedding announcement in the *Post*."

"You're lying," Bennett snarled.

Troy smiled and shook his head. "I find that being truthful works best."

Marie walked over to Captain Bennett. "I'm Mr. Mondale's lawyer. Can you tell me what this is about?"

Bennett looked in her direction with a derisive half smile and returned to Troy. "If you want to go back to prison, I can arrange it."

Marie pushed her way between the two of them. "I demand to know what this is about. You can either explain yourself or leave."

The captain took a step back. "Your client has started harassing a woman he raped sixteen years ago."

"I know about the rape. My client knows better than to contact that woman. He is not harassing her."

"He sent her a package and was stupid enough to put this address on the envelope."

Troy shook his head. "I haven't sent anything to Mrs. Foster."

"It has your address."

"I'm a registered sex offender. My address is readily available to anyone with access to the internet."

"Why would anybody else send her a DVD and use your office address?" Bennett demanded.

"I don't know. I haven't talked to anybody about her. But I can think of some obvious answers," Troy retorted.

"Such as?"

Marie put a hand over Troy's mouth. "My client has no way of knowing who might have sent that package. Have you asked Mrs. Foster who has been giving her trouble lately?"

Bennett sneered but said nothing.

Marie said in her best lawyer's voice, "This interview is over, Captain."

Bennett glared at her but turned and walked out of the office.

Eve had stood frozen, afraid to move, throughout the encounter. Now she was trembling. As soon as the door shut, she let out a soft "Shit."

Marie brushed a hand across Troy's cheek. "Are you okay?"

He nodded. Hurt and anger were written on his face.

Eve cleared her throat. "I'm leaving. I'll call you tomorrow if that's okay."

"Sure. Do that." He looked and sounded drained.

32

Adan was in a deep funk when he entered the Boundary Line as Peter Baeker a little after eight. Anticipation and fear burned like fire in his gut. The fear was stronger. It made him numb to everything. It left him weak and empty. His legs seemed ready to give out. He pushed on so he could get home and light up a joint or two or three.

Greg spotted his mark out of the corner of his eye and turned slightly. They made eye contact. He turned back and signaled the bartender.

Adan trudged to his table and collapsed onto his seat, his body numb, his mind blank.

The waitress, the short, dark-haired one, came over. "The usual?"

Her voice roused him from his stupor. He needed a moment to come up with an answer. Greg arrived with two beers before Adan could say anything. He smiled at the woman and shook his head. He nodded toward Greg and mouthed, *Not right now.*

Her lips curled up into a tight, half-smile. She nodded and walked away.

The big man set the beers down and took his seat. "You look a little pale."

"Must be something I ate. I'll be all right in the morning."

Greg nodded sagely. "Good."

Adan slid an envelope from his back pocket and handed it under the table. Greg folded the envelope twice with his right hand and slipped it into his pocket. Adan watched in horrified fascination. He took a swig of his beer. "Aren't you going to check it?"

A scowl played across the ex-con's face. He relaxed. "If anything is missing, our deal is off," he growled. "Ya wouldn't want that, would ya?"

Adan shook his head.

Greg smiled and winked. "Good."

He leaned back and sipped his beer while he studied the man sitting across from him. His eyes narrowed. "Maybe you should go on home and get some rest. You don't look so good."

Adan nodded and rose. He drifted out of the bar, head down and hands in his pockets.

33

The sound of breaking glass shattered sleep at four in the morning. People struggled to get up to find out what was going on. Eric and Cindy bolted from their bed. They were young and in good shape. He sprinted through the living room and out the front door. She raced to the picture window to survey the street.

At first, everything looked normal. It took Cindy several seconds to realize that her car's windows had been smashed out. Eric saw that the tires had been slashed by the time he was halfway down the sidewalk.

Cindy would later recall seeing a dark-colored car speeding away from her house.

The first PG County police unit arrived thirty minutes after the attack. Two more showed up at the scene five minutes later. The police went door to door on the Fosters' block and one block farther in each direction. No one had seen what happened. Only a few of their neighbors had heard the windows being smashed. Some reported a black car fleeing from the scene of the crime. Others said the car was blue. Half of the homes on those three blocks had security cameras that captured pieces of a vehicle approaching the Foster residence and trashing the burgundy Ford Edge. Segments of video from cameras near the scene captured details. Two figures hopped out of a dark car. In less than a minute, they smashed the Ford's windows and slashed the tires. They piled back into their getaway vehicle and drove off.

When Cindy gave her statement to the police, she volunteered that Troy Mondale, a D.C. resident, was probably responsible for the attack. She told police he gone to prison for an earlier assault and had been harassing her since he got out of jail.

Crime lab technicians pieced together snippets from the home security camera footage. They used advanced editing software to combine multiple views of the car and the perps to create an enhanced 3D version of the event.

The two thugs wore bulky clothes, including hoodies that hid their faces. They appeared to be wearing Halloween masks in the glimpses of their faces caught by the cameras. Police used the car as a benchmark to estimate that they were six feet tall. Probably male. Their vehicle was identified as a dark blue 2005 Toyota Corolla. License plates had been removed from the front and rear. Oddly, the car did not speed away.

Troy Mondale was only five-foot-ten according to his driver's license. But he could not be ruled out because he could have worn thick-soled shoes that made him taller. There was no way to figure out who his companion might be.

A vehicle registered to Troy matched the description of the getaway car.

PG Police notified Jack Edwards that Troy Mondale and an unknown companion were persons of interest. Jack tentatively identified the partner as Troy's associate, Marie Moretti, and dispatched his detectives to take them into custody. He would later regret naming the lawyer as the likely companion.

Detectives went to Troy's home and office. Neither he nor Marie was at either location. An area-wide alert went out just after one p.m. The police were looking for a man and a woman driving a dark blue, late model Toyota Corolla. They were assumed to be armed and dangerous.

* * *

Troy looked over at his passenger. Marie gave him a puzzled look and shook her head. Everybody on the highway with them had just been alerted that they were armed and dangerous and on the run from police.

Minutes after the alert appeared on the overhead signs, a state police car pulled up behind the couple with its lights flashing. They pulled to the shoulder. The trooper sat in his car and watched them until his backup arrived. When PG County police showed up, they took over. A sergeant took charge. She had the suspects step out of their car and place their hands on the roof so they could be searched. No weapons were found. She had them handcuffed and put in her car for transport to the PG Corrections Department in Upper Marlboro, Maryland. A tow truck hauled their Corolla to impound after a search for weapons and drugs turned up nothing.

Troy and Marie demanded legal representation at any interrogation. They both wanted William Golden, an associate professor of law at GWU and the third principal in Troy's consulting firm. He had become interested in Troy while the younger man was still in prison.

He had also been Marie Moretti's adviser in law school.

Marie went first. She was a prominent attorney in the District of Columbia with no prior arrests.

The flight charge was patently ridiculous. She and Troy had been driving west toward D.C. when they were arrested. They were returning from a meeting with a client in Leonardtown, Maryland. The meeting had lasted over an hour, and they had started back shortly before one. Trip data from the GPS in the car would support those statements.

The vandalism charge was a problem. Marie had been home alone at the time of the crime. No one could verify her statement. But she had no reason to cause harm to Mrs. Foster. The two had never met. When Marie threatened to bring a false arrest suit against the PG police, they decided they didn't have sufficient grounds to hold her. She was released.

Troy gave the same story as his partner. But the car used in the crime matched Troy's blue 2005 Toyota Corolla. Golden called an investigator to confirm that his client's car had been in a parking garage all night.

When the police asked Troy why his car was at the scene of the crime, he said, "I don't know anything about that incident. I was in bed asleep all night. As far as I know, my car was in the garage."

"We have a video that places your car at the scene of the crime."

"A video that places *my* Toyota at the scene of a crime in Bowie, Maryland, at four a.m.?" Troy asked incredulously.

"Your blue 2005 Toyota Corolla," the officer insisted.

"With the dented fender and the broken taillight?" Troy shot back.

"Yes. With the dented fender and the broken taillight."

"That's not my car," Troy smirked. "Mine doesn't have any damage."

The officer glared at him.

Nickey Arnold arrived just in time to interrupt the standoff.

The investigator spread her stack of papers on the table. "These are copies of the parking garage logs from noon yesterday until noon today." She pointed to a circled entry. "Mr. Mondale's car entered at 4:43 p.m. yesterday." She indicated a second circled entry. "It left the garage at 10:27 this morning. There are no log entries for that car in between those two times. That car does not show up on security footage at any time during the night. Mr. Mondale's car was parked there all night."

Golden gave the police time to study the material before asking, "Are we free to go?"

"Mr. Mondale will have to spend the night with us." The detective grinned as he delivered the bad news.

"Why? There's no evidence tying him to the crime."

"Mrs. Foster has accused him of making threats against her."

"Does she have any proof? My client has not had any contact with Mrs. Foster."

"Her complaint is credible. He has a history of violence."

"That was sixteen years ago, and Mr. Mondale has served his time."

"I can hold him for twenty-four hours while we investigate Mrs. Foster's complaint, and that is what I am going to do."

Golden turned to Troy. "Hang in there. I'm not finished."

Two hours later, Golden returned with Marie Moretti in tow. He had an order for Troy Mondale's immediate release signed by Judge Greg Turner of the Prince George's County Circuit Court. Turner had been a prominent attorney when Bill Golden worked for him as a law student. Those kinds of relationships could be important in some situations.

Troy got back to his condo after midnight. His car was still in impound. The situation was still up in the air. It felt like he was back in prison. The only thing he could do was try to get some sleep.

34

Captain Bennett walked up to Troy's table. He was sitting alone in The Café, an eatery in the Cap Gallery mall area. The plastic dish that had held his omelet was pushed to one side. He sipped coffee while reading online newspapers.

She sidled up to him to see what was on his iPad. Her thigh brushed against his elbow. The scent of honeysuckle and wildflowers wafted over him.

He ignored the provocations and continued reading.

"Good morning, Mr. Mondale. Awfully far from home, aren't you?"

Troy looked up. She wore dark slacks and a matching blazer over a white blouse. He scrunched his nose and shook his head. "Nah."

"Don't you live over by the zoo?"

He nodded.

Bennett asked suspiciously, "Why are you eating breakfast over here?"

"Why not? At least I have a reason for being here."

The captain stepped back, folded her arms, and stared down her nose at her quarry. Her foot began to tap. "I have a reason for being here."

"What is that?"

"I'm trying to figure out why you came all the way over to Cap Gallery to eat."

"I get to start the day with a nice walk and a good breakfast. Habits I picked up in prison."

"You could get the same meal near your condo on Connecticut Avenue."

"But I wouldn't get my walk."

Bennett rolled her eyes and shook her head. "Maybe you like this place because Cindy Foster works here."

Troy looked around. "I don't believe I have ever seen her in here."

The officer pointed to elevators in the corridor just outside the eatery. "Upstairs."

He looked out toward the elevators. No one was using them. The Saturday morning crowd did not have the same manic energy as the weekday crowds. "You learn something new every day."

"You expect me to believe that you just happen to frequent a restaurant in the building where the woman you raped works?"

"Yes."

"You're lying," Bennett snarled.

"As far as I know, Captain, I am free to move about this city and patronize whatever businesses I choose." Troy paused for a sip of coffee. He pressed his lips into a line and exhaled through his nose as he studied the officer. "Unlike you, I have served my time for my crime."

Bennett's face turned a bright red. "Unlike you, I haven't committed any crimes."

"You don't consider beating a prisoner in your custody a crime?"

"I was found not guilty," she snapped.

"Because you are a member of the police fraternity. If I handcuffed somebody and beat them with a pipe, I would get prison time." He paused to watch her react then sneered. "You would make sure of that."

"I was found not guilty because he was resisting arrest," Bennett fumed.

"What made him stop resisting? The broken arm? The shattered knee? The cracked skull?"

"He kept fighting, so I kept fighting."

"I spent a lot of time in the prison infirmary tending to men who got the worst end of a confrontation with the guards. They all said the same thing: 'He didn't give me any choice.'"

"That's because you animals all behave the same way."

Troy pursed his lips and nodded. "You hate men, don't you?"

Captain Bennett pulled herself together. "My job puts me in contact with some despicable men. I have to protect women from them."

"But you love that job because it gives you an excuse to beat men into submission."

"The men I deal with are criminals like you. They have to be dealt with harshly."

"Some of them," he conceded. "But you enjoy besting all of them. You never get tired of going after them. As soon as you put one down, you go after the next."

"There is a large population of perps in this city."

"You and Adan Jackson are two sides of the same coin," Troy suggested. "He has never met a woman he didn't want to rape. You have never met a man you didn't want to emasculate."

"That's enough, Mr. Mondale. You are way over the line."

"Just like you went over the line coming in here to harass me."

"Stay away from Cindy Foster."

Troy glared at the policewoman. "Stay away from me. Abuse of your police powers is a punishable offense."

Her eyes opened wide in disbelief. "Are you threatening me?"

"Are you abusing your police powers?"

Bennett answered with a tight-lipped stare.

Troy bit on his lip and nodded. "I would like to finish my breakfast in peace."

She sighed and shook her head. But she walked away.

35

Captain Lydia Bennett marched straight to Sergeant Jack Edwards's office, as soon as her desk was cleared on Monday morning. He had not been involved in the 1993 rape case, but he would know about it. He would understand how important it was to make sure that Troy Mondale did not hurt Cindy Foster again. This was his city. It was his responsibility to keep it safe.

Jack looked up when she stepped into the doorway. He scowled but stood to greet her. "Captain Bennett, please come in and have a seat."

"Thank you."

He watched with a grim smile as she crossed the room to his desk. "What can I do for you, Captain?"

She sat with her hands folded in her lap. Erect posture. Shoulders pulled back. Gaze direct and challenging. She smiled quizzically. "I know you're busy, Sergeant, but I think we need to discuss a case that affects both of us."

Jack took his seat. "By all means."

"I'm not sure whether you remember, but there was a particularly violent rape on the Georgetown campus back in 1993."

"There was a lot of talk about it at the time."

"One of the attackers was sent to prison. He is out on the streets now and living in D.C."

Jack nodded but said nothing.

Bennett continued, "He seems to be going after the victim again. It looks like he is stalking her."

"Why doesn't she file a complaint?" he rumbled.

"I'm not sure. She called me." The captain pursed her lips. "I suppose she remembers me from the rape investigation."

The sergeant was grave and concerned. "She needs to come down here and talk to us."

"She's afraid," Bennett objected. "This man is a violent, dangerous criminal."

"We'll protect her. But we need to get her statement. For one thing, she needs to tell us what he is doing."

"He sent her a package of suggestive material, and he has parked himself outside her office," she snapped. "That should be enough to open an investigation."

"I am sure it will be if she gives my detectives a statement," Jack insisted.

Bennett rose abruptly and paced over to the window. When she turned back to face the sergeant, she began, "He locked her in a room and raped her. You can't let him get away with that again."

Jack leaned back and stroked his chin. "Has he threatened her?"

Bennett took one step toward him. She paused with her hands on her hips and glared at him. Jack tilted his head to one side and raised his brows. "So, he hasn't made any overt threats."

"He was sitting outside her office the last time I talked to him."

"Why didn't you arrest him?"

"I couldn't."

"Because ...?"

Bennett walked back to her chair. "Put a tail on him and find out what he is up to."

"On what grounds?"

"Probable cause," she snapped. "He's a rapist, and he's stalking this woman."

"He is stalking her? Or you suspect he is stalking her?"

"Do something before he attacks her again, Jack."

Jack grimaced. He picked up his desk phone and dialed a number. "Smith, could you step into my office?"

The captain sat down and folded her arms. Moments later, a dishwater blonde with angular features walked through the door. "Have a seat, Liz."

The sergeant turned to Bennett. "Okay, Captain, who is this man, and what does he look like?"

"Troy Mondale. Medium build, red hair, blue eyes. He gets breakfast every morning in The Café in Cap Gallery so he can watch the elevators."

"Wait a minute," Jack objected. "You told me he was sitting outside the woman's office. The Cafe is in a public shopping area on the first floor."

Bennett snarled, "He watches the elevators that go up to the offices. Mrs. Foster has to pass right by him whenever she comes to work."

"As do hundreds of other office workers. The Cafe is a restaurant open to the public. I can't do anything about anyone, including Mr. Mondale, patronizing the business."

"He's dangerous."

"This office doesn't work that way," the sergeant growled. "I am not going after people without a good reason."

"You're just going to wait until something happens to Mrs. Foster?"

"Mondale has been out of prison for five years. If he was going to do something to Mrs. Foster, he would have done it already."

Bennett was quizzical. She put a finger across her lips. "Have you been checking up on him?"

"I checked him out when I got wind of someone harassing Mrs. Foster."

"That was probably Mondale."

"It was Adan Jackson."

"You're sure?"

"Mrs. Foster hired a private detective to confront Jackson and tell him to stay away."

"Mondale put him up to it."

Jack sat back and chuckled. "Troy Mondale couldn't get Adan Jackson to leave a burning building. The consensus among cops I have talked to is that Mondale was a patsy. The Jackson boys set him up, and he took the fall."

"He led the assault," Bennett snarled.

"Is there anything else, Captain?"

"What about the attack on Cindy Foster's car? The PG police have Mondale on video."

The sergeant shook his head. "The County prosecutor has decided that there isn't enough evidence. He's dropping the charges."

Bennett stared in amazement. "The video shows the two of them slashing tires and breaking windows."

"No one witnessed the crime. Even Mrs. Foster said they had fled the scene before she got to her door." Jack shrugged. "Home security cameras caught two people. They wore hoodies and bulky work clothes that could have been purchased anywhere. There is no way to identify them."

"What about the report on the tip line?"

"That call is a problem, Captain," he said in a low, threatening voice. "The caller claimed to be a witness and said the vandals were driving a blue 2005 Toyota Corolla. The caller gave a license number that belonged to Mondale's car." He paused to get her reaction. She stared back, poker-faced. "There were no witnesses, and the vehicle didn't have license plates." The big man put his elbows on his desk and leaned toward his visitor. "The police did not give out any information on the car except to say that it was either black or dark blue. It looks like the caller had access to inside information and added some details to lead police to Mondale." He pulled his body erect and narrowed his eyes. "So, we're wondering how the caller knew the make and model of the vehicle and how she came up with the license number."

Bennett rose. She stood staring down at Jack. "If you can't back that up with facts, Sergeant, you better keep it to yourself."

The captain was almost to the door when Jack said, "Just a friendly tip."

She turned and eyed him.

A faint smile played across his face. "Make sure you don't overstep your boundaries, Captain."

"What is that supposed to mean, Sergeant?"

"I heard that you marched into Mondale's office and threatened to put him back in jail."

"Where did you hear that?"

"I have my sources."

"Good day, Sergeant," Bennett said as she walked out of the office.

Liz said, "Eve?"

"Get back to work, Detective."

36

As the week wore on, Adan noticed things. He did not see or hear anything that told him Cindy had reacted to the Delilah videos. But there was a subtle response to the attack on her car. Her eyes followed him. She stared at him when she thought he couldn't see her. Adan sensed that Cindy was feeling suspicion and fear. He guessed that at some level she remembered his promise to make her pay if she went to the police. That made him feel powerful, and he liked the feeling.

Adan began thinking seriously about dealing with his enemies. When he thought of Cindy, he raged over the bitch detective she had sicced on him. He stewed over the dressing-down in Agarwal's office. *A little damage to your car scares you? Wait 'til you see what's coming next.*

As for that whore who had embarrassed him in his hotel room, *you'll get yours, sister.* He had the goods on her. She was a private detective who specialized in divorce cases. Her condo was off Crain Highway between D.C. and Baltimore. That was a dark and deserted road at night when she drove home. Adan hadn't figured out how to predict when and where to ambush her. But he was working on it.

He sat in his office mulling over that problem and realized he knew a woman who should be looking into a divorce. She had never complained about her hubby, but she obviously did not care much for him. Adan had found her online at the Ashley Madison website, where she called herself Polly Andry. Her real name was Gertie Gelberger. She could have been Adan's twin sister. A six-foot-tall, blond amazon with incredible sexual prowess. Just thinking about her made Adan so hard he couldn't sit still. He called Gertie about meeting him for lunch. He didn't have to ask twice. She was ready for a good fuckfest.

* * *

They went straight to Adan's room. A little waltz brought them to the edge of the couch. Shoes came off as they danced across the room. They undressed each other while they kissed and caressed.

She opened his pants. His cock stood straight up like a dagger. She went down on her knees and flirted with his erection while she pushed his pants to the floor.

He pulled her back to her feet and opened her slacks. She wiggled out of them and pushed his shirt open to reveal brawny pecs. She slid out of her blouse and drove her chest against his, pushing him back to the wall.

She fondled his shaft while he helped her out of her thong. This was a bothersome ritual, but she insisted on it. She did not want to have to buy new underwear every time they hooked up.

Adan grabbed her butt and hoisted her. Gertie dutifully wrapped her legs around his waist. He carried her to the doorway leading to the bedroom with his cock pushing against her clit. He forced his way in and began pounding her. Heavy breathing and moans said she was utterly lost in the act.

A knock on the door broke the spell. "Room service."

He pulled free and set her on the floor. She paused to fix him with a murderous stare. This was not the first time he had pulled that stunt. Gertie spit in his face before racing to the bed and yanking a cover over her naked body. He laughed and smacked her on the rear end as she spun away from him. He hustled over to grab his trousers as if they would hide what he had been up to.

A young woman pushed the cart into the room, staring straight ahead with a stony expression, but her cheeks were red. Sex smells hung in the air. Adan followed her into the room. When she turned to hand him the bill, the bulge in his crotch brushed up against her arm. She became visibly uncomfortable while she waited for him to examine the tab and pull his wallet from his pants. When he handed her a couple of twenties, she looked up at him. He smiled playfully.

A smile played across her face for an instant before she beat a hasty retreat. His boyish grin caught her fancy, but his eyes were scary.

He dropped his pants as he walked back to the bed. He pulled the cover off Gertie. "Where were we?"

The meal consisted of fruit, cheese, cold cuts, bread, and wine. It would keep. Their lust would not. They locked in sexual combat, battling to be on top while remaining locked at the hip. He humped while she worked her hips to bring forth the magic sensations.

When they needed a break, they sat naked across from each other at the table by the bay window, which looked out onto Calvert Street, and ate. Then they went back for more. It was almost two when they reluctantly agreed they should be getting back to the office.

Adan said casually, "I need a small favor."

"I don't pay for sex," Gertie retorted.

"Of course not." Adan chuckled. "But I would like to ask a favor as a friend."

She grabbed a towel and headed for the shower. "What is it?"

"I need some help with a woman."

Gertie stopped and turned. She eyed Adan. "You need help with a woman? What kind?"

"It's nothing really. I just want you to make an appointment with her at your office."

"An appointment? Is she interested in some property?"

"She's a private investigator who works on divorce cases."

"I'm not getting a divorce. I certainly wouldn't get one to marry an asshole like you."

Adan walked over to her and put his arms around her. "I'm not asking you to get a divorce. I just want you to talk to this woman about investigating your husband."

The suggestion brought a disdainful, suspicious squinch from Gertie. She pushed free of his embrace and went off to shower.

When she came out, she said, "You're setting her up."

It was an accusation.

"I just need a few minutes alone with her car."

"You are not thinking of planting a bomb, are you?"

"No." He raised his hands. "I'm afraid of bombs."

"You had better not because I won't be part of murder or anything like that," she said sternly.

"I just want to put a tracker on her car."

"Why?"

Adan exhaled in frustration. "I want to get her alone so I can give her a piece of my mind."

She grinned. "Your mind? Or your cock?"

"My mind," he snapped.

"You're not going to hurt her?"

"Absolutely not. She's butting into things that don't concern her, and I want to let her know that I don't appreciate it."

Gertie eyed him suspiciously. "Why don't you just call her and tell her?"

"She won't listen. I want to get her alone and tell her face-to-face just how I feel about the situation."

"Don't expect me to help you in any way if something goes wrong."

Adan grimaced. "Does that mean you'll do it?"

"How do I get in touch with her?"

37

Adan showered, dressed, and paced around the room to give Gertie a good head start before going to his car. He stopped in front of the portrait on the living room wall, *Matador and Bull* by Sanchez. A man narrowly avoiding a bull's charge drives his sword deep into the beast's neck. The vivid depiction of the violent, desperate, life-and-death struggle of a bullfight in brilliant color spoke to the executive.

It was a copy, but Adan used to love it. Now it reminded him of that woman: Cindy or Nickey or whatever her name was. *A bullfighter finishing off his victim. Is that your style?*

He bared his teeth in an angry sneer. *You're damn right, bitch.*

Adan tore himself away and left the room, his whole body vibrating. He could not go back to his office and sit.

Instead, he walked into the Marquee Bar and ordered a scotch on the rocks. It didn't help. He drove over to the Tahiti and ordered another one. The place was practically empty at that time of day. He found a table against one wall and surveyed the room as he sipped his drink. The girl dancing on the stage had light brown hair and a figure that reminded him of Cindy Smith. Adan ordered another drink and asked about the stripper. Could she visit with him at his table after she finished her set?

The waitress's butt held his attention as she made her way back to the bar. An African American woman stepped into his line of sight and followed the waitress. He turned his attention back to the dancer, who was starting to dress. His waitress went up to her and said something. She looked at Adan, smiled, and waved. She stopped at several other tables to thank her admirers as she worked her way over to him.

When she reached his table, she smiled and extended her hand. "Hi, I'm Sally Ride."

"Adam Smith." He took her hand. It was so petite he was afraid of crushing it.

She pulled a chair around to sit next to him. "So, you liked my number?"

"Yes. You are a very sexy woman."

Sally laughed. It was deep and hearty. "So, are you playing hooky or on vacation?"

He rocked his head. "Ah have flexible hours."

"So, what do you do when you're not being naughty and hanging out here?"

Adan grinned fiendishly and whispered in her ear, "Make money."

She laughed again. "I bet you're good at that."

He chuckled. His hand slid to her thigh. She covered it with her hand. Sally asked questions and smiled as she listened intently to his answers. She leaned closer and raised her eyebrows when she asked in a shy voice, "Would you like a private dance?"

Adan wrinkled his nose and shook his head. "Ah'm not in the mood for that."

"What are you in the mood for?"

"Right now? Ah would really like to be fucking you."

She turned her head slightly to look at him sideways. Her eyes went wide with shock. But she grinned when she said, "We might be able to arrange that."

"Really?"

"Really." Sally raised her right hand and waved. A middle-aged woman standing at the bar chatting with the young black woman turned and nodded. Then she turned back to her companion and held up one finger before walking toward Adan's table. He studied her as she crossed the room.

She was a big woman. Tall. Broad at the shoulders and hips. Black hair and a dark complexion. As she got closer, he could see that she applied her makeup generously. Her eyelashes were long and thick, her lips bright red.

"Carla, this is Adam Smith," Sally said when the woman reached their table. "He wants to take me out for a couple of hours."

The shift manager smiled. "Very good. Mr. Smith, could you come over to the bar with me? I will need to get some information while Sally changes. Then you can be on your way."

The Nubian princess captured his attention as he approached the bar. She was focused on her cell phone. A study in unconscious beauty. Her long, slender nose descending from her forehead to her pouting lips. The prominent jaw and slender neck. Her silky black hair was trimmed halfway down her ears and tapered along the back of her neck. *How does she manage that?*

He felt sensations in his hands as though he was touching her smooth coffee skin. He imagined himself in bed, holding her naked body close to his.

Carla asked for his cell phone number, the make and model of his car and the license number, and his home address. He looked up while he invented his answers. Two surveillance cameras stared down at him. It didn't matter what he told her. The police could use the surveillance footage to find him if they needed to. Carla explained that the fee for two hours was $100, and "a generous tip would make the date go a lot better."

Adan handed over a C-note.

Sally suggested the Courtyard Marriott a half-mile away. Adan said he didn't have his car. Carla called a cab and got the couple on their way a little after four.

* * *

The shift manager went back to her office for a job application and handed it to the African American woman. "Fill this out. You can mail it to me or bring it back. However, at the moment, we are fully staffed. I will keep your application on file and contact you when something opens up."

Rhonda Johnson smiled politely. "Thank you, ma'am."

She knew she would never hear from Carla Mitchell. It didn't matter. She had no intention of working at the Tahiti. Her job was to keep an eye on Adan Jackson. Johnson walked out of the club and straight to Adan's

SUV in the parking lot. She placed a tracking device under the car near the rear bumper. Then she called Detective Liz Smith to set up a connection to the tracker she had just planted.

Liz asked, "What's our boy up to now?"

"He's at the Marriott up the street with a hooker."

"Without his car?"

Johnson rolled her eyes. "They took a cab."

"Did he make you?"

"He undressed me, but he already had a date."

"Take the rest of the night off. I'll keep an eye on him."

* * *

Sally was worth the price of admission. She called herself "Ride" because that was what she loved to do. She also enjoyed being ridden. And just about every other imaginable form of sexual engagement. She even gave her client a quick introduction to erotic asphyxiation. Adan called a cab a little after six and took Sally back to the Tahiti. He gave her an extra $100 when he dropped her off. She was good, but she wasn't Gertie.

38

Peter Baeker strode into the Boundary Line and took his regular seat a little after eight. He smiled and nodded as the waitress approached his table. She turned and went off to get his beer. Greg strolled over and sat across from the executive, who ignored him and concentrated on the game. He did not even glance over to acknowledge his friend's arrival.

When his beer arrived, he paid but kept his focus on the TV.

The Nats were playing the Arizona Diamondbacks at home. They were in the bottom of the fourth with no score. Peter barely smiled when Davis, the Arizona pitcher, loaded up the bases, and Zimmerman stepped to the plate. But he pumped his fist when Zim sent a line drive deep into left field, scoring two runs. Then he ordered another beer. Greg watched the game and waited.

After the inning ended, Peter said casually, "My friend was pleased. The woman's attitude has changed."

Greg turned to look at him. "How did your friend know about that? It was supposed to be between the two of us."

"We had lunch today," Peter said. "He brought it up. Said something about how she was acting differently. One thing led to another. No big deal. He doesn't know anything about you."

"That's good."

"The thing is," Peter continued, "we got to talking and thinking that another message, something a little stronger, might be needed."

Greg's eyebrows shot up. "*We*?"

"Yes. We were talking. We agreed that there was an improvement in her attitude, but we felt like she was still a problem."

"Is that right?" the big man growled.

Peter's head snapped around. "What's the matter?"

"It sounds like you're talkin' too much. I don't know your friend. I don't trust him." Greg shook his head. He chugged a drink of beer. "He could tell the police all about that conversation when they come askin' about what's been goin' on with that woman."

"He can't tell them anything," Peter insisted. "We just had a conversation. One that he started, by the way."

"But he knows that somebody trashed her car to send her a message," Greg countered.

"No." Peter shook his head. "I think I said it was odd the way that happened."

"You need to be careful," Greg warned. "The next thing you know, the police will be askin' you why you thought it was odd."

Peter grimaced and gulped his beer. The fifth inning had ended. He had missed most of it, but the score was still two zip in favor of the Nats. "It's no crime to wonder about things like that."

Greg glared.

Peter turned back to the TV. He raised his voice to regain control of the conversation. "The thing is, I agree with him. Something more needs to be done."

"Be careful. Some things you can get away with. Some will get you into trouble."

Peter pursed his lips. He leaned back and looked up at the ceiling. "I think she would finally get the point if something happened to her husband."

"That could get you into real trouble."

"Not if the mugger disappeared."

"What're you talkin' about?"

"If I came up with enough money," Peter suggested, "somebody could rob the guy and skip town before the police tracked him down."

The ex-con nodded sagely. "That might be possible."

"The thing is, I want the guy to work for me this time."

Greg finished his beer and ordered another. He rested his hands on the table and leaned back. "Two problems," he said solemnly. "First, you can't trust somebody who'd do somethin' like that." He paused. "And second. You would be puttin' yourself in a dangerous situation."

"Not if he does the job and disappears."

"That's a big if."

They let the waitress serve Greg's beer and go back to the bar. Peter said, "Find me somebody, and I'll take care of the rest."

"I like you," Greg said thoughtfully. "Let me handle that kind of stuff."

"I want to do this one. I just need to know who to talk to."

Greg sipped his beer. He looked at Peter and shook his head. "I'll see what I can do."

Peter handed him a slip of paper. "I can be reached at this number."

Greg scanned the note before slipping it into his pocket. "OK."

The TV caught their attention. The crowd was on its feet, cheering. The Nats had won.

Peter stood to leave. "Thanks. I appreciate your help."

He strolled out of the bar. Greg smiled as he watched a rich, arrogant fool walk away satisfied

39

Gertie and her husband, Max, started Gelberger Real Estate in 1989.

She had been a nineteen-year-old college student working as an assistant manager at a Dairy Queen when Max spotted her. He fell instantly in love and talked her into coming to work for him at his real estate business. Once she got her real estate license, she proved to be as talented at selling as she was at managing. She quit college and married him. That was in 1988, on her twentieth birthday.

Gelberger Real Estate was still doing well twenty years later. Their offices were in a high-rise on Pennsylvania Avenue. The marriage was still on the books, but it existed in name only.

Gertie called Nickey as soon as she got back from her rendezvous with Adan. The conversation was brief. Gertie mentioned her marital problems and said she would like the detective to investigate her husband. She could not explain how she got Nickey's name and number. A friend had made the recommendation, but Gertie hadn't thought to ask how he got the information. Nickey let it go and said she could fit Gertie in on Friday afternoon.

* * *

The detective arrived shortly before three and parked on a side street two spots south of Pennsylvania Avenue. She found her prospective client alone in her office. Gertie stood and walked over to greet the detective with a handshake and a winning smile. The room was spacious but equipped only for the manager and one other person. It had a sofa and a conference table with chairs to accommodate meetings with clients. The décor emphasized color and flowing lines at the expense of standard office furniture. Subdued colors suggested a pleasant fall day. One large window looked out onto the city.

Gertie explained that she and her husband had been leading separate lives for a few years, and she had decided it was time to end the marriage.

"Why don't you get a no-fault divorce?" Nickey asked.

"He doesn't want a divorce because a marriage, even a token marriage, helps his image. A divorce would be a disaster for him."

"You can still file for divorce. If he wants to contest, he would be looking at a very public trial. That would be the disaster he's trying to avoid."

Gertie answered with a faint, dismissive smile. "I have been led to believe that I will make out much better if I can prove he is cheating on me."

They talked for several minutes about the husband and his habits. The woman gave the detective some clues about her husband's probable girlfriends. Nickey explained that she would need a two-thousand-dollar retainer. Gertie wrote the check without hesitation. The two women shook hands, and the detective was escorted to the door.

* * *

The meeting felt like a setup. Nickey didn't like it. Too neat. Too quick. She circled her Lexus, looking for something out of place. Nothing suspicious. She checked the underside. A small object inside the right rear wheel well came loose when she gave it a slight tug. It was a cheap satellite tracker about the size of a cigarette pack. A magnet on one surface held the device in place. She put it back and drove off.

40

Nickey walked out of the motel just before two in the morning and sat in her car. It would have been a good time for a cigarette, but she didn't smoke. The man in the room was Ben Chapman. She was his Natalie, an oasis of peace, calm, acceptance, and pleasure.

His problems were common in American society. The people in Ben's life were angry and demanding. He was well paid, but he was expected to put in an eighty-hour workweek. Every project was oversold, understaffed, and underfunded. It was up to the Ben Chapmans of this world to somehow pull off a win and deliver on the promises.

His wife was angry and frigid. She had her own job issues, and she was tired of household responsibilities. A steady stream of stories about the mistreatment of women stoked her anger. The one thing she seemed to enjoy was complaining about men in general and Ben in particular. He could never do enough to live up to her expectations.

He wasn't up for much pleasure these days. The booze and the coke he used to escape from the hell that was his life were destroying him.

Ben Chapman did not know that his wife had hired a divorce lawyer to end their marriage. Neither of them knew that the lawyer had hired Nickey Arnold to investigate. He had a reputation for being successful in his work and in his marriage. Nickey discovered the demons lurking just below the surface. Booze, drugs, sex. Women. Many women. Some eager. Others yielding to pressure.

Nickey would put all this in her report to the lawyer. He would use that report to get a favorable settlement for his client. Ben Chapman, the brilliant engineer and debauched womanizer, would be ruined.

It had been four hours since she had picked Ben up at National Airport for their assignation at the Marriott Courtyard in Greenbelt, Maryland. In that time she had defused the frustration and anger that made him unbearable at the end of trips like this one. She had listened patiently as he gave a blow-by-blow description of his three days on the road. They finished off a bottle of scotch and showered together in the room's tiny stall. After the shower, she fucked him until he could no longer keep his eyes open. She kissed him and told him she had an early meeting that morning. He rolled over and dropped off into a deep sleep while she dressed.

Nickey fired up the Lexus and backed out of the parking space. At the parking lot's exit, she turned left onto University Boulevard heading south and east because there was no direct route to her condo.

Her radio was tuned to WMZQ. Cole Swindell was singing "Even Though We Break Up in the End." She sang along in spite of herself as she passed Goddard Space Flight Center. After that, it was a dark, empty, tree-lined, four-lane road. Blake Shelton belted out "She Wouldn't Be Gone." *Ben should listen to this. Not that it would do any good.*

It took her ten minutes to reach the juncture with Annapolis Road. She turned left toward Crain Highway. More dark, lonely, tree-lined road. Gordon Lightfoot was halfway through a haunting rendition of "The Wreck of the Edmund Fitzgerald."

The only sign of anyone else on the road was a pair of headlights following her at a comfortable distance. She passed a large building complex that housed Bowie High School and the Bowie Library. The light at Racetrack Road was red. She stopped. A Ford Crown Victoria rolled up behind her. She couldn't see much. It was an older model. Probably some hotshot in an old police cruiser he bought at auction. There was no license plate on the front. She looked back up at the light. The guy behind her gunned his engine. She studied the car in her rearview mirror.

Suddenly, it hit her like an electric shock. *The tracking device. He's coming after me.*

The engine behind her roared again. She jammed down on the accelerator. Her Lexus shot away from the Vic. It tore after her. It wasn't as quick, but the driver pushed it as hard as it would go.

The road narrowed to three lanes as it wound through an unlit wooded section. She let up on the gas when she hit a hundred. It was less than half a mile to the next stoplight and the end of Annapolis

Road. She would have to make a sharp left turn onto Crain Highway.

The Ford's lights blinked and the car smacked into her rear end. She sped up and moved to the right-hand lane for the widest possible turn. But she would have to brake. She couldn't make it around the corner at that speed. *I'll be a sitting duck in the middle of the turn. He'll ram me.*

That was the trap. If she turned left onto the highway, she would be driving over the Patuxent River Flood Zone, with steep embankments on either side of the road.

The right turn lane was a narrow passage between the curb and a six-inch, high, triangular concrete lane divider. Nickey aimed for the opening. At the last second, she slammed on her brakes and skidded through the turn. Her tires squealed as they fought to hold the road. The old Vic was not nearly as nimble, but the driver was reckless. He missed the alley for the right turn and jumped the divider, landing on the highway with a loud thump. His exhaust clanged when it hit the pavement. The Vic turned sharply and roared off in pursuit of the Lexus. It had a lot of ground to make up.

The two cars tore down a dark, deserted, six-lane highway as fast as they could go. The old patrol car was heavier than the Lexus. But it had a bigger engine. Nickey had to push her car to its limits to have any hope of outrunning the hunter.

Her eyes flicked from the road to the rearview mirror to the speedometer. They were doing 130. He wasn't gaining. Neither was she. It was insane. Too many things could go wrong. She could run out of gas before he did. There was no way to win this one.

Change of plans. Counterattack. She reached into her purse for the cold, reassuring steel of her Beretta. *You want a rematch? You got it.*

Nickey let up on the gas. The Lexus slowed imperceptibly. The Vic kept coming. The gap between them began to close. Her speed dropped below one hundred as she eased her foot off the accelerator. The gap closed faster.

She watched her pursuer bearing down on her. He was getting close. The Vic's front end dipped. Its tires began to scream. The driver had slammed on his brakes to avoid crashing into her Lexus.

Nickey grinned. *Too late.* She jammed down on her own brakes and gritted her teeth, bracing for the impact. The old Crown Vic rammed her. A shock wave ripped through Nickey's body. Her purse hit the floor with a thud. The Lexus's rear bumper slid up over the Ford's front bumper and crushed the engine compartment like an empty beer can. A second shock wave slammed against Nickey's body.

Momentum kept the two vehicles skidding along the highway. Nickey pulled her purse back up on the passenger seat. She took a deep breath and jammed down on her gas pedal. Her rear wheels spun angrily against the front of the crippled patrol car. The Lexus ripped free and shot forward.

She slammed on her brakes again and pulled into a sharp turn. Her car skidded around, tires squealing as they slid over the pavement. When Nickey came out of the skid, she was heading back toward the Vic. She opened her window and pulled the Beretta from her purse.

As she closed on the old Ford, her first shot hit the front tire on the driver's side. Her second shot hit the driver's side window in the corner near the doorframe. Her third and fourth shots punctured the rear tire. The tire was designed to survive a nail puncture and give the driver time to come to a graceful stop. The nine-millimeter rounds punctured the sidewall, much like a nail on entry but left big, jagged holes on exit. They destroyed the integrity of the tire, causing a blowout.

The Vic weaved back and forth wildly as the driver struggled to bring it safely to a stop on the shoulder.

Nickey came around again and filmed the disabled Ford with her cell phone as she drove past it. She stopped a few feet past the front end, got out, bowed, and waved before driving off.

A mile down the road, she turned around and came back to a private lane where she could watch the salvage operation. About forty minutes later, a tow truck arrived to rescue the Vic and its driver.

Adan Jackson emerged from the driver's seat. The tow truck operator chatted with him before securing the disabled heap. Adan hopped aboard the truck, and they headed south.

The detective followed at a safe distance with her headlights off. The tow truck descended onto Route 50 in the direction of Annapolis, where the Jacksons had a large estate. She watched discreetly as the disabled Ford was moved to the back of the house, where it could be hidden until repairs had been made. Unless someone tipped off the police.

When she reported the incident to her insurance company, she told them that the other car sped away after rear-ending her Lexus. She had not gotten the number from the license plate.

She told Jack a different story when she talked to him. He said it was out of his jurisdiction. She would have to file a complaint with the PG Police.

Nickey laughed. "That's not going to happen, Jack. I don't need the hassle. I just wanted you to know that Adan is escalating."

41

Troy and Marie spent Sunday afternoon in the office, getting ready for seminar night. Shortly after six, they locked up and took the elevator to the lobby. They walked out to the street and turned right onto 22nd toward the parking garage where Troy kept his car.

Two tall, rangy men met them before they reached the garage entrance. One of them said, "Wussup, homey?"

Troy said, "Same old. Same old."

The show of indifference did not hide his wariness. Marie picked up the vibe and shot a sideways glance at him.

"Lotta muthafuckas talkin' bout you."

"Good things, I hope."

"Mos'ly."

"What can I do for you?" Troy asked. "Do you want to come up to my office?"

"Too busy. Word's out a cracka muthafucka lookin' fo' some help."

"Anything in particular?"

"Wants t' teach some bitch a lesson."

Troy scowled and shook his head. “Not my concern.”

The big man raised his hands. “Okay. Dat’s cool.” He grinned. “Alls I’m sayin’ is, you knowed the bitch back in the day.”

Troy turned to Marie. She arched her brows. He turned back to the informant. “Maybe I should talk with this dude. How do I get in touch with him?”

The man passed a slip of paper to Troy. “Thought you might ask. Stay safe.” He and his partner turned and walked away, blending in with the crowd on the sidewalk.

Marie put a hand on her partner’s arm. “Cindy?”

“I don’t know who else it would be.”

* * *

Around midnight, Troy placed a call.

A man answered, “State your business.”

The voice hinted of the old South. Troy was sure he was about to talk to Adan Jackson for the first time in over fifteen years. He said in his low, throaty, Tom Jones voice, “I heerd ye was lookin’ for some help with a problem.”

“Who told you that?”

“Don’t rightly know. Black dude tipped me cuz I work odd jobs.”

“Ah need to know who Ahm dealing with,” the man insisted. The drawl was less pronounced than Troy remembered, but it was still there.

“Gittin’ lotsa interest, are ye?” Jones chided.

“Doesn’t matter. Ah need some credentials befo’ we can talk business.”

"Here it is, mate. Yuh put the word out. It got to me. That means yer people figgered I was the man for the job."

After a long pause, Adan drawled, "Ah'll make that call. Meet me at the Jefferson tomorrow night at eleven."

"Too snazzy. I'm in room 110 at the Super Stay on H Street. Meet me there. Nobody'll bother us."

Another long pause. "How will Ah recognize you?"

"I'll ask if ye're feelin' lucky. You say ye're not Eastwood. I'll say I'm Tom Jones."

Another pause. "Ah'll see you tomorrow night."

42

Troy had picked the Super Stay on H Street from a Google search and a drive-by to case the motel. It was a three-story high, L-shaped structure with a dimly lit parking lot nestled between the building and H street. An island with bushes and trees ran between the lot and the road.

The office was on the first floor at the west end of the building. Room 110 was at the far end of the long edge of the L next to a small alleyway between the two sections.

The ex-con considered several elaborate plans for the meeting before deciding to go simple. Tom Jones had been locked away in the closet for six months and might not ever come out again. He could pull this off and disappear.

The vagrant showed up at the Super Stay at nine looking for a room. The one he got was on the second floor. Adan would show up at eleven. Troy was banking on that. He went down at ten-thirty and set up three sports video cameras he had picked up while looking into a "People's Surveillance System." They would record the meeting from three different angles and hopefully give him the evidence he needed to go to the police.

Tom Jones walked over to the island and picked a spot between a tree and a bush where he could watch and wait. It was 10:47.

A Lincoln SUV pulled in front of room 106 at the Super Stay on H Street at eleven p.m. sharp. Minutes passed. The doors opened, and two tall, well-dressed men emerged. Adan stepped out on the passenger side. The lookalike who got out on the driver's side would be his brother, Beau.

Jones stood and started toward the men.

They walked to the door and knocked. Nothing happened. Adan banged on the door and called out, "Tom. Tom Jones."

Jones was five feet away near the front of the SUV when he answered, "Are ye feelin' lucky?"

The two men turned and stared in disbelief at the scruffy figure in ill-fitting clothes from the Salvation Army. A black wool knit beanie was pulled down to his ears. His unbuttoned navy pea coat was a size too big.

The vagrant repeated in his low, throaty voice, "Are ye feelin' lucky?"

Adan managed to get out, "You're not Clint Eastwood."

Jones walked up to the men so they could see the mark on one cheek and his oddly mismatched eyes. "No, mate. I'm Tom Jones."

"We've decided to take you up on your offer to help," Adan stammered.

Jones folded his arms and nodded. "I'll be needin' more info."

"How much is this going to cost?" Beau demanded.

Jones grinned, revealing a glittering gold tooth. "Depends on wucha want done."

"We want a man mugged and roughed up," Adan said.

"Roughed up? 'Ow bad?"

"Roughed up," Adan snapped.

"Does he need an ambulance, or can he drive?" Jones asked patiently.

"Put him in the hospital," Adan said.

Beau objected, "No. It doesn't have to go that far."

Adan glared at his brother. "Okay, he doesn't have to end up in the hospital, but it better be more than a bloody nose."

Jones said, "A grand."

"I can get somebody to do it for fifty," Adan snarled.

Jones nodded. "Aye, and when the cops catch him, he'll lead 'em straight t' ya."

"What about you?" Beau challenged.

"They won't catch me."

"Five hundred," Beau said.

Jones's lip curled into a sneer. "Five hundred it is. But I need 'alf now."

Beau pulled two hundred-dollar bills from his wallet and held them out. The vagrant studied the offering with a look of disgust. He looked up at the tall, well-dressed stranger. They stared at each other. Jones spat at the man's feet and snatched the money from his hand. "What do ye have in mind?"

Adan handed over a photo. "His name is Eric Foster. He will be at a meeting at the Fairfax tomorrow evening from seven to nine. You will be able to jump him when he walks back to his car."

The vagrant stuffed the picture into a coat pocket but said nothing.

Adan looked over at Beau, who was impassive. He turned back to Jones. "Will you do it?"

He nodded. "Aye, mate. Consider it done."

Awkward silence followed. Adan shoved his hands in his pockets and looked down at his feet.

Beau nudged him. "Let's go."

He jostled Jones on his way to the SUV. Adan shrugged and followed but avoided contact with the vagrant. The two men got in and drove off. Jones watched until the Lincoln had left the parking lot, then he went up to his room.

At four a.m., the vagrant retrieved the three GoPro cameras he had set up to capture the meeting. He put them in a fanny pack and began walking toward downtown DC. An hour and twenty minutes later, he reached the building where Troy Mondale had a condo. He circled to the back. At 5:33, a maintenance man opened a back door to take trash to the dumpster. Tom Jones entered the building through that door.

Troy took off the hat and coat and removed the gold cap as he ascended to the third floor. He discreetly entered his condo, cleaned up, and changed. Then he set out on his morning walk to Cap Gallery for breakfast.

43

Troy made it to the office by nine. Marie was waiting. "Did you talk to him? What does he want?"

"I talked to *them*. Adan and his brother both came to the rendezvous last night. They..." Troy paused and shook his head. "Adan wants somebody to put Cindy's husband in the hospital."

Marie's eyes widened in shock. She shook her head. "They just came out and told you that?"

"They told Tom Jones."

"Do they have any idea who Tom Jones is?"

"They're clueless. They have no idea what they're getting themselves into." Troy started toward his seat at the conference table. He stopped and turned back to Marie. "I don't know how they got the word out on the street. They certainly don't know how to hire a hit man."

"What do you mean?"

"Jones offered to do the job for a grand. That's pocket change. Beau made a counteroffer of five hundred."

"You agreed to do it?" Marie gasped. "Are you crazy? What were you thinking?"

"I didn't have a choice. I have to nail them."

Marie slumped back into her chair behind the desk. "Tell me exactly what happened."

He grinned triumphantly and produced his fanny pack. "I can do better than that. I captured the whole meeting on video."

He emptied his bag on the desk.

Marie pointed to the C-notes folded around a small photo and demanded, "What is that?"

"Beau gave Jones a down payment."

The lawyer glared at him. "And of course, you took the money." She shuddered. "You're an idiot." She pointed at the pile. "Three cameras?" Her voice was withering.

"Different angles," Troy explained. "I didn't know how it would go down, so I set up three cameras to make sure I got at least one good view."

She picked up one of the cameras and removed the memory chip. "Let's see what you've got."

Each camera had a 32-gigabyte MicroSD chip that could be inserted into a slot on Marie's laptop. The cameras stored the video in 2-gigabyte chunks. The first three chunks recorded dead time before the Jacksons' SUV showed up. The meeting took up the next segment. Marie stared intently as the action unfolded and a deal was agreed to. Occasionally, she shook her head and let out a tsk. She did not like what she saw. The rest of the recording was dead time following the meeting.

The lawyer looked up at her partner. Her lips pressed into a grim line.

"What's the problem?" Troy demanded.

"You agreed to commit a felony and accepted a cash tender."

"I collected evidence of a conspiracy to commit a crime," Troy objected. "I plan to turn that evidence over to the police so they can make an arrest."

"But you did it on your own. You did not coordinate with the police. They did not sign off. You were not authorized to commit a crime as part of an investigation."

"They would have," Troy contended.

"They would have assigned an undercover cop."

"This is cheaper and more efficient. They don't have to go through a lot of paperwork, and they don't have to pay me."

"You are an ex-con. Not a cop," Marie rebutted in her best courtroom voice.

"I'm trying to help," Troy retorted. He turned away and ran his fingers through his hair.

Marie folded her arms across her chest. "You raped a woman." Her voice was harsh. "Adan and Beau helped you. You went to prison." She laid out the case against him like a prosecutor. "Now you are talking about beating up the woman's husband. That looks bad."

"*They are* talking about beating him up," Troy shot back. "I'm trying to prevent that from happening."

"Or..." Marie paused. She fixed a damning stare on Troy. "You are trying to lure them into committing a felony so you can send them to prison."

"They put the word out on the street. You were with me when I found out about it."

"From two men that neither of us had ever seen before. And by the way, there were no witnesses to that conversation."

Troy stared at Marie. He looked as if he might cry. He closed his eyes and dropped his head.

"I thought you were on my side." He sounded broken and defeated.

"I am," Marie consoled. "But right now, I have to help you figure out how to deal with this mess. If I were the Jacksons' lawyer, I could argue that those videos prove nothing. The two men look like Adan and Beau, but they could be actors."

"Adan's prints have to be on that photo."

"So are yours. That's enough to send you back to prison." The photo of Eric Foster was still stuck in the fold of the C-notes. Marie flattened out the bills and studied the picture. "I know him."

Troy stopped pacing and turned to look at her.

She was smiling. "A couple of years ago, we buddied up on the Southern Maryland Century. We were together on our bikes for six hours."

"What are you thinking?"

"I don't know. I haven't quite put it together yet." Marie drifted around the room, deep in thought, rubbing her hands together. She stopped abruptly and turned to Troy. "Tom Jones conspired to commit a felony." She pumped her fist and said triumphantly, "He's a vagrant who could disappear at any time."

"But my fingerprints are on the evidence."

Marie pursed her lips. "Because I brought it into the office, and we were careless with it."

"How did you get the evidence? Are you friends with Tom Jones?"

"He's a client. He had second thoughts about the job and came to me for help."

The office phone rang. Troy walked over to the desk and answered. "Hi, Eve." He looked over at Marie. She nodded vigorously and gave him a thumbs-up. He said, "Today? Let me check my schedule."

The lawyer held up an index finger. Troy said, "I have some free time this morning. Can you come in about an hour?" He listened. "Great. See you then," he said and hung up. He looked over at Marie. "What now?"

She grinned. "We verify that your friend is working with the police."

"And then ..."

"We wipe the chips and the photo clean and put them in a package with the money. The evidence is dropped on her doorstep. She delivers it to the police and tells them in all honesty that she has no idea where it came from."

"What about tonight?"

Marie sighed. "We had better be there to make sure nothing bad happens. The Jacksons might have a Plan B. I'll meet Eric and escort him to his car. I'll be carrying. Jones should be nearby in case I need help."

"Then he disappears?"

"Vanishes into thin air." She laughed and gave Troy a kiss. "We can do this, baby."

44

Eve's arrival brightened up the tense atmosphere at Mondale Consulting. She was happy to see Troy again. The brush up with Captain Bennett seemed to have blown over. Even Marie's presence couldn't dampen her spirits.

When they were seated, she said, "What is the major issue with the prison system?"

Troy laughed. "Confinement."

"Duh! That is the point: punish people by locking them up."

He nodded. "Yes. Exactly. Confinement is unnatural and uncomfortable, whether it is in a prison or in a hospital or in a corner. So, let's punish people by locking them up. We'll take away personal choice. We'll limit physical and intellectual activity. We'll prohibit sex. That should teach those fools not to go around committing crimes."

Eve gasped. "Sex?"

"Sex is officially illegal in prison," he assured her. "Of course, there are ways to satisfy your needs. I'm sure you have read about conjugal visits. The vast majority of men in prison do not qualify. For those who do, a visit is another humiliating reminder of their situation." He paused to watch her absorb what he was saying. "Prisoners are not even allowed to get affectionate with wives or girlfriends during authorized visits." He paused to look up at the ceiling. His right hand went to the back of his head. He looked at Eve again and smiled. "Masturbation is technically prohibited. But that rule is generally not enforced. As a matter of fact, most prisons have a private area with porn to accommodate the inmates' needs." He paused to watch Eve scribble her notes. "Women guards and staff, even lawyers, will sometimes make themselves available for a price. Unsanctioned sex is a dangerous option. The penalties can be severe for everybody involved, but …" He paused and pressed his lips into a silly grin. "Some people will do anything for sex or money. One of my fellow inmates got connected with a female lawyer. You could always tell when she came by to discuss his case. He came back from the meetings lit up like a neon sign. Then, one day, it stopped. I never heard what happened. My best guess is that she ended it because someone said something to her."

Eve looked up at him as she mulled her next question. "What about homosexuality?"

"Prohibited but tolerated."

"You were raped. Is that tolerated?"

He took a deep breath. "Rape in prison is like rape everywhere else, except that you have a bunch of men with nothing to lose. The rapists are already doing time. The guards aren't there to help inmates. Filing a complaint can get you ostracized, beaten, or even killed. Victims have no real recourse."

Eve opened her mouth to say something but changed her mind.

Troy stood and stretched. "Confinement has become a serious concern because of our space programs. It takes a little over three days to get to the moon. A week to get there and back. Add in time for touring the place, and you are up to ten days. A trip to Mars takes at least six months. How will astronauts be affected by six months of confinement in a space capsule?" He paused and took a few steps toward the back of the room. He stood with his back to Eve. "The crew members on a mission to Mars will face the same issues as prison inmates. They will be confined in a small space for a long time. But they will be highly educated, goal-oriented, and equipped with all kinds of interesting things to do. They will be on a great adventure." He took a deep breath and blew it out. His head nodded as he continued. "Still, they will be imprisoned, and that will take a toll on their personalities."

Troy turned back to face Eve. He clasped his hands in front of his chest, his index fingers pointing at the reporter.

"By contrast, the population of any prison consists of a large group of generally uneducated, poorly motivated humans thrust into an intentionally perverse situation." His hands moved up and down to emphasize the words. "A six-month trip to Mars will be more challenging than anything attempted since ocean travel in the old wooden sailing ships. But it cannot begin to compare to six months or sixty months or sixty years in prison." Troy looked down at the floor and shook his head. "I was in there for 4,396 days."

He shook off the reverie.

Eve felt like she was going to cry. "I don't know how you did it."

"I was lucky." His voice was husky. "I found some good friends and mentors. They steered me away from trouble." He returned the table and stood leaning toward Eve with his hands on the back of his chair. "It takes a great deal of strength to survive a prison term. You need support. You need people who will have your back. That usually means becoming part of a gang. Many prisoners already have connections when they enter a facility because they belong to the Crips, Bloods, Mafia, or skinheads. In my case, the bible study group found me. It functions much like a gang, but it has a strong Christian ethic. That was important to me. I had to stay out of trouble because I wanted time off for good behavior."

"How do you stay out of trouble in a situation like that?"

Troy straightened, closed his eyes, and tilted his head back. His fingers raked through his hair. "Life in prison is incredibly regimented. You are given standard-issue clothes. Meals and mealtimes are dictated. You can only shower and use the toilets at certain times of the day. Every prisoner has to return to his bunk for census three times each day. The guards can order everybody back to their cells whenever they want. The cells are locked at 2100 and opened again at 0600. That gives inmates a lot of time to figure out ways to game the system."

He took a deep breath and forced the air out through his pursed lips. "I trained myself to get up at 0300 to clean up and to wash my clothes in the sink. Then I studied until the cells opened at 0600. I hit the chow line early and ate while everyone else was showering. I worked out while others were eating their lunch or taking an afternoon nap." A sardonic grin crept across Troy's face. "Those nap times become habitual for most inmates because there is so little stimulation in prison." He tapped his index finger against his chest. "I challenged myself to stay awake and focus on productive activities—reading books, magazines, and newspapers, whatever I could get my hands on. College courses. I helped other inmates with their mail and volunteered in the clinic." He paused and waited for Eve. When she looked up at him, he continued in a low, solemn voice. "Prisons have a suicide epidemic, so there is a big need for reasonably sane inmates to sit around on suicide watch." Troy bit on his lip and looked away. When he turned back, his lips were pressed into a grim line. He studied the reporter with a distant, narrow-eyed stare as if he was still caught up in the memory. He put his hands on the back of his chair and leaned toward her. "All of that was hard work. It paid off. My needs are simple, and I have the tools I need to make it on the outside. I left prison in good shape physically and mentally and I have a college education."

Eve made some quick notes, then looked up. "Why would the guards order you to go back to your cell?"

Troy took his seat. "A prison is a war zone. Fights break out all the time. Guards use a lockdown or the threat of one to control the violence. If something is not accounted for, the guards have to find it. Razor blades are carefully monitored because they make good weapons. A razor blade is doled out to a prisoner at shower time and must be returned and signed in before the guy leaves the shower. If that doesn't happen, the entire prison is shut down until the missing blade is found." He stopped and stroked the stubble on his chin. "The warden has to deal with an arms race. Every once in a while, he orders a search to find and confiscate weapons. Inmates have to be in their cells during the entire search. When it's your cell, you are handcuffed to the bars while the guards go through your stuff." His face twisted into a bitter smile. "You get to clean up the mess after they leave."

Eve watched with a forlorn look as Troy wandered toward the back of the room.

Marie stood and came around to the front of the desk. "Have you decided where you are going to publish this piece?"

"I have sent out some query letters. *Washingtonian Magazine* is interested."

"I'll bet the police are interested," Marie observed.

Eve stared at her. "What are you saying?"

"I'm thinking the police sent you here to keep an eye on Troy."

"I'm here to get a story. That's what I do for a living."

"So, you aren't connected to the police at all?"

"Some of my friends are police officers."

"Did one of them put you up to this?" Marie pressed.

Eve blushed.

"I see."

"You asked me who suggested that I talk to Troy, and I said I didn't know." Eve looked down at her right foot and crushed out an imaginary cigarette. "That was a fib. My friend Nickey Arnold told me about the story. She said I would find it interesting."

Marie stared impassively. "How did she find out? Is she a cop?"

Eve shook her head. "She's a private detective."

"How did she find out about Troy?"

"Cindy Foster hired her."

"To find out about Troy?"

"No. Adan Jackson was bothering her. She wanted Nickey to make him back off."

"Why didn't she go to the police?"

"He wasn't doing anything illegal. He was being careful."

"You still haven't told me how you found out about Troy." Marie was poker-faced. Her stare made Eve squirm.

"Nickey had to do some background investigation because Cindy wouldn't tell her what was really going on."

"And?"

"She ended up talking to Detective Ed Twomey. She brought me along."

Eve stopped abruptly when she saw Troy whip around and glare at her. His sudden fury shocked her. She looked over at Marie, who was still staring at her. Eve said, "He told us about the rape and said that the Jacksons got off because of some videos Cindy had made."

Marie walked over and stood looking down at Eve. "Are you sure you told the truth this time?"

"Yes."

"I think you are still lying," Marie challenged. "Your cop boyfriend put you up to this."

Eve looked into her purse. She pulled out a letter from the editor of the *Washingtonian*.

Marie scanned it and handed it back. "That doesn't prove you aren't working for the police."

Troy walked over to Eve. "I think you had better leave."

She picked up her things and started for the door. "Can I please finish this story? I am convinced the *Washingtonian* will publish it and that it will be good for you and your business."

"I'll have to think about it," Troy said in a low, solemn voice. "I'll let you know if I decide to continue."

45

Jack spent the night with Eve. When he left for work in the morning, he found a plastic sandwich bag stuffed under the windshield wiper on his cruiser. A note on the baggie read, "*Urgent: About Last Night. Open ASAP.*"

A quick inspection told him the bag contained a hundred-dollar bill folded around a three-by-five photograph and a small memory card.

* * *

Jack stopped by Detective Bill Andrews's desk when he reached the office and asked, "Where's your partner?"

Bill looked up and deadpanned, "She worked late."

"I want to see the two of you when she gets in." The sergeant dropped the bag on the desk. "See what you can make of this."

The detectives trudged into their boss's office two hours later. Bill led the way. Liz dawdled a few steps back, looking irritated as if the meeting was an imposition. Jack growled, "What took so long? Just how late did you work, Detective?"

Liz responded with a tight-lipped grin.

Bill said, "We had to wait for a copy of the video file."

"Do the words 'Urgent' and 'ASAP' mean anything to you?"

"Yes, sir. But the computer guys had to make sure the chip wasn't dangerous before they would check it out. Then it took a little while to figure out what was on it. In the meantime, we had the lab look for prints." He shook his head. "Whoever gave you this wiped everything."

"What have we got?" Jack demanded.

"It looks like two men, Adan and Beau Jackson, hired a vagrant named Tom Jones to assault a man named Eric Foster."

"How do you know it was the Jacksons?"

"The Lincoln is registered to Adan Jackson. Facial recognition confirmed the ID."

Liz added, "According to the video, Foster was going to be lured to a dinner meeting at the Fairfax Hotel last night. Jones was supposed to jump him after he left the meeting." She shrugged. "No assaults like that were reported last night. I called the Fairfax. The manager assured me that there was no incident. We are getting ready to go out and look at footage from their security cameras."

"Any idea what they have against Foster?"

"No, sir. We haven't found any connection between the Jacksons and Foster."

Jack said, "See if he's married. Adan Jackson has been harassing a woman named Cindy Foster. She may be the connection. Talk to the Fosters, but don't tell them about this video. What about Jones?"

"Nothing," Bob said. "Facial recognition turned up some possibilities, but none of them has mismatched eyes."

"I want to see that video."

Bob handed him a USB stick. "It's too big for email."

Jack escorted the detectives out of his office and shut the door. He pulled up the video and hit play.

The camera was looking out toward the parking lot. Two metal columns were visible. *Probably attached to the underside of the second-floor balcony.*

Headlights came into view. A Lincoln MKX pulled up and parked directly into a parking spot ten feet from the camera. Nothing happened for over a minute. Two big, well-dressed men got out and walked to the motel. Their faces were plainly visible as they converged on the motel room in front of their vehicle.

This was the first time Jack had laid eyes on either of the Jacksons. He shook his head. *How could Nickey take down one of those guys?*

One of the men banged on the door and called for Tom Jones. *That must be Adan.* A man moved into the picture near the Lincoln.

"Are ye feelin' lucky?" The voice was a low growl, but the words were distinct.

Adan said, "You're not Clint Eastwood."

The man answered, "No, mate. I'm Tom Jones."

Challenge and response. Very nice.

Jack paused the video and zoomed in. *Jones is an alias. He carries himself like he's done time.* The sergeant had a sharp, punch-in-the-gut feeling. *Troy Mondale.*

But the man in the frame was a vagrant who looked nothing like the pictures of Mondale. He had a boxer's pug nose and a mark of some kind on his right cheek. His eyes were disconcerting even in low light. No one would ever mistake him for Mondale. Except Jack couldn't shake the feeling that Mondale was Jones. He considered calling Eve but nixed the idea. *She'll see through the disguise. She won't quit until she's figured it out.*

Jack hit play.

The vagrant approached the brothers.

The Jacksons wanted somebody beaten up. Adan was aggressive. Beau was constrained. Jones was aloof and professional.

"Does he need an ambulance, or can he drive?" he asked without a hint of emotion.

He named a price. Beau haggled. Jones agreed but demanded half up front. Beau proffered cash. Jones was offended but accepted the money. *That must be the money that was in the bag.* Adan produced a picture and identified the man as Eric Foster.

Almost certainly Cindy Foster's husband. Another hunch. *They wanted to send her a message.*

The vagrant took the picture but said nothing.

Adan pressed, "Will you do it?"

Jones responded, "Aye, mate. Consider it done."

Jack shook his head. *Why the fuck did you agree?*

46

The phone on Adan's desk rang around two. Troy was responding to one of the messages Adan had left for Tom Jones.

"It's about time," the executive snarled. He desperately wanted to know what had happened the night before.

"Sorry, mate. I just got around to checkin' for messages," Troy answered in his raspy Tom Jones voice.

"What have you been doing all day?"

"I been busy. Look, I know ye're upset about last night, but it couldn't be helped."

"What couldn't be helped?" Adan spun his chair away from the door and looked out the window.

"Your man Foster got away."

Adan clenched his teeth and hissed, "How?"

"He met some bird, and the two of them walked to the cars together."

"You let a woman stop you?"

"Aye, mate. Ye paid half price for one. Ye can't expect me to throw in a second one for free."

Adan jumped to his feet. He stood in front of the window, eyes closed and phone pushed up against his forehead. When he had regained some control, he said, "You took our money and promised to get the job done."

"I will," Troy assured him. "But it has to be done right. Let me pick the time and place."

"When?"

"A few days. A couple of weeks at most. I know where he works. He'll make a mistake pretty soon."

"Bullshit. You've got three days."

"What's the rush, mate? Ye should take yer time. Make sure it's done right," Troy scolded.

"Three days," Adan repeated sternly. "And don't call me on this number again."

"Sorry, mate. It was an honest mistake."

"How did you get my office number anyway? Have you been checking up on me?"

"I like to know who I'm doing business with. It won't happen again."

Troy ended the call before Adan could answer. He snapped the vagrant's phone in half and pulled the battery. With any luck, the police would be monitoring Adan Jackson's phones by now.

He was in a small park across from Union Station, one of the genuinely fascinating places in Washington, D.C.

The station had opened in 1907. During World War II, it handled as many as 200,000 people per day. A century later, it was still one of the busiest rail facilities in the nation. A shopping mall added in the eighties multiplied traffic. The venerable landmark attracted millions of tourists and shoppers every year.

The day was warm and sunny. Troy had a rare moment to enjoy peace and satisfaction. He walked past a trash can and disposed of the cell phone battery as he made his way to the magnificent old building. The phone itself went into another nearly full trash can in the mall's food court. He bought a hamburger, fries, and a drink for a rare leisurely lunch before walking back to his office.

* * *

Adan tried to get Jones back on the line. His call went straight to voice mail. He was so furious he could not sit down. *The asshole turned his phone off.* Adan sneered. "I know people who can whip your sorry ass, *mate*."

He paced around his office, palms pressed against his head. Visions of revenge flashed across his mental screen. He had no idea what he was going to do, but his hit list now had three names: Cindy, the bitch from his hotel room, and Tom Jones.

The call had scared Adan as much as it had angered him. He could not understand how a bum like Jones would know his direct number. He did not realize how easy it would be for Jones or anyone else to use the license number from the SUV to get that kind of information. It never occurred to the executive that the vagrant had spent time in the America First offices and sat at his desk as part of a cleaning crew. Instead, Adan convinced himself that Tom Jones was an undercover cop posing as a hitman. He wanted to discuss the situation with Greg, but he was afraid the police were monitoring his phones. Besides, he did not want to give Greg his real name. He would drive over to the Boundary Line Bar for the conversation.

47

Adan picked up a new phone for Peter Baeker on his way home that evening. He left his apartment at seven forty-five so he would get to the bar by eight-thirty. Early but not too early. The game would be underway. He could ease into the discussion.

He arrived at the Boundary Line at 8:21. But he had no memory of the drive. He was barely conscious of the world around him. His plan to remind Cindy of their situation had ended in disaster. Now the police were out to get him. The weight of it all threatened to crush him.

Peter Baeker trudged to his usual table, his eyes glued to the ground in front of his feet.

The waitress asked, "Are you OK?"

He forced a smile, nodded and mumbled, "Could you bring me a beer?"

"The usual?"

"Yes, please." Her presence lifted his spirits a bit. But he still sounded anemic.

The game was on. The Nats were at home, playing the Cubs. No score yet.

Greg came over, beer in hand. He sat and watched the game until the end of the inning. "What's up? You don't look so good."

Peter pressed his lips together and shook his head. He turned to face Greg. "You were right. You can't trust people like that."

Greg turned toward him. "People like what?"

"The guy you put me in touch with."

"I didn't puchya in touch with nobody."

"A guy called me, so he got my number from you. He said my people told him to get in touch with me," Peter retorted. He was careful not to raise his voice.

"You insisted on pickin' your man. You gave me the number." Greg's words were measured, threatening. "I put the word out just like you asked. I got no control after that."

Peter pressed his lips into a tight line. He shook his head. "The guy said the word got to him because he did odd jobs."

"Who?" Greg demanded. "Who was it?"

"Tom Jones."

"Never heard of him. Probably got the info because nobody wanted t' work for somebody like you."

"What is that supposed to mean?" Peter grumbled.

"Nobody knows you. They ain't gonna trust you. You could be setting them up."

"I paid cash."

Greg's eyebrows shot up. "How much?"

"Two hundred."

The ex-con sneered. "Chicken feed. A man that'd work for that is garbage. A bum." He leaned back and regarded his companion with half-shut lids. "If you still want the job done, I can help."

Peter turned back to the game. It was the bottom of the fourth. Two out. Still no score. Zim was at bat. He went down swinging. Peter shifted his eyes toward Greg. "I don't know. Like you said, they don't trust me." He added somberly, with a shake of his head, "And I don't trust them."

"Do you trust me?"

"Yes."

"I know people. Good people. I trust them, and they trust me." He smiled. "If I say you're okay, you're okay."

Peter took a drink of his beer. It was getting warm. "So, I use you as a subcontractor."

Greg grinned. "Yeah. It's like puttin' up a building. I hire the men, and I make sure the job is done right."

Peter took another drink. Two Cubs sprinting around the bases caught his attention. Willie Harris fielded the ball deep in center and launched it toward home. Zambrano and the ball reached the plate at the same time. He dove and touched the bag before the catcher could bring his glove around to make the tag. Fox reached third easily. Peter looked up at the ceiling. "I don't know." He turned back to Greg. "I just don't know."

Greg nodded. "Maybe you should let it go." He pressed his lips together and drummed his fingers on the table. "I just hate to see all your hard work go to waste."

"What do you mean?"

"We've been talkin' about this woman for a month now. She's obviously a pain in the ass, and you've taken extraordinary steps to straighten her out. That's all going to waste if you quit now."

Peter bit his lip and played with his beer. "I could see how it was all going to work out," he mused. "I thought it'd be a piece of cake." He looked over at the ex-con. "Now I just don't know."

"Getting shafted like that hurts," Greg empathized. "It's happened t' me. That's why I've put a lot of time into developing relationships. I need to have friends I can work with."

Peter's shoulders slumped wearily. He took a drink of his beer. The Cubs were heading into the field up one zip. The Nats were getting ready for another turn at bat. He turned toward Greg with a forlorn expression. He shook his head and went back to the game.

"I took care of her car. Didn't I?" Greg said. Peter did not answer. The ex-con continued, "I can help you with her old man."

Peter looked over at him.

Greg said, "Let's get a couple of friends to join us. We can at least talk about it." Peter shrugged. Greg pulled out a cell phone and sent off a text message. "They'll be here in about fifteen minutes. Let me get you another beer."

The game dragged on. The Cubs drove in a couple of more runs. The Nats' bats were mostly silent. Zim hit a solo home run. In the middle of the seventh inning, two men entered the bar and walked over to Greg. The leader was dark-complected, with a full head of black hair combed back like a young Elvis Presley. A big, light-skinned black guy with his head shaved bald followed a couple of steps behind. They were both about six feet tall, but the second guy was a little taller and heftier. Peter guessed he had played football and lifted weights when he was younger.

The Elvis look-alike was Tony. Baldy was Mo.

An African American woman entering the bar right behind the men caught Peter's attention. She peeled off and took a table on the other side of the room.

Greg put a hand on his arm to bring him back to the moment. "Peter is looking for somebody to take care of some business. He needs someone to send a message to some people who are making his life miserable."

"How do we find them?" Mo asked.

Peter said, "He works downtown."

Greg added, "The idea is to rough the guy up. The woman is off-limits." He turned his attention to the executive. "Peter, is there some time when this guy might be on the streets by himself?"

"He stays late on Friday nights to back up the system."

"Where does he work?" Greg asked.

"America First in Cap Gallery."

"Where does he park his car?" Tony wanted to know.

"I'm pretty sure he takes the Metro."

"Pretty sure?"

"I've left the office with him a couple of times. He didn't go to the parking garage. He went out to the street."

"Okay," Greg said. "He works at Cap Gallery and uses the Metro. That means L'Enfant Plaza Station. Peter, if you could find out which route he takes to the station and tell us when he will be leaving the office this Friday, we could take care of him before he gets to the Metro."

Peter looked bewildered.

Greg said, "Can you do that, Peter?"

The executive nodded. "Yes. If you give me a number, I can call you when he's leaving the office."

"Ya havta get us the money if we're gonna do it Friday," Mo said.

"What money?" Peter demanded. "How much?"

"Ten grand," Mo shot back.

Peter was stunned.

"Ten grand each," Tony snarled.

Greg could see the deal was about to collapse. He held up his hands. "Wait a second. This is a small job. Mo could do it by himself."

"It's me 'n Tony. That was the deal," Mo objected.

"All right," Greg soothed. "But let's keep it to ten grand. I don't need to be paid. I'm just makin' the introduction." He looked at Mo and then at Tony. "This is just a small job." He turned back to Peter. "Ten grand. Okay?"

"That's a lot of money. I don't think it's worth that much. I could beat that turd up myself."

"You could," Greg agreed. "But you don't know what yer doin', and if you get caught, you'd be lookin' at serious time."

Peter's face screwed up into an ugly sneer.

Greg almost laughed. He nodded. "If yer thinkin' your lawyer can get you off, you should also think about how much that'll cost. Ten grand is cheap."

"Maybe I'll just forget about it," Peter scoffed. But he already knew Greg was right. Ten grand was pocket change.

The ex-con protested, "You don't want to do that. Think of the time and money you've put into this."

"Sunk costs."

"True. But there may be other problems we can help you with."

Peter looked down at his lap.

"Who is it?" Greg urged.

"That asshole Jones, and there is a detective."

"Police detective?"

"Private."

"We can help you with that," Greg assured his friend. "And that would sweeten the pot for us."

"Let's see how this goes." Peter glanced at the others to get a reading. "I'll give you five K tomorrow and five K when the job is finished."

Tony and Mo were about to object.

Greg jumped in. "We can do it that way. Give me a number where I can reach you."

"You give me your number," Peter countered.

Greg rattled off a phone number. Peter pulled out his new phone and sent a text: *Noon tomorrow. OK?*

Greg's phone vibrated. He pulled it out and checked the message. "OK."

Peter rose. "Greg, Tony, Mo."

He spotted the African American woman as he strolled out of the bar. She was eating and texting with her eyes locked on her phone. She looked familiar. He kept walking and tried to focus on the door. But she remained in his peripheral vision. He fretted. *Is she tailing me? Have the cops figured out who Peter Baeker is?*

Tony and Mo followed a minute later. As Greg walked back to the bar, the African American woman caught his attention. *Cop. That ain't no coincidence.*

48

Edwards called the team back into his office for a progress report early on Thursday morning. Smith brought along another cop. "This is Officer Rhonda Johnson. She is on loan to help with our surveillance on Adan Jackson."

The sergeant said, "Good to have you on our team, Rhonda." He rose and extended his hand. "How come you're available?"

She shook his hand. "I don't have an assignment yet. I have been filling in for officers who are sick or on leave."

"That's a good way to learn the ropes."

She smiled. "I volunteered for this assignment because I wanted to do some real police work."

"How do you like it?"

"It's boring. But at least I get out of the station."

"Police work is boring," Edwards agreed. "Surveillance is about the most boring thing you can do. But it's important." His lips pressed into a tight line. "Adan Jackson is a dangerous man. We need to know what he is up to so we can stop him before it's too late." He winked. "Thanks for volunteering and welcome to our team."

Edwards stepped away from his chair and turned to face Andrews. It was back to business. "What have we got, Bob?"

"The video appears to be legit. There's no evidence of tampering. We have confirmed our identification of the Jackson brothers. We haven't come up with anything solid on Jones." Andrews paused to look over at his partner, who stood a few feet away with her arms folded across her chest. He turned back to the sergeant. "We have reason to believe he is actually Troy Mondale. Basic facial recognition characteristics match up, but the bum in the video is a piece of work. No jury would believe he was Mondale." The detective shrugged. "And we don't have any evidence to put him at the scene, so it looks like a dead end."

Edwards nodded. "We don't have enough to justify an investigation. What about the dinner meeting?"

"Eric Foster, the man in the photo, showed up for dinner at the Fairfax." Andrews checked his notes. "His companion was a man named Abraham Jacobs. The waiter said they talked business for a couple of hours. Foster left around nine." The detective checked his notes again. "Jacobs stayed and was joined by another man. The waiter identified the second man as Beau Jackson based on a photo we showed him. We were able to identify Jacobs as Adan Jackson wearing a pretty good disguise."

Edwards stroked his chin as he took a long breath. "Eric Foster showed up at the Fairfax and had dinner with Adan Jackson from seven to nine, just like the video said he would. But he wasn't beaten, and there was no sign of a vagrant matching the description of Tom Jones. Is that where we are?"

"A woman joined Foster as he was leaving the restaurant." Andrews glanced over at his partner. "They paid their bills and walked out together."

"The woman was Marie Moretti, Mondale's business partner," Smith interjected. "That's one reason we think Jones is actually Mondale."

"What about the Fosters?"

Andrews flipped through his notes. "Eric Foster is married to Cindy Foster." He paused and looked at his boss. The sergeant gave a slight nod. "He said it was a job interview. Jacobs claimed to be the US representative for Muenster Data Systems, a German company. Foster thought he was interviewing for a position as VP of Data Operations. He gave us some details about the dinner, but he didn't say anything about the woman who left with him."

Smith, who had been staring intently at Andrews, broke in. "He didn't recognize Beau Jackson or Tom Jones. Mrs. Foster said they didn't look familiar." She pursed her lips and shook her head. "But she reacted strongly to both Beau Jackson and Abraham Jacobs. She probably realized it was Adan,"

Andrews nodded. "If Jones is Troy Mondale, his disguise has Mrs. Foster fooled."

Edwards paced to the window. He came back to the side of his desk. "It looks like the Jacksons tried to hire somebody to rough up Eric Foster, but the perp never showed. Why was Moretti there? What's the connection?"

"She's a public defender. Maybe Jones got cold feet and told her about it," Andrews offered.

"Why didn't she just notify the police?" Smith demanded. "She was probably protecting Mondale. She had to make sure nothing happened to Foster."

Edwards held up his hands. "I don't want to dig into this right now. Nothing happened, so we have nothing to investigate."

"I think I have something," Johnson interjected.

Three heads turned in unison. Three sets of eyes focused on her. She panicked and froze momentarily. Edwards nodded. "Okay. What have you got?"

"Adan Jackson spent about thirty minutes with three ex-cons last night."

"Go on."

"About an hour after Jackson went in the Boundary Line Bar, a couple of bruisers showed up. I followed them inside on a hunch. They went straight to the table where Jackson and Greg Jantzen were sitting." She paused for a reaction from the sergeant. He nodded. "I didn't get close enough to hear what they were saying, but the conversation was pretty heated. They must have worked things out because they seemed to be on friendly terms when Jackson left."

Smith said, "Adan puts on a disguise and goes bar hopping at night. He has spent a lot of time at the Boundary Line in Shepherd Park. Whenever I checked in on him, he was sitting with Jantzen, watching a game on the TV."

"I was able to identify the thugs," Johnson continued. "Mo Adoyo, a small-time drug dealer with a couple of assault convictions, and Tony DeLuca, another small-time drug dealer who's been convicted of car theft and transporting stolen goods."

Edwards folded his arms and looked up at the ceiling. "The hit is still on. Jones failed. Jantzen and his men are going to take care of it."

"Why does he want Foster beat up?" Andrews wondered.

"He's crazy," Smith snapped.

"But what's the connection?" Johnson demanded.

"Sixteen years ago, Adan Jackson, his brother Beau and Troy Mondale raped Cindy Smith, who is now Cindy Foster. Mondale went to prison. The Jacksons got off with a slap on the wrist."

"Could Mondale be looking for payback?"

"I can't rule that out," Edwards conceded. "But he seems to have other priorities. Jackson is the one who has been acting aggressively. A week ago, he attacked a woman on Crain Highway in the middle of the night. A month earlier, he tried to rape her in a hotel room. Now he's hanging out with violent ex-cons." The sergeant shook his head. "It's only a matter of time."

49

Greg called Peter Baeker at eleven. “Meet me at a bench on the mall side of the Air and Space Museum in forty-five minutes. Bring the money. Small bills split between two mailers.”

“Kinda late for those instructions,” Adan retorted. “Fortunately, I have some small bills on hand.”

“I’m serious,” Greg threatened.

“So am I.”

Baeker strode along on Seventh Avenue past the museum and turned onto Jefferson. Greg Jantzen rose from a bench twenty feet away and walked toward him. The ex-con handed over one of the two identical bags he had purchased from a food truck. “I hope you’re okay with a gyro. I got ya a bottle of water to wash it down.”

Baeker nodded. Jantzen led the way across the Mall toward the National Gallery of Art. An active lunchtime crowd was out enjoying the weather. Tourists trudged from museum to museum and crisscrossed the vast open green. Some of them picnicked. Office workers took their daily walks. The more ambitious jogged around the perimeter. Scattered groups threw

Frisbees around. This pair stood out. One wore blue slacks and leather loafers. He had on a short-sleeved white shirt and a blue tie with thin gold stripes. He carried a leather briefcase. The other wore a tee that showed off his prison tats. His jeans had seen a lot of miles, and he wore steel-toed boots that belonged at a construction site.

Greg found a bench. "Put yer mailers in the empty bag and leave it for me," he ordered as they sat down to enjoy their lunch.

Peter nodded. "The Nats aren't doing all that well. They might grab a wild-card spot, but they aren't going anywhere."

"Naw," his companion agreed. "Their pitchin's weak."

They talked baseball for twenty minutes. The exec placed the trash from his meal inside his empty food bag. He opened his briefcase and handed Greg some papers before putting two mailers into the bag with the refuse. "That's information on offshore accounts," he explained. "As your financial adviser, I recommend that you get one."

"Don't need it," Greg objected.

"You could use the flexibility," Peter urged. "And the security. I've studied your plans. You need an offshore account, given the amount of money you're looking at."

"I been doin' business for a long time. Never saw a need for anythin' like that."

"You should give it a try. I can set one up for you," Peter suggested. "If you aren't happy, you can go back to using local banks."

Greg rubbed his chin as he considered the proposal. "Ya think it will make that much of a difference?"

"I wouldn't have suggested it if I didn't."

The big man sat looking at his companion for a long time. "Okay. I'll give it a try. But I'll expect you to cover my losses if anythin' goes wrong."

Peter picked up Greg's food bag and stood. "You have my word."

He walked back to his office. The ex-con watched him for a while before reaching into the remaining food bag and pulling out the two mailers. He hefted them to make sure they had money inside, then he shoved them into his jeans and walked away.

50

Eric Foster left work shortly after eight on Friday. He had been running some backups and reviewing activity logs. On his way to the Metro, he encountered a homeless man, a big guy in ragged clothes, looking for a handout. The panhandler's coffee can held a few small bills. His crude cardboard sign read, "Homeless Out of Work Need HELP."

Eric usually had no problem helping such people. But something about this man set off alarm bells. Eric shook his head and tried to walk past the vagrant.

The man stepped sideways to cut him off. They were almost touching. "Please, sir. I'ze really hungry. A dollar would help. Any change you could spare. Please."

The hackles rose on the back of Eric's neck. He felt weak and nauseous. His mind refused to function. His hand reached for his wallet as if it had a mind of its own. Getting the billfold out of his pocket was a struggle. He was taking out some small bills when a blow to the back of his head stunned him. Two men started beating on him.

The attack lasted a minute or less. When it was over, Eric was lying semiconscious on the sidewalk.

His wallet, cell phone, and ID badge were missing. The attackers raced from the scene in opposite directions.

A woman coming from the Metro station saw the whole thing. She called 911 and hurried to help the victim. But she was across the street and half a block away. The attackers had knocked Eric to the ground, grabbed a few items, and fled the scene by the time she got through to the 911 operator.

The woman, a middle-aged receptionist, stayed with Eric until the ambulance arrived. She told police that she had not gotten a good look at the men. The one who attacked from behind was white but dark-skinned, with black hair. She thought he had used a stick or something to beat Eric while he was on the ground. The beggar, an African American, had his back to her during the attack. When he took off running, she caught a glimpse of a beard. His hair looked false, like a wig. Both men were bigger than their victim.

After he was stabilized at the hospital, ER staff and police were able to identify him and his wife from a couple of rings. A class ring told them his alma mater and the year he graduated. His initials were etched on the band. They were able to use that information to determine that his name was Eric Foster and look up his driver's license. "Cindy" was etched on his wedding band. The attending physician called the Foster residence.

* * *

Cindy was already anxious by the time she got the call. Eric was late, and she hadn't heard from him. She answered her phone immediately.

A strange woman said, "Mrs. Foster?"

The question alarmed her. She hesitated. "Yes. This is Cindy Foster."

"I am Doctor Asa Harbir. Your husband, Eric, has just been admitted to the Emergency Room at Providence Hospital." Dr. Harbir was calm and commanding.

Cindy fainted. The sound of a voice calling, "Mrs. Foster, are you okay?" brought her back.

She picked up the phone. "Yes, I'm okay. What happened?"

"Your husband was mugged a short time ago. I need you to come to the hospital as quickly as possible."

"Where are you?" Cindy asked in a dazed voice.

"Providence Hospital, on Varnum Street in Northeast D.C. Can you make it down here?"

"Yes," Cindy said as firmly as she could. "Yes. I just need to get my keys, and I'll come right down."

"Where are you?" Harbir asked.

"Bowie, Maryland."

"That's a bit of a drive. Are you sure you're okay?"

"Yes." *Eric needs me. I have to be okay.*

"Drive safely," the doctor urged. "Don't panic. He is going to be all right."

But you said as quickly as possible. He's not all right. "I'm on my way, Doctor."

As soon as Cindy got off the phone, she called Ellen, who said she would go straight to the hospital.

51

The blows to Eric's head had caused critical injuries. Immediate action was required to prevent permanent damage or even death. He was in surgery by the time Cindy reached the hospital.

She exploded. "Why didn't somebody ask me? You can't just operate on my husband without my permission."

Ellen hugged her friend. "They had to," she explained. "They tried to reach you, but the calls went straight to voice mail. They couldn't wait for you to get here and give them permission. I told them to go ahead."

"On whose authority?"

The lawyer met Cindy's glare with unblinking resolve. "Mine," she said in her best lawyer voice. "I'm your attorney. I'm also your friend. Eric needed immediate care because of the damage to his brain." She caressed her friend's cheek. "I did what I would want you to do under the circumstances."

Cindy blinked. She gasped. "They're going to operate on his brain?"

Ellen led her to a chair. "It's going to be okay," she soothed. "Someone saw the attack and reported it. An ambulance came right away and brought him here."

"But they are going to operate on his brain."

"Dr. Harbir said they had to. His brain was swelling." Ellen smiled warmly. "She will come down and explain it to you as soon as she has taken care of him."

"Oh God, Ellen, what's happening?"

The lawyer pulled her friend's head into her chest and held her. "I don't know."

They were sitting in a large corridor with swinging doors at each end. A wide aisle ran between rows of seats along the wall on each side. Another aisle intersected ten feet away. One branch led deeper into the hospital. The other led to a stairwell. A nurse's station was positioned at the intersection of the two aisles.

A man and a woman in matching blue suits emerged from the stairs and walked toward Cindy and Ellen.

"Mrs. Foster?" the man began. "I'm Detective Rick Sanchez. This is my partner, Detective Shane Bailey. We would like to ask you a few questions if you don't mind."

Ellen smiled in recognition. "Detectives."

Cindy studied the pair suspiciously. Sanchez was Hispanic. Medium height and build. Bailey was about the same size but with creamy white skin, blue eyes, and blond hair.

The distressed wife pulled herself erect. "What do you want?"

"I am sorry about what happened to your husband," Sanchez said. She nodded. The detective continued, "We have just begun our investigation into the assault. It appears to be a random attack. But we need to rule out other possibilities." He grimaced. "Can you answer a few questions?"

Cindy shuddered. Her eyes narrowed. "Can you tell me what happened?"

"We are still trying to figure that out," Sanchez said with a slight toss of his head. "Probably one man posing as a panhandler engaged your husband from the front. A second man approached from behind and hit him over the head. They delivered a quick beating and took off with his valuables. We were able to identify him from his college ring."

Bailey added, "That's a pattern we've seen in other attacks."

Cindy nodded. She still looked dazed.

Sanchez moistened his lips. "Where does your husband work?"

"America First Financial Services in Cap Gallery."

"Do you know why he stayed late tonight?"

"He is the senior systems manager. He stays late on Friday nights to oversee system maintenance and backup."

"So, this is his normal routine?"

"Yes."

Bailey asked, "Can you think of anyone who would want to hurt your husband?"

Cindy jerked around to face the detective. Her eyes opened wide in terror. "Why? What's going on? I thought Eric was robbed."

"It looks like a robbery," Sanchez acknowledged. "We just want to make sure it wasn't something else."

Cindy held her hands to her temples and shook her head. She said in a sad voice, "The only person I can think of is Troy Mondale."

The detectives looked at each other and turned back to Cindy. "Who is Troy Mondale?"

"He raped me, and now he's out of prison. He has been making my life a living hell."

"I see. Do you know where we can find him?" Bailey prodded.

"No." Cindy shook her head. "I think he lives in D.C. Ask Captain Bennett. She knows."

"Captain Bennett?" Sanchez echoed.

"She's head of the Sexual Assault Task Force."

"Right. Captain Bennett," Bailey said.

Sanchez handed a business card to Cindy. "If you think of anything else, give me a call."

He winked at Ellen as he turned to leave. "Counselor."

She frowned. Her lip curled into a sneer. The detectives didn't notice. They were on their way to the stairs.

Shortly after eleven, a dark, slender woman in hospital garb walked up to Cindy and offered her hand. "Mrs. Foster, I am Dr. Harbir. We talked on the phone earlier."

"What's happening? Is Eric okay?"

"Your husband is resting. I removed part of his skull to ease the pressure from internal bleeding. I have put him in a medically induced coma to keep him stable."

Cindy closed her eyes and shook her head. "That sounds bad."

"I am sure he is going to be okay. Your husband received a severe beating. Luckily, help arrived right away."

"But the brain damage could be permanent," Cindy countered.

"I don't think so."

"Why not?"

"We have seen cases like this before. He has broken bones and brain trauma, but nothing that will not heal."

Cindy buried her head in her hands and twisted it from side to side while mumbling inaudibly. She looked up at the doctor. There were tears in her eyes. "When will I be able to talk to him?"

Harbir smiled reassuringly. "It should be sometime next week. I am hopeful that we will be able to bring him out of the coma in a couple of days. He will need a couple more days before he is ready for visitors. In the meantime, I suggest you go home and get some rest. We will keep you informed of your husband's progress."

"Thank you." Cindy stood and hugged her.

The women regarded each other for a long moment before the doctor turned to leave. "I have to get back to work. Go home and rest."

Cindy stood motionless as she watched the woman walk away.

Ellen broke the spell. "Do you want to come back to my apartment? Or I could drive you home."

The distraught woman turned to her friend and frowned as she considered her options. "I want to go to the chapel and pray."

It was a brief visit. After a few minutes, Cindy stood and stalked out.

Ellen raced to catch up. "Are you all right?"

"I have to go check on Eric."

52

As they were leaving the hospital, the two women encountered another couple coming into the atrium from the street.

Ellen recognized the man and brightened. "Troy?" she called. Then, as if she realized something must be wrong, she asked, "What are you doing here?"

Cindy suddenly recognized the man who had raped her all those years ago. "What are you doing here?"

Troy and his partner stopped a few feet from the women. His hands slid to his hips. He bit on his lower lip while he appraised the slender brunette. "We just had a visit from the police."

"Then you should be in jail," Cindy snapped.

"No," the ex-con said mildly. "I had nothing to do with what happened to your husband. I came down here to try to straighten things out."

Cindy glared. Troy continued. "I have admitted that what I did was wrong, and I have tried to apologize to you." He lifted his hands, palms up. "I don't expect those things to change how you feel about me. But I do expect that you will take me at my word on this." He touched his fingers to his chest. "I have no intention of causing you trouble of any kind." He turned his palms toward Cindy. "I have no reason to bother you. I have every reason to stay out of your life." His eyes widened as he lowered his hands. He spoke in a calm, measured voice, each syllable enunciated distinctly. "Please do not send the police after me every time something goes wrong."

"Why not?" she snarled. "You get out of prison, and all of a sudden, I start having problems."

"When did I get out of prison?" Troy challenged.

"You got a fifteen-year sentence, so sometime in the past year."

"Wrong," he sneered. "I've been out for five years. Time off for good behavior. You knew nothing about it because I've stayed away from you."

Cindy turned to the woman with Troy. She extended her hand and said in a friendly tone, "I'm sorry. I didn't get your name."

The woman reached out and shook hands. "Marie Moretti."

Cindy smiled maliciously. "Did you know your boyfriend is a rapist?"

"Yes," Marie answered calmly. "And I know he served time. He's turned his life around."

"He's still a rapist," the woman hissed.

"And you're still a pathetic whore," Marie shot back.

Ellen jumped in. "Be careful. Don't say things you can't back up."

"Your client has admitted to accepting payments for performing lewd and lascivious acts," Marie pointed out. "That makes her a prostitute."

"My client?" Ellen snapped. "Where did you get that?"

"You're not denying it." Marie grinned. "She's a whiny piece of shit with the brains of a gerbil. She needs to grow up and stand on her own two feet."

"Back off. Her husband is upstairs in a coma with half a dozen serious injuries."

"And you're taking care of her while he's out of commission." Marie turned her intense, unnerving stare on Cindy. She scanned the woman from head to toe and back up. "I don't know which is worse," she said in a cold, cutting voice. "Being beaten within an inch of your life or being married to her."

Cindy burst into tears. She screamed, "Shut up."

Troy held his hand up to cut his partner off. "Why don't you go wherever you were going?" he suggested. "But stop siccing the cops on me."

"What are you talking about?" Ellen demanded. "The detectives asked if she could think of anyone who might want to harm her. Your name came up."

"An undercover cop has been assigned to keep an eye on me. Bennett has dressed me down twice. Where did she get the idea I was harassing Cindy?"

Ellen looked at her friend. She looked at the floor.

"Somebody filed a false report to the police that got us arrested," Marie interjected. "I haven't found the culprit yet. It was either your client or Captain Lydia Bennett. You can count on one thing: When I do find out who it was, I'll be coming after her."

Ellen's jaw tightened. She glared at Marie. Then she took a deep breath and grabbed Cindy's arm. "Come on. Let's go."

53

Ellen led her friend to her car. They walked in silence, seething at the unfairness. Ellen felt betrayed. Troy Mondale wasn't surprised to see her with Cindy. He must have known they were friends. That bitch lawyer was just perfect for him. Rude. Insensitive.

Ellen's adversarial instincts made her shake the anger and get on top of the situation. She could not let that encounter throw her off her game. She called Nickey and told her to come over first thing in the morning for an emergency meeting.

Back at the apartment, Ellen curled up on the couch with her besieged client. They watched romantic movies, sipped wine, and snacked on cake and ice cream. Cindy fell asleep with her head on her friend's lap. Ellen dozed off some time later. They were still sleeping when Nickey knocked on the door.

The three women rehashed the assault over breakfast.

"That sounds like a pretty severe beating for a simple robbery," Nickey observed.

"Yes," Ellen agreed. "But it is not unheard of. There is no reason to believe Eric was targeted."

"It was probably Troy trying to intimidate me," Cindy groused.

The angry outburst caught the other women off-guard. Ellen recovered and scolded, "Troy hasn't bothered you since he got out of prison. Why would he start now?"

"You believed that BS?"

The lawyer grimaced. She turned to Nickey and explained, "Troy and his girlfriend caught us as we were leaving the hospital last night. He wanted Cindy to stop blaming him for what was going on."

"He put on this big act like he's been avoiding me for the last five years," Cindy scoffed. "I think he just got out of prison and it took him a while to find me."

"You have to take it easy," Ellen warned. "You don't have any proof."

"He blames me for sending him to jail. He wouldn't hesitate if he saw an opportunity."

Nickey shook her head. "He walked right past you, and nothing happened."

"When? What are you talking about?"

"The last time I came here for a meeting. I was behind you. You were on your way to the elevator. Troy got off the elevator and walked past you on his way to the door. Nothing happened."

"He's here in this building?" Cindy howled.

Ellen nodded. "Yes."

"How long have you known this?"

"A few months. I ran into Troy at the elevator last December. But I didn't realize he was the man who raped you until last night."

Cindy jumped up and stormed across the living room, muttering, "What do I have to do?"

Nickey called after her, "Get a grip, Cindy. You have a problem, but it's not Troy Mondale."

The woman halted and whirled around, her eyes blazing.

"Adan Jackson has been harassing you, and he is becoming more violent." The detective continued in a firm voice. "That is your immediate problem."

Cindy's body relaxed a little, but she was still grim.

Nickey walked over and placed her hands on her client's shoulders. "Adan Jackson might be the man behind the attack on your husband. You can't rule him out."

"Shit. I thought I got those people out of my life fifteen years ago." She shook her head angrily. "But here they are, fucking with me again."

"He's becoming more violent? What do you mean?" Ellen demanded.

Nickey turned to face the lawyer. "He tried to run me off the road the other night."

"You reported him, didn't you?"

"Sort of," Nickey said with a shrug. Ellen arched her brows. "I downplayed it in my report to the insurance company. I did talk to the police about it. They are watching him, but they want to nail him on something big."

"Like putting a man in the hospital?" Ellen asked ruefully.

"I'm sure they didn't expect that."

"But that might have been what happened."

"Yes," Nickey agreed. "That's why we have to keep a close eye on Cindy. We don't know what Adan is up to, and we can't depend on the police."

"What about Troy?" Cindy insisted.

"I'll check him out," the detective assured her. "Can you stay here for a few days?"

"That's a great idea," Ellen said.

Cindy looked doubtful. "I suppose."

"Do you need anything from your house?" Nickey asked. "Why don't I drive you out there to get your things?"

"I have to pick up my car from the hospital."

"I'll take you over there and follow you home."

"That's not necessary."

"Either Ellen or I should be with you twenty-four-seven," Nickey urged.

"What about when I'm at work?"

"I'll go with you to the office," Ellen said. "One of us will meet you after work. Make sure you're not alone with Adan. If he gets out of line, report him."

Cindy looked down at the floor and shook her head.

54

Sanchez and Bailey stopped at a nearby McDonald's after interviewing Troy and the woman he introduced as his lawyer. They each ordered a cup of coffee but abstained from the fattening stuff. Sanchez was a nervous snacker. Bailey challenged him to give up snacks while they were on duty after he complained about putting on weight.

She broke the silence. "Mondale had nothing to do with it."

Her partner smiled. *Too damned good-looking to be a criminal?* "He had an alibi, and he doesn't match our description of the attackers. But that doesn't mean he had nothing to do with it."

"Get serious," Bailey smirked. "He answered our questions. He didn't hold anything back."

"He raped the woman."

"That was a long time ago. He pled guilty and served time. He knows what would happen if he got caught doing something like this."

"Why did he need a lawyer?" Sanchez smiled triumphantly. *Chalk one up*.

His partner grimaced and shook her head. “Do you think he lied to us?”

He shrugged. “I didn’t see any tells.”

She took a drink of coffee. “So, where do we go from here?”

He screwed his face into a thoughtful expression. “We dig.”

Bailey drank her coffee and waited for more. Sanchez looked off to his left toward the counter. When he turned back, he said, “I’ll run a background check and see what we’ve got first thing in the morning.”

“I want to hear what Bennet has to say.”

* * *

The assault on Eric Foster might have slipped through the cracks if Cindy had not mentioned Troy Mondale and Captain Bennett. Andrews and Smith were too busy with Adan Jackson to notice that the victim of a random mugging was Eric Foster.

Captain Lydia Bennett guessed what had happened when she saw the item in the Saturday morning paper. She made plans to pay a visit to Mondale that afternoon.

Bailey had little use for the captain, and she did not want a vice cop interfering with her robbery investigation. The captain had a reputation for an unusually high arrest and conviction rate. Her detractors said she relied on coercion to push suspects into plea deals. But no one openly challenged her tactics. She was getting vicious sex offenders off the streets.

Bailey had a reputation too. Some said “Bailey” was short for Barely Legal, referring to her approach to police work. But she was smart enough to lay a solid foundation before she went after a suspect.

The detective placed her call to Lydia Bennett at almost the same time Nickey knocked on Ellen Magee's door.

"Do you have a minute, Captain?" Bailey asked.

"What can I do for you, Detective?"

"Do you know Cindy Foster?"

"Why?"

"Sanchez and I investigated a mugging last night. Mrs. Foster's husband was the victim. When we interviewed her, she named Troy Mondale as a person of interest. She also said that we should talk to you about him."

"He served time in prison for rape. He's out. He has a condo on Connecticut Avenue near the Woodley Park Metro station and an office in Foggy Bottom not far from the Metro."

"Yes. I was wondering if you have information that would help us with our case."

"Nothing concrete."

"But you have contacted him recently as part of an investigation?"

"Cindy came to me with a complaint that he was harassing her. I paid him a visit and asked him to stop."

"Did you find any evidence that he had been bothering her?"

"What's this about?"

"Mr. Mondale doesn't match either of the attackers described by our eyewitness." Bailey sighed. "But that doesn't rule him out. He may be involved in some other way." She waited, but Bennett did not respond. "If you have any information that would point to him as a person of interest, I need to know about it." Bailey was pissed. She was getting belligerent, but she didn't care.

"He was extremely hostile," a sullen voice responded. "He seems to harbor feelings of anger toward those who put him in prison. I intend to keep an eye on him to make sure that he doesn't do anything to Cindy or anyone else involved with that case."

"So, you're going on a gut feeling at the moment?" Bailey prodded.

"I don't have enough to lock him up," Bennett replied. Then she added, "Yet."

"All right, Captain, thank you for your time. I hope that you will let me know if something does pop up."

"Of course," she said. "You might want to check with Jack Edwards. I believe that Mr. Mondale is on his radar as well."

Bailey called Sergeant Edwards immediately. Her name and photo must have popped up on his phone. He answered with, "Detective Bailey, what can I do for you?"

"Lydia Bennett told me that you have an interest in my case."

"What case is that?"

"A mugging. Eric Foster was beaten and robbed last night."

"I saw that in the paper," Edwards said. "What makes you think it's related to a case I'm working?"

"Mrs. Foster identified Mondale as a possible person of interest and referred us to Captain Bennett. She told me he was on your radar."

"I am keeping tabs on him, but I have no reason to believe he has been involved in any criminal activity."

"I don't either. He doesn't match the description of either of the assailants. Rick and I talked to him. He has an alibi, and he doesn't seem to be hiding anything."

"My money is on Adan Jackson. We got a tip that he was trying to hire somebody to put a hit on Eric Foster."

"What happened?"

"Nothing. Foster wasn't assaulted."

"So what? It has taken Jackson this long to find somebody?"

"It's possible. That would explain the mugging."

Bailey pursed her lips. "I've got a mugging. You've got a threat. Neither of us has enough for an arrest."

"Are you going to work with me?" the sergeant asked.

Bailey nodded. "Sure. Why not?"

"Talk to Liz. She can help you."

55

Adan was up before dawn on Saturday morning. By eleven, he had finished the morning paper and was plowing through his clients' financial data. The folders stacked to the left of his laptop were completed. Those on the right would be completed before he called it a day.

A cell phone interrupted his concentration. He pulled it from his pocket and checked the caller ID. He answered, "Greg."

The ex-con growled, "It's taken care of."

Adan summoned Peter Baeker. "Yes," he replied. "I saw the item in the paper."

"Come by the bar tonight with the money. Small bills in two mailers."

"I've already transferred your money to your new account."

"What new account?"

Baeker looked up and shook his head in despair. "The one we talked about in the park the other day."

"Bad idea," the gruff voice snarled. "They ain't gonna be happy."

"As I explained to you, the offshore account is the best way to do business."

"Not this time. Not with these boys," Greg warned. "They ain't on board with it. Best you give them the cash tonight."

"I've already given you the money."

"Do they have it?"

"It's in a bank account. They can withdraw it any time they want."

"Right now?" Greg jeered.

"No. Not at the moment. They need the account number and password."

"Which you have. You're the only one can take that money out. So, you haven't paid them yet."

"I have put the money into the account. Once they have the account number and password, they can do whatever they want with it." Baeker pressed his lips together and exhaled forcefully. "They can change the password and lock me out."

"Think about it, Peter," Greg prodded. "That's a lot more trouble than cash."

"For a single transaction, yes."

"How many are we talking about?"

"I don't know, Greg. The other night you were looking for more business."

"You got something in mind?"

"We can talk about that when I give you the account information."

"Okay. Show up at 8:15 with the cash. You pay the boys off, and we can go inside for a beer."

"I'm just going to hand the money over to them at the bar?"

"Sure. We'll do it discreetly out in the parking lot before we go in. It'll be fine."

56

Adan Jackson was congenitally precise and prompt. He put on Peter Baeker at 7:30 p.m. and drove to the Boundary Line, arriving at 8:13. Three men were standing around with lit cigarettes at the rear of the building. Peter parked and walked over to them. The smell of weed assaulted his nostrils as he approached.

Greg was overly friendly. Almost jovial. "You're right on time, as usual, Peter."

Mo and Tony met him with icy stares.

He nodded at the three men. "Greg. Mo. Tony."

"You brought somethin' for the boys, right?" Greg prompted.

Peter stuck his hands into the pockets of his jacket and pulled out two mailers. He handed one to each of the "boys." Tony ripped his mailer open and pulled the stack of bills halfway out. He cocked the tops back and scanned them to make sure everything was in order as he let them slide past his thumb. Mo watched and then checked his stack of bills. The two men looked at each other and shrugged.

Greg said, "Let's go inside for a beer."

He led the way to a table in a far corner. The men sat watching one another while they waited for the beers to be served. No one said a word. Greg broke the spell. "Peter, you said you had some ideas that we might be interested in. Stuff we could help you with."

Baeker stared at the ex-con. His eyes narrowed and his mouth opened. He couldn't make himself put those thoughts into words. He was afraid to share them with this particular group.

Greg egged him on. "You wanted something done about that bum who stiffed you. What was his name? Jones? That's it, Tom Jones."

"Yes. Um, Tom Jones. That was his name." He swallowed. "I'd like to, um, make sure he doesn't do anything like that again."

"Permanent?" Mo asked.

Peter hesitated. Rage over the last phone conversation with the bum built into an explosion. "Yeah. Permanent." A vision of Mo and Tony kicking and beating on Jones flashed through his mind. "Beat the shit out of him and throw his body in a dumpster."

Greg tensed at the unexpected outburst. He recovered and urged, "What about the dick?"

Peter looked puzzled.

The ex-con prompted, "You said something about a detective."

"Oh yeah. Her."

"What about her?"

Peter pursed his lips. The knife attack ran through his consciousness once again. "She's a vicious bitch. Always pushing people around and telling them what to do. The world would be better off without her."

Greg stroked his chin while he thought. "You got two different cases there, Peter. Jones is a bum that nobody cares about. The fuzz ain't gonna waste a lotta time trying to figure out what happened to him. Then you got a detective with clients and all. That job has to be done carefully. Even then, the cops might track down her killers."

Peter had not considered this turn of events. The word "killers" hit him like an electric shock. He shuddered. His eyes widened, and his lips pressed into a grimace. He stammered, "What are you saying?"

"Jones ain't worth the trouble. We could handle the dick, but it's a big job and it's high risk. If you ask us to take care of her, we could throw in the bum."

The exec felt himself being pulled under. He pushed back against his seat. His eyes closed. Baeker shook his head as he struggled for an answer. He inhaled deeply and forced air out through his nostrils. "Bottom line. What is your proposal?"

"We'll take care of the bitch, but it has to be done right." Greg pressed his lips into a line, arched his brows and shrugged. "The real problem is getting away with it. Like I said, she probably has connections, so there will be pressure to find out what happened to her." He rocked his head back and forth. "That means we'll need some time to make preparations."

Tony jumped in. "We have to be careful how we do it and what we do afterward." He added ominously, "One of us might end up back in prison. That'd be extra. You'd have to put up some insurance money."

"How much are you talking about?"

"Three hunnert grand," Tony snapped without hesitation.

Peter recoiled in shock.

Greg hissed, "Careful. We got company." He nodded toward a table at the other end of the barroom. A couple of dykes were downing shooters and smoking something. Probably weed. Whatever they were talking about, they were having a good time. The ex-con continued in a low growl. "The black one was here the other night. Cop for sure. The white one is most likely her partner."

Mo snarled, "What're we gonna do about 'em?"

"Let 'em be. They already reported on us. We'll just need to be careful," Greg rumbled. He turned to Peter. "Do we have a deal?"

The exec hesitated. "I need to think about it."

"You need to decide," Greg challenged. "We can't keep playing around."

"All right. Let's do it. But I need to know your plans before I fork out that kind of money."

"Put half in that fancy account and text me the info. When I see the money, we'll put the plan together. Then we can meet and make arrangements."

"How long? A week?" Peter asked.

Greg rocked his head. "We could get ready in a week." He added, "But not here."

"There's a resort in Vermont that is quiet and out of their reach."

Greg nodded. "Alright, Vermont. Gimme that info as well. And you'll need to reimburse us." He took a moment to assess the exec. "What's so special about the week?"

"I'll be out of the country this week. I get back next Saturday."

"What time?" Tony demanded.

"Saturday morning. I'll arrive in New York early and drive up there. Should be there before noon."

"Okay. Get outta here," Greg ordered. "We'll sit here and keep an eye on the cops. Make the down payment and get the info to me by noon."

Peter finished his beer, and walked out to his car.

57

Adan Jackson arrived at the Courtyard Marriott in Vermont's Green Mountain Wilderness area two days late. He had returned to New York on time, but he stopped off in the city for an extended visit with Beau. When he did show up for the meeting, he found Greg, Tony and Mo anxious and out of sorts.

Greg grumbled, "This ain't natural. It's like being in prison. We belong in the city."

"Worse," Tony said. "I'd rather be in the pen."

Adan, who had put on Peter Baeker, tried to conciliate. "It won't happen again. If this is done right, you will finish this job in a few days and get your money. Then we can go our separate ways."

Greg nodded sagely. Then he casually dropped, "Things have changed."

Peter raised his eyebrows. "How so?"

The ex-con grinned. "The price has gone up. It's three million."

"We have an agreement, and I expect you to honor it," the exec replied indignantly. "I can't be shelling out more money every time you decide to up the price."

"How do you feel about a few years in prison?"

"If I go, you go as well."

"We've been there before. We know how to do the time," Greg countered. "Besides, the DA will cut a deal for our testimony."

"And if dat kid in da hospital dies, yer lookin' at serious time," Mo threatened.

Peter's jaw tightened. His head began to throb. He suddenly hated these men.

Tony slid a piece of paper over to him. "That's our corporate account. Wire one and a half mil. I'll confirm that we have the money and I'll send you a signed contract. That'll make it legal."

The exec was astounded. *Two weeks ago, these thugs knew nothing about offshore accounts. Now they had a sophisticated system in place.* He shook his head. "All right. One million apiece. Half now. Half when the job is done."

Tony warned, "You have one hour to transfer the money. If it ain't in our account by 1:15, we shove off, and you're a dead man."

Thirty minutes later, Peter called Greg's room and got the answering machine. He called Tony. When he picked up, Peter said, "I've sent the money and confirmed the transfer."

"I see that. I'm taking care of a few details," Tony answered. "We can get back together at 1:30." He hung up.

When the meeting reconvened at a table in the hotel restaurant, Peter got right down to business. "What's going on with Foster? What's his status?"

"They removed part of his skull and put him in a coma," Greg said.

"I saw that in the paper. I also read that there was a witness. Any chance you will be recognized?"

Mo sneered and shook his head. "She can't identify us. She was across the street."

Peter moved on. "You said he might die."

"He seems to be recovering okay," Greg replied with a grin. "He should be fine as long as nobody messes with him."

Peter shivered involuntarily. "Then he'll be able to talk to the police."

"He was out before he knew what hit him," Tony boasted.

"What about Tom Jones?"

Mo shrugged. "Disappeared. Coulda skipped town."

"He's a ghost," Greg jeered. "He doesn't exist."

Peter recoiled and sputtered, "What do you mean? I've talked to him on the phone. I met with him at the motel."

"He's like Batman," Tony retorted. "You don't find him. He finds you."

"Nobody knows nothin' about him. Nobody even remembers seeing him," Greg said.

"That asshole cheated me out of two hundred dollars," Peter groused.

"A cheap lesson in the school of hard knocks," Greg observed. "We have real problems."

"What kind of problems?"

"The police are watching us."

"I figured that," Peter scoffed. "You take care of that bitch detective. You get your money and get out of the country. There's nothing they can do."

"Remember those two bitches in the bar the last time we met?" Greg asked.

"Yes."

"The black one tailed us when we left D.C.," Tony said. "But we took care of her."

A wave of nausea swept over the exec. "You took care of her?"

The thug gloated, "We snuffed her and tossed her body in the woods. Her car ended up in a lake. Problem solved."

"Until the cops realize she's missing and come looking for her," Peter shot back.

"Exactly," Greg said. "We're in a bind."

"What does that mean?"

"It means," the big man intoned, "the situation has changed. If you want that dick bumped off, it's got to be tomorrow."

"You have a plan? Good. What's the problem?" Baeker smiled contemptuously. "Wait. Don't tell me. She's doesn't have a fixed routine."

The ex-con grinned. "She always ends the day at home."

"For Christ's sake. That's all there is to it? You wait for the lights to go out and then march in and bang."

"Simple? Yes. Smart? No." Greg laughed. "She likely has a great alarm system. She likely sleeps with her piece. Going after her like that would be dangerous." He smirked and shook his head. "I don't know what the cops have on you and her. But they know about you and me. And I have a record. It wouldn't take them long to come after us."

"I just gave you a million and a half," Peter growled. Heads turned to see what was going on.

Greg leaned back and smiled. "We're gonna do the job, Peter." He nodded slightly for emphasis. "But there's something you need to do." He leaned toward the exec and rested his forearms on the table. "We can snatch her, but we need a quiet place to work. Someplace where we can finish her and leave the body undisturbed while we disappear."

"I have no idea where that would be. I certainly don't own a place like that," Peter protested. "And again, she's unpredictable. How are you going to snatch her?"

"You're gonna love this," the ex-con beamed. "She's guarding your princess. She drives the bitch over to the hospital every night for a visit with her poor old man then drives her to an apartment in D.C. We'll grab her when she leaves the hospital."

The exec needed a minute to digest that plan. "What about Cindy?"

"Cindy? Is that her name?" Greg sneered. He shrugged. "Collateral damage."

Peter looked off to his left, a grim expression on his face.

"Are you getting cold feet?" Tony demanded.

"No." Peter jerked back, forcing himself to meet the thug's eyes. "It sounds like a good plan. I'm on board."

"Good," Greg said. "You need to find us a place tomorrow."

"How am I supposed to do that?"

"The housing market is in bad shape. Lots of properties are up for sale. Make a down payment on some dump in Northeast D.C. and tell the agent you need keys so your crew can come in and estimate the cost to fix it up."

Baeker looked doubtful. "I'll see what I can do."

"We just need one night," Greg insisted. "Best if it's tomorrow, but we'll give you until Wednesday afternoon."

"Whether the bitch lives or dies is up to you," Tony said. "Either way, we get paid. Is that clear?"

Peter jerked to attention. He wanted to tell them to go fuck themselves. His gaze darted from Mo to Greg to Tony. He wilted. "Perfectly."

Greg stood. Mo and Tony followed his lead. Greg said, "We'll be taking off now. Call me when you've got the place. Noon Wednesday at the latest. We get paid Wednesday, no matter what."

They turned and marched out of the restaurant.

58

Adan was afraid for the first time in his life. He had always been confident that no matter how things looked, he would emerge safe and sound. His immortality was a given.

Now he was caught in a trap by three thugs who had killed a cop and who were getting ready to murder two women they had never met. He did not doubt they planned to kill him. For the time being, his safety was guaranteed by the remaining million-and-a-half-dollar payment. He might not live very long after he gave them the money.

"There's only one way out," Adan said, "Ah have to give them what they want and get out of the country. Ah have business connections in China. Ah should be safe there."

He had driven at high speeds for six hours with only one pit stop to make it from Vermont to the Omni Shoreham for dinner with his brother.

Beau sat across from him in a semi slouch. "What were you thinking?"

"Ah was just pushing a few buttons to get a rise out of her," Adan complained. "She didn't have to send that dick after me." He paused and grinned. "Dickless dick." He laughed.

Beau scowled. "Now you're running for your life from a gang of killers you hired to take care of the detective."

"It's not a gang," Adan corrected. He bit his lip and shook his head. "It's three mercenaries. Ah pay them, and that's the end of it." He shrugged. "The trip to China is just a precaution."

"You don't think they have figured out the Jacksons are rich?" Beau sneered and picked up his wine glass. He paused to ask, "What's to stop them from pushing *our* buttons?"

Adan sat back and folded his arms. He glared across the table.

Beau looked down at his plate while he chewed a bite of steak. He took a drink of wine and wiped his lips. He raised his head and fixed Adan with a cold stare. "Get rid of those men."

"How? Tell them, 'The deal's off. Goodbye and good luck?'" Adan leaned forward. "You don't say things like that to people like that. They told me they would kill me if I didn't pay them."

Beau leaned forward, hands clasped between his legs. He moistened his lips. "Kill them before they kill you."

"You're crazy," Adan blurted in a hoarse whisper.

Beau was unmoved. "You brought this on. You put us in this situation. It's up to you to clean up the mess."

"Ah didn't," Adan stammered. "It just happened."

"Nothing 'just happens,'" his brother taunted. "It was your job to keep the situation under control."

The exec's breath was coming in short, heavy bursts. "Doesn't matter. We can't kill them."

Beau finished a bite of salad and sipped his wine. "And why not?"

"They're the killers. We don't have any weapons," Adan shrieked.

Beau tapped his head. "We have these."

Adan nodded and sneered. "But they have guns."

His brother raised his hands. "Calm down." He tapped his head again. "Start thinking."

"Ah am thinking," Adan snapped. "Ah'm thinking it's a dumb idea to try to kill those thugs. Ah have to pay them off and get them out of the country."

Beau grimaced. "How are you going to get them out of the country?"

"It's either that or go to jail."

"For what?"

Adan rattled off the crimes. "Beating up Cindy's old man. Killing a cop. Killing the detective and Cindy."

"Do you have any evidence that they did any of those things?"

Adan opened his mouth but said nothing. Beau continued, "As a matter of fact, the detective is still very much alive, isn't she?"

"Yes."

"On the other hand, they can testify against you. They probably have enough evidence to put you away for a long time."

Adan stared down at his plate. He nodded.

"As long as they are out there with that kind of leverage, we are all in trouble," Beau warned. "If anything happens to the detective or Cindy, your life is over. The rest of the Jacksons may very well be paying for your stupidity for a long time."

"That bitch embarrassed me," Adan growled. "I'm not going to let her get away with it."

"She's a nobody," Beau snarled. "It would not have occurred to Cindy to go after you if you had left her alone like I told you." He stabbed a bite of lettuce with his fork and chewed it savagely while he glared at his brother. "You are a boorish, overreaching clown. You have no sense of proportion. You can't distinguish between your fantasies and your real life."

"What are you talking about?"

"A long time ago, you fantasized about raping that woman. Then you did it, and you dragged Troy and me along for the ride. I'll bet you are fantasizing about Cindy's death. I'll bet that in your fantasies, you watch her writhing in pain while she slowly succumbs to your torture."

Adan stared glassy-eyed for a second or two. The image of the woman suffering at his hands had hit a nerve. He shook it off.

"Well, that is not going to happen," Beau said. "But your friends are dangerous, no matter how this plays out. They cannot be allowed to live with the knowledge they have."

"Ah'm deluded?" Adan sneered. "That is the craziest statement Ah have ever heard."

"It is a cold, hard fact."

"How do you plan to do it?"

"We are going to lure them into a trap and shoot them."

"What kind of trap?"

"They want you to find a place and pay them by five tomorrow. Right?"

"Tomorrow or the next day," Adan corrected.

"Tomorrow," Beau insisted. "There are some old properties in Northeast that an enterprising realtor could buy cheap, fix up and sell for a nice profit. Peter Baeker is going to arrange to buy one tomorrow. Your friends will show up expecting their money. We will take them out before they know what hit them."

"There are three of them, all armed. We don't have any guns."

"I have some," Beau said coolly. "We drop two of them as soon as they walk in the door. Then we have the numerical advantage."

"I've never even held a pistol. What are you doing with guns?"

"I like them, and I enjoy shooting. I have one for competition and a couple of Sigs I picked up over the years."

"Can I see one?"

"They are out in my car, along with some ammunition. I'll take you out in the woods where we can fire some practice rounds. There is nothing to it," Beau assured his brother. "You just point and pull the trigger."

Adan shook his head. "This is crazy."

"Sometimes, you have to be crazy to survive."

Adan stared at his brother, awed by this unsuspected aspect of his character.

"Let's get out of here," Beau said with forced enthusiasm. "We have a lot to do."

59

Jack scanned the report quickly. He had seen enough of them that he could grab the essentials without wading through all the nitty-gritty. What he got was the disturbing details of rookie officer Rhonda Johnson's death. What he did not get was a plausible explanation.

He looked up at Detective Liz Smith, who was standing in front of his desk. "How did this happen?"

"She was keeping an eye on the three ex-cons because Adan was out of town," Liz began in a matter-of-fact tone. "On Friday, they got together at the Greyhound bus terminal and then went their separate ways. She followed Mo Adoyo. He went straight up 95 north through Baltimore and kept going. She texted me at that point to inform me of the situation. I told her to stay in contact but out of sight."

The detective stared poker-faced, waiting for a comment. Jack stared back but said nothing.

She continued, "Johnson reported seeing all three cars in close proximity on 95 between Baltimore and New York. She reported in when they crossed the George Washington Bridge into the Bronx and again when they headed north on 87. Her last report said that they had turned off 87 onto 32, heading west into the Catskills."

Liz took the report from Jack and tried to scan through it. That was a chore. She knew what it said because she had helped the New York State trooper put it together.

Officer Rhonda Johnson's body was discovered in a shallow grave near a trail in the Kaaterskill Wild Forest Area by a cadaver dog. The golden retriever named Sunshine was on a walk with her owner and handler Charlie Wilson when she picked up the scent and insisted on investigating. They discovered a fresh grave and uncovered human remains before notifying the police.

The victim, a black female, was transported to the morgue, where it was determined that the cause of death was asphyxiation. Bruises and lacerations showed that she had struggled with her attacker or attackers. She had suffered a bullet wound to the right hand.

They were able to identify her because her fingerprints were in the database. When the team learned she was a police officer from Washington, D.C., they got in touch with her supervisor, Detective Elizabeth Smith.

In the meantime, police in the field located the crime scene about 1000 meters from the grave. The investigators pieced together what had probably happened. The officer drove into a

> *trap. She got out of her car and drew her weapon to confront the killers. A bullet struck her right hand and caused her to drop her service weapon. Her attackers overpowered her and pinned her down while a plastic bag was held over her head.*
>
> *The perps stripped her and transported the body to the trailhead. They carried it up into the woods for quick burial. Then they drove her car to a nearby reservoir and pushed it in. Her clothes were in the trunk. A helicopter pilot spotted the vehicle during a search of the area.*

Sergeant Edwards studied the detective from behind his desk. "Why didn't she have backup?"

Liz put the report down and shook her head. "She was supposed to find out where they were going. Her orders were to avoid contact."

"Did you order her to follow them?"

Liz struggled for control. She did not scare easily, but Jack could put the fear of God in anyone. "Officer Johnson was on the other side of Baltimore when she reported in. I had to make a decision. I chose to let her keep going."

"Without backup?"

"They had a fifty-mile head start."

Jack stood and walked over to the window with his hands behind his back. *Liz made the call. That was her job. It just didn't work out the way she had hoped.* He turned around. The detective was staring at the floor with her back to him. "Were they planning to meet somebody in the Catskills?"

She turned to face him. "I don't know. It's possible."

"What do you think?" the sergeant demanded.

Liz glared at her boss. She snarled, "They were going someplace else. When they made her, they lured her into a trap in the middle of nowhere."

"Because?"

"They did a half-ass job of covering it up. It was a shallow grave in the woods, not a permanent hiding place."

"So, they didn't care if we found her body?"

"What the hell do you want?" Liz demanded. "You've been doing this long enough to figure it out."

"Okay. I agree with you," Jack rumbled. "They detoured into the mountains to get rid of Johnson. They may have believed that would throw us off the trail. You realized something was wrong when she went silent. But there was nothing you could do about it."

"I did notify the New York State Police of the situation."

"They never got the message," Jack pointed out. He shrugged. "They couldn't have done anything anyway. They wouldn't have known where to look."

Liz shuddered. Her jaw tightened. She clenched her fists and looked down at the floor.

"You still can't do anything about it," Jack said. "We know who did it, but we can't prove it. We have to continue our investigation. Who was she focusing on?"

Liz walked toward the door. She stopped halfway, interlocked her hands, and pushed them toward the ceiling. She arched her back. Then relaxed. Turning back to face Jack, she said, "The big guy, Greg Jantzen." She nodded. "He seemed to be the leader."

"You need to find him ASAP. I'll get Sanchez and Bailey to go after the other two."

"She was a goddamn rookie," Liz said bitterly.

"She was an adrenaline junkie. She volunteered for this assignment because it was dangerous," Jack countered. "She was doing her job. If she had thought she needed help, she would have asked for it."

Liz turned to leave.

Jack asked, "What about the Shoreham? Did you follow up on that situation?"

"Jackson is a regular. There has never been any trouble."

"Except the night Nickey Arnold was his guest?"

"Yeah. Except that night. But neither of them has filed a complaint." She continued to the door and stopped. "Eric Foster is conscious and receiving visitors. Bill and I are going to drop in on him."

"Sanchez and Bailey are handling that."

"We want to ask him about the mystery woman who accompanied him to his car. He didn't want to talk about her in front of his wife."

The sergeant shook his head. "She's not important."

"Is there something I should know?" Liz asked suspiciously.

"Just a gut feeling."

60

Troy sat at the dining-room table, his laptop open in front of him. He was preparing for a panel discussion on prison sentencing practices. He had reduced his talk on life behind bars to cues scribbled on a set of three-by-five cards. His attention was focused on cards containing memory jogs for other presentations when the doorbell rang.

He opened the door to Cindy Smith Foster. Her cold fury contrasted starkly with the pleasant, flowery scent of her perfume. He noticed for the first time that she was using highlights to darken her honey-brown hair.

"Would you like to come in?"

"Get out. You don't belong here," she snarled.

"Actually, I do."

"You were told to stay away from me."

Troy shook his head. "You came to my condo and rang the bell."

"I came here to tell you that you have to get out," she retorted. Her voice rose, along with her fury.

"You should leave." Troy's lips pressed into a grim line. He pushed the door shut.

Her hand shot out and held it open. She repeated fiercely, "You were told to stay away from me."

"That was an unofficial warning by a cop butting into something that doesn't concern her." He smirked. "You don't have a restraining order."

"I'll get one."

"No." He shook his head. "You have no basis for a keep away order. But if you did get one, it would require you to stay away from me."

She put her hands on her hips and glared at him.

"I haven't done anything to you, and I'm not going to." He shook his head. "I don't even want to talk to you. As long as you don't come around bothering me, we shouldn't have a problem."

"My friend lives here. I come to visit her."

Troy shrugged. "I know. Ellen used to be friendly. Now she doesn't speak to me. She just glares. That's her prerogative. I have to live with it."

"You're a rapist. Your very presence is revolting."

"I understand how you feel…"

"Do you?" she cut him off in midsentence. "You have no idea what it was like."

"I do know, and I don't expect you to forgive me."

"You're a man. How would you know?"

"I felt it when I watched you struggling on that bed. I felt it when I was raped. Now please go and don't come back." Troy pushed on the door, but she blocked it.

She eyed him suspiciously. "*You* were raped?" Her lips twisted into a sneer. "I'll bet."

"Good night." He pushed on the door.

Cindy pushed back. She studied his face. "You're serious."

"Yes. Good night." He turned to walk away.

She called after him, "Is there any record? Did you report it?"

Visions of violence and terror flashed through his mind. His body began to shake with hurt and anger. He turned on her in a rage. "You fucking idiot. Leave."

"Why didn't you report it?"

His face reddened. His breath came in short puffs as his hands curled into white-knuckled fists. He managed to keep his voice under control. "I was locked up with very bad people. They would have beaten the shit out of me if I had reported it. I could have been killed. So, I learned to live with it."

Troy turned and took a few more steps to the center of the room. He stood there trembling, his fists clenched and his head bowed.

"What happened?" Cindy asked as she stepped into his apartment. She took another step and halted.

He felt an odd connection with the woman. It reminded him of feelings he experienced the night of the rape. He was suddenly aware of the odor of his roast beef and potato dinner lingering in the air. He could feel her taking in the bare living room. The lack of furniture suddenly struck him. The room was empty except for a futon and a recliner in a far corner. Her attention turned to the dining area where a laptop sat open on the table covered with books and magazines. She was struggling to understand his lifestyle. What did he do? How did he fill his nights and days?

A darkened hallway caught her attention for a moment. Her focus came back to him. The man whose attack had destroyed her life. She repeated her question in a soft voice. "What happened?"

Troy didn't move. "Please leave and don't come back."

She walked over and took his hand. "Troy, I," she stammered, "I don't know what to say."

"There's nothing to say. You got what you wanted. Just leave and don't come back."

"What is that supposed to mean?" she demanded angrily.

"You wanted me to pay for what I did. I was imprisoned and tortured for twelve years." He shuddered violently. "One year for each minute you suffered. I paid for my crime. It's time to let me live my life in peace."

Cindy clapped her hands to her head. "I didn't want that. What you did was wrong, and you deserved to be punished. That's all I wanted."

He turned to his tormentor. His face twisted in hurt and anger. "What you did wasn't right either."

"It was just acting, for God's sake," Cindy squawked. "I just acted in some stupid videos."

"Stop kidding yourself," he growled. "You were promoting gang rape. You starred in movies meant for sick, dangerous men. People were hurt."

"What do you mean? Who was hurt?"

"You and at least five other women." He glared. "All raped by men inspired by those videos." He touched his chest. "I was hurt. The difference between us is that I accepted responsibility for my actions. I went to prison because what I did was wrong. It was a stupid mistake, but it was wrong. So, I paid the price."

She clasped her hand over her mouth. Troy took her arm to escort her out.

Ellen called from the doorway, "What's going on?"

"Your friend can tell you about it when you get back to your apartment," Troy said.

The lawyer seemed alarmed by his demeanor. "Take your hands off her."

"She's trespassing. I have asked her to leave three times. She refuses."

"That doesn't give you the right to assault her."

"She assaulted me. I'm defending myself. If you want to take it to court, fine. But you are in my home without an invitation."

"Your door was open."

"That won't hold up in court."

"I'm going." Cindy yanked her arm free and stalked out of the apartment.

61

Adan woke with a start on Tuesday morning. Monday had a been a long, stressful day that ended with Beau's hour-long Introduction to Handguns. As he sat on the edge of his bed, gathering himself, he realized this would probably be the most dangerous twenty-four hours of his life.

Greg Jantzen had ordered him to get an old house that could be used to dump bodies. According to the ex-con, it had to be delivered tomorrow at the latest or else. Beau had decided it would have to be tomorrow because he needed time to prepare an ambush for the three thugs.

As Adan dressed for work and plotted out his course of action, he managed to push worries about police surveillance to the back of his mind. For their part, the police had pushed him down on their list of priorities. Sergeant Jack Edwards had just ordered Detective Liz Smith to find Jantzen and put a tail on him.

But as soon as Adan pulled away from his condo, a tracker alerted Detective Bill Andrews that he was in town and on the move.

He parked in his assigned spot in the Cap Gallery garage. The props and makeup for creating both Abraham Jacobs and Peter Baeker were in his briefcase. Identity changes would have to be made in public restrooms. On the way up to the office, he bought a new burner phone for Jacobs, the alter ego who would procure the house for Greg.

Adan got busy calling real estate brokers as soon as he finished his routine daily chores. He did not call Gelberger Real Estate. He didn't want Gertie in on this deal. She could be a big help, but she could also be a liability. There were plenty of other brokers. Adan got lucky on his third call. The man had a property on H Street in Northeast, and he was willing to make a deal. He wanted $250,000, with twenty percent down.

"Dot can be arranged," Dr. Jacobs assured him.

"How soon are we talking about?"

"I vould like to close today. I fly back to Germany on Friday."

"That's not possible," the broker objected. "I will need time to prepare the paperwork."

"So Tursday, da?" Jacobs urged.

"We might be able to do it Thursday afternoon. What's the rush?"

"I come back in September to teach course. I need a place to stay."

"The property we're talking about is going to need quite a bit of work before anybody could move in."

"Da. I vill have dat taken care of."

"Well, you're going to have to close on it before any work is done."

"Da. I get loan Tursday."

"Sounds good."

"Tomorrow contractors come look around and make estimate," Jacobs said.

"I'll have to be there," the broker insisted. "What time are they coming?"

"Ve haf to talk. Maybe pretty late. But I make sure dey don't break anyting."

"I have to be there."

"I come today and bring check for fifty tousand. I sign papers. You give me du keys, da?"

"No. I don't know," the broker demurred.

"I bring check for hundred tousand, and you get du rest on Tursday. You give me du keys so ve can look around. Da?"

"I need cash," the broker squeaked. He was stressing. "Your check is going to have to clear the bank."

"Da. Cashier's check," Jacobs said dismissively.

The broker paused to consider. "You bring me a cashier's check for one hundred K today and sign a promissory note for the remaining one hundred fifty K by Thursday noon, and we have a deal."

"Da. I come after lunch."

"I'll be out of the office until 1:15," the broker said. "Can you make it around 1:30?"

"Da. Das iss goot."

That was a great start. Adan called to reserve a rental car at Reagan National Airport. Then he went downstairs to the public restroom and put on Abraham Jacobs. The trip to the airport took twenty minutes on the Metro. Waiting in line and filling out the paperwork for the car took another twenty minutes. Jacobs was getting ready to board a shuttle to the car lot when Peter Baeker's phone rang. It was Greg Jantzen.

Adan took a breath so he could switch characters. "What's up?"

"We need to meet," Greg growled. "I want to know what's going on."

"Everything is fine," Peter assured him. "I located a place. I am making arrangements."

"Meet me at the Monocle. I'm in the parking lot."

"I can't come right this minute," Peter said, sounding calmer than he felt. "I'll be there by twelve."

"Don't be late," Greg warned and hung up.

Adan rushed to the nearest restroom to shed Jacobs and put on Baeker. He grabbed the next shuttle to the rental car lot and picked out an unobtrusive gray Sonata.

The Monocle started life as the American Cafe. The new owners kept a reference to the old title in the full name of their establishment—The Monocle: An Old School American Bar and Grill. Peter spotted Greg's car in the parking lot just behind the restaurant. He pulled up next to the ex-con's Dodge Ram and parked so they could talk without getting out of their cars.

Greg demanded, "What's goin' on?"

"I have a meeting with the realtor. I am going to hand him a check and sign the papers."

"So, we can do it t'night?"

"No, he won't give me the keys until sometime tomorrow morning."

"What the fuck?" Greg bellowed. Face red and eyes bulging, he bared his teeth as if he was about to jump out of his car and attack.

Peter remained calm. "He has to make sure my check is good before he will give us unsupervised access to the house."

"Give 'im a cashier's check," Greg snarled.

"I am," Peter smirked. "But he has to make sure it isn't forged. We're talking about a substantial amount of money."

"Fuck! Where is this place?"

"I'll tell you after I pick up the keys."

"Tell me now," Greg demanded.

Peter threw him a bone. "It's on H Street in Northeast. I'll give you the specifics tomorrow."

He closed his window and drove off but checked in his rearview mirror to make sure Greg wasn't attempting to follow him. At a McDonald's a half-mile away, Peter Baeker walked into the restroom. Abraham Jacobs emerged. He got a Big Mac and fries for lunch. Then he drove to a nearby branch of the HSBC Bank, where he had a checking account with more than enough money to buy the house on H Street outright. But Adan had no intention of purchasing the place. He would close out the account as soon as business was taken care of.

Jacobs arranged for a cashier's check in the amount of $100,000 and drove to the realtor's office. His timing was superb. He sat down with the broker at precisely 1:30. He handed over the check, completed the paperwork, and took possession of the keys.

The plan was going perfectly. The next item on his agenda was a get-together with Beau at the Patriot Club, a gun club and shooting range in Prince George's County, Maryland. Adan put his disguises in his briefcase and checked a traffic app before starting the Sonata. The preferred route, 395, was shut down because of a major accident. He opted for New York Avenue, which became Route 50 in Maryland. He had forty-five minutes, but the new route was going to make him late.

62

Liz walked from Jack's office to her partner's desk. Bill looked up. "Adan is back at work." He pointed to a display showing the Lincoln SUV sitting in the Cap Gallery parking garage. "We should check him out."

She crossed her arms and nodded. "I want to talk to Moretti."

"Because?"

"She's involved in this, and I want to find out how."

"Aren't we supposed to be tailing Jackson?"

"Jack just told me to find Greg Jantzen and tail him." She shrugged. "You take Jantzen. He knows me. I'll take Jackson."

Bill stood. "Sounds like a plan."

"But Jackson is in his office," Liz said, "and according to Johnson's notes, the best way to locate Jantzen is to check his favorite restaurants at noon. We have a couple of hours to kill."

Bill arched his brows.

Liz continued, "I know Jantzen's car. I'll help you locate him. But first, let's drop in on Moretti."

Her partner shrugged and grabbed his keys.

* * *

They stopped by Cap Gallery to confirm that Adan's Lincoln was in its assigned parking space before proceeding to the lawyer's office. When they walked in, Mondale was working on a laptop at the small conference table. Moretti was at the desk. She looked up. "Can I help you?"

"I'm Detective Bill Andrews, and this is my partner, Detective Liz Smith." They flashed their badges.

Mondale cleared his throat. "What can I do for you?"

Andrews turned his focus to Moretti. "Can you tell us where you were on the evening of July 14?"

She pursed her lips and shook her head. "No."

"You had dinner at the Fairfax. Does that help?"

Marie looked up at the ceiling and then grinned. "That's right. I did."

"And you met with Eric Foster."

She studied the ceiling again. She scowled and pursed her lips. "I ran into Eric when I was leaving."

"You're sure that's all it was?"

"Yes. Why?"

"You walked out to his car with him," Smith said.

Marie screwed up her face and then smiled. "I asked him to walk me to my car. I felt safer with a male companion at that time of night."

"Just any man?" Andrews asked.

"Eric is an acquaintance. I wouldn't have asked somebody I didn't know."

"You didn't go there to meet with him?" Andrews pressed.

"No."

"You did not know in advance that he was going to be there?" Smith asked.

"No."

"It seems odd that you would pick that night to go to dinner at the Fairfax," Andrews observed.

"Why is that?"

"You have never eaten at the Fairfax before."

"Is that a fact?" the lawyer challenged. "How would you know that?"

"We had a tip that Eric would be there and that he was being set up for an attack," Smith interjected.

"And that gave you probable cause to search my background?" Moretti asked incredulously. "Are you at all familiar with a document called the Constitution of the United States of America?"

"We are conducting a criminal investigation," Andrews insisted.

Moretti fixed him with a cold stare. "What crime are you investigating, Detective?"

"The assault on Eric Foster."

"There was no assault."

"He was severely beaten," Smith countered.

"Not on the night in question."

"But you know that he was mugged and is now in the hospital in critical condition," Andrews said.

"Of course."

"How?"

"I read about it in the *Post*," Moretti sneered. Her face screwed up in contempt. "Besides, that twit, Cindy Foster, accused Troy of being responsible. Detectives Sanchez and Bailey tracked him down and grilled him the night it happened."

The detectives looked at each other.

"They didn't know about the threat, and they didn't know about your meeting with Foster at the Fairfax," Andrews said.

Moretti jumped to her feet and leaned over the desk glaring at the detectives. "I did not meet up with Eric Foster at the Fairfax. I ran into him as I was leaving to go home. It was a coincidence."

"I don't believe in coincidences," Smith objected.

Marie grabbed a Post-it from her desk and scribbled on it. She folded the paper and held it out to Smith. "What day were you born?"

Smith pulled back as if the sliver of paper might explode.

"It's a simple experiment," the lawyer assured her. "I can find out if I really want to know. But this will be painless and interesting."

The detective turned to her partner. He shrugged. She said, "April 30, 1974."

"That was exactly one year before the fall of Saigon. George Washington was inaugurated on that day in 1789, and, coincidentally, I was also born on April 30, 1974."

Smith opened the paper. Marie had written "4/30/74." The detective crumpled it up and flipped it back. "That proves nothing."

"It demonstrates that coincidences are real," Moretti objected. "My running into Eric at the Fairfax is no more significant than my being born on the same date as you. He and I are friends, bicycle buddies. I am upset about what happened to him, but I had nothing to do with it."

Mondale rose and walked to the door. "Detectives, this interview is over."

Andrews whirled around. "What's your hurry?"

"We have work to do."

"We are investigating a felony. We would like you to answer some questions," Andrews growled.

"But I don't have to answer those questions. So please leave."

Smith said, "It would help clear up some things if you cooperated."

"It won't help at all," Moretti snapped. "Neither of us had anything to do with the attack on Eric Foster."

Andrews pointed at Mondale. "You had a motive."

"I have never met Eric Foster. I have no reason to do him any harm."

"But Cindy Foster sent you to prison."

"Cindy Smith—that was her name at the time—had almost nothing to do with my going to prison. She was the victim of a brutal rape. I was one of the rapists." Troy shuddered. "I went to prison because I committed a crime." He paused to assess the detectives.

Smith started, "But—"

"Now that I am out," Troy continued, "I have no reason to have anything to do with Mrs. Foster. I have every reason to avoid all contact with her and most especially to avoid causing her any pain or suffering."

The detectives stared at him but seemed unable to come up with another question.

Moretti said, "You need to leave."

After they were gone, Troy turned to his partner. He cocked his head and chewed on his lip for a moment before asking, "How did you know that?"

"I'm psychic. I get it from my gypsy ancestors." She grinned mischievously.

He shook his head and exhaled audibly. “This is probably a good time to go for a workout.”

Marie nodded. “That was pretty intense.”

63

When they returned from their workout, a man was waiting at the door to their office. Marie grabbed Troy's hand. He squeezed but kept walking.

The man stepped back when they got close. He broke into a faint, tight-lipped smile and nodded. "Troy."

"What do you want, Beau?"

The visitor glanced sideways at Marie. "I need to talk to you."

"Marie, this is Beau Jackson, the other member of our rape gang. Beau, this is my partner, Marie Moretti."

"Can we have a few minutes alone?"

"No. I wouldn't feel comfortable talking to you without a witness."

"Can we at least go inside?"

Troy shrugged and led the way into the office. He circled behind the desk and deposited his gym gear before plopping into the boss's seat. Beau followed over to the front of the desk. He stood calm and erect, waiting for a cue, an invitation to speak. He held his hands crossed in front of his groin. Troy stared poker-faced, except for a slight downturn at the corners of his mouth.

Marie stood just inside the doorway, watching.

After several seconds Troy demanded in a low, angry voice, "What do you want, Beau?"

"I need some help, and you could probably use some money."

"I don't need money that badly."

"You don't even know what I want," Beau protested. "It's a small favor. No risk. I need your help for a couple of hours, and I am willing to pay you ten thousand upfront."

Troy leaned back and folded his arms across his chest. "That's a lot of money for a few risk-free hours."

The visitor raised his hands, palms toward Troy. He shook his head. "I feel like I owe you. I want to make things right."

"The Jacksons don't have that much money."

"Name your price," Beau insisted.

Troy studied the man without a hint of emotion. "I don't know what you have in mind, and I don't want to know," he growled. "My advice to you is forget about it, whatever it is. Walk away."

"Relax." Beau tamped down the volume with his right hand. "It's not that big a deal, but I do need your help."

"You're lying," Troy roared. "It's so bad you're scared shitless." He put his hands on the desk and stood. "There is nothing to discuss. Take my advice and quit while you're ahead."

"Troy…"

"Get out."

Beau recoiled. Troy stared fiercely. His visitor turned and walked out of the office with his head down and shoulders drooping.

64

Adan rolled into Maryland on a beautiful July afternoon. Selections from Wagner's epic opera *Siegfried* filled the car. *Good omen.*

He reached the Patriots Club, a shooting range located in a wooded area just east of the NASA Goddard Space Flight Center, a half-hour late because of the accident on 395. He cruised around the parking lot, looking for Beau's car. No luck. But that didn't worry Adan. He couldn't imagine it would take that long to learn to shoot a gun.

Adan checked for calls or messages on his phone. Nothing. The exec went into the foyer and killed ten minutes looking around. He called Beau. The call went straight to voice mail.

He rented a Sig 229 and a shooting lane. Over the next forty minutes, he emptied three clips, firing at three different targets. The results were consistent. He couldn't hit the broad side of a barn.

Adan wandered back to the front, looking for Beau. His brother had not arrived yet, and he hadn't called with an explanation. He tried reaching him again. The call went straight to voice mail again.

A good-looking brunette wearing a blue polo shirt with "Patriots Club" emblazoned over her right breast came up to him and asked, "Is everything okay?"

Adan spotted a tag on her left breast that gave her name as Jill. He flashed his boyish grin. "Ah was told shooting a gun was easy, but Ah'm not having any luck,"

"First time?"

"Yes. Ah have been encouraged to get a weapon for self-defense, but Ah don't think it's going to work."

Jill smiled. It was a broad smile that displayed lush lips and near-perfect teeth. Her brown eyes sparkled. "Would you like me to work with you?"

"It's worth a try."

"Training costs one hundred dollars per hour. You can purchase half-hour increments."

"Do you think you could teach me to shoot in thirty minutes?"

She pointed to the targets he was carrying. "You already know how to shoot. I'm sure I could help you with your aim. I have had pretty good success with other rookies."

"All right, let's start with a half-hour."

They went back to the lane Adan had rented.

Jill walked him through the procedures. "You want to establish a good grip when you pick up the gun."

She was hot, and she smelled like roses. The Sig rested comfortably in her hand. She loaded a clip and fired off eight rounds. Eight holes appeared near the center of the outlined torso. Adan could cover all eight of them with one hand.

He tried it. A few rounds hit the torso, but his shots were high and to the right. Jill stepped behind him and adjusted his stance. She told him to load another clip and bring his weapon into position but hold his fire. When he was ready, she readjusted his posture. He emptied another clip. Better, but still high right. The instructor had him load and take his shooting position but count to three before he started firing: Set his feet on one. Breathe and relax on two. And shoot on three. His shots hit the torso most of the time.

He loaded another clip.

Just before he fired, Jill said, “Stop.”

She stepped behind him and adjusted his feet with her feet. Her body pushed up against his. She placed her hands on his and said, “Fire away.”

It was delicious. Adan added another half hour. By the end of the hour, he was hitting the torso almost every time. His swollen cock made his pants bulge. Jill checked it out furtively. Her cheeks were a little red.

“Ah don’t think Ah am quite ready for a shootout.”

She chuckled. “It probably doesn’t matter. A gunshot will take the fight out of almost anybody. Just get off a couple of rounds in the general direction, and you’ll be okay.”

He took her left hand and kissed it. *No ring.* “Thank you, my lovely. You are truly gifted.”

Her cheeks turned bright red. “You are welcome, sir. If you want any more instruction, you can ask for me by name.”

You’re interested, aren’t you? He started cleaning up the area.

She said, "Don't worry about that. We'll take care of it. Just bring your Sig back to the front desk and I'll get you checked out."

Adan picked up his gun and turned to walk away from the shooting lane. As he did, he brushed up against the woman. His hand slid across her butt. She didn't flinch. She kept her arm in contact with him as she escorted him to the front desk.

There was no sign of Beau. Adan checked his phone. Nothing from his brother or from anybody else, for that matter.

He handed a credit card to Jill. "Ah need to make a call. Could you go ahead and ring me up? Ah'll be right back."

His call went straight to voice mail. Beau was two hours late. Something had gone wrong.

Adan went back to pay. Jill handed him his card and a slip of paper to sign. "Here you are, Mr. Baeker. Just sign our copy."

He had handed her the wrong card. He took a deep breath. Set his feet and adjusted his posture. Then he let the air out and signed his name: Peter Baeker.

She smiled. "It was a pleasure working with you, Mr. Baeker."

"You can call me Pete. Ah can honestly say, this has been the best part of my day." He gave her a broad smile. "By the way, Ah may have some free time later this evening. Is there a number where Ah can reach you?"

Jill picked up a business card and scribbled a number on the back. She smiled as she handed it to him.

Adan sat in his car and regrouped. His brother's disappearing act left him dangling in the wind. It was time to disappear.

I've got everything I need. I could drive up to BWI or out to Dulles and grab a flight to China. He shook off the thought. *I've already paid Greg a million to get rid of the bitch detective. I should take care of that before I go.*

He pulled a business card from his pocket and studied it. "Jill Watson, 301 555 5555."

And she drew a little heart. She wants to get together. All I have to do is give her a call.

Adan shook off that thought too. *If I stick around, I have to give Greg the other million and a half. He won't take care of the dick unless I'm holding that money over his head. But there's nothing to stop him from killing me once I give him the money.*

In the end, the lure of hot pussy won. Adan decided he could enjoy one last fling and figure out his escape plan in the morning. He needed a quiet place where he could put it all together.

* * *

Adan booked a room for Peter Baeker at the Hilton Inn in the heart of D.C. As soon as he was settled, he checked airline schedules. American had a 9:30 flight from Dulles to Beijing. Greg would be busy with the bitch at least that late. The exec started to book a seat but realized he would want a new identity, and he couldn't get it until morning. He went down to the pool for a quick dip and a short visit to the sauna before dinner.

He read through the newspaper and watched TV while he ate. An accident involving several cars and trucks on the 395 in D.C. had claimed the lives of at least two people. Names of the victims were being withheld, pending notification of the next of kin.

Adan called Jill, using the hotel room phone. When she answered, he said, "Jill, this is Peter Baeker from the shooting range this afternoon."

"Pete, what are you doing calling from D.C.?"

"Ah'm renting a room for the night. Ah have a big day tomorrow, and Ah don't want to be driving back and forth to Annapolis."

"Must be nice. What are you doing?"

"Nothing. Ah have finished getting ready for tomorrow, and Ah'm ready to relax. Ah was wondering if you would like to join me. Ah have a big bed."

"Sounds wonderful. But I have a big day tomorrow too. I can't spend the night in D.C."

"That's too bad. Ah was looking forward to spending some time with you."

She giggled. "I live in Glenn Dale. That's a lot closer than Annapolis."

"Are you asking me to come to your place?"

"Sure. Why not?" She giggled some more.

"Ah would do that, if I knew where you lived."

Jill gave him her address and some landmarks to help him find the place.

Adan scribbled it all down on the pad by the phone. "It might take me an hour to get there."

"So, you are going to come?"

"Yes, ma'am. Ah'm getting ready to leave right this minute."

"Okay. I'll be waiting. See you in an hour."

Adan checked directions using Google Maps. He cut eyeholes in a pillowcase and picked up a Nats ball cap and a windbreaker from the gift shop. On his way down to the parking garage, he donned the pillowcase, cap, and jacket. He strolled around the parking garage. When he found a Camaro with the windows open and key in the ignition, he got in and started the engine. Plenty of gas. He was on his way.

65

The phone rang late in the day at Mondale Legal Consulting Services. A deep, rumbling voice said, "Troy, this is Sergeant Jack Edwards. I would like to talk to you."

"Go ahead. Talk."

"Face to face."

"I've used up my cop time for the day."

"You are going to talk to me," Edwards retorted. "If you want to make it in this city, you will have to get along with me. Let's get off on the right foot. I'll meet you somewhere for a beer if you would like."

"I don't drink."

"Pizza?"

Troy looked over at Marie and shook his head wearily. "As you probably know, I spent over a decade in a state penitentiary. I found the best way to get along with prison guards was to have as little to do with them as possible. I imagine it's the same with D.C. cops."

"Fair enough. But you did have to deal with the guards sometimes, right?"

"Yes. Unfortunately."

"I heard about the visit this morning. Something else has come up. It may be a matter of life and death. So, right now would be a good time," the sergeant insisted. "I am on my way over to your office. I can be there in fifteen minutes. Unless you would prefer to meet somewhere else."

Troy looked imploringly at Marie. She winked and mouthed, *Yes.*

"I'll be here working, Sergeant."

"Thanks."

Seventeen minutes later, the door opened, and Jack Edwards stepped into the office. He was physically big enough to fill a doorway. His personality was big enough to take over a room as soon as he walked in. He strode to the table where Troy was sitting and offered his hand. The ex-con shook hands. "What can I do for you, Sergeant?"

Jack took a seat and removed his sunglasses. "You can call me Jack."

"What can I do for you, Jack?"

The sergeant tilted his head. He squinted and pursed his lips. "Beau Jackson is dead."

Jack smiled at Troy's shocked expression. "I assume that means he was fine when he left here a few hours ago."

"I had nothing to do with it."

"So, it was just a coincidence that he died right after talking to you."

Troy glared.

The sergeant laughed. "Lighten up, Troy. Beau was killed in a traffic accident. Nobody suspects foul play."

"Why are you here?"

"He was heading east through D.C. That's why the accident came to my attention. He had three silencers and two handguns in his trunk. One was an unregistered Sig. I suspect we will discover it was lost or stolen and put on the black market." Jack stared intently at Troy, waiting for a reaction. He got nothing. "There is another gun out there. And I'm willing to bet it's unregistered."

Troy stared at the sergeant in poker-faced silence. He had trained himself to hide his thoughts and feelings.

Jack continued, "I want to know where the other gun is, and I want to know about the plan."

Marie's stare was making Troy uncomfortable. He knew she wanted him to cooperate. "I can't help you, Jack."

"Can't or won't?"

"I can't. This is the first I've heard about a gun or a plan."

"What did you two talk about?"

"We didn't talk about anything. He came in, said hello, and left."

"Why would he do that?"

"He and his brother are assholes."

"His GPS indicated he was here for about thirty minutes. Hello and goodbye doesn't take that long."

"Ms. Moretti and I were out of the office for about an hour. Beau was waiting at the door when we got back."

"Troy, this is serious. As soon as I saw this stop on his GPS log, I knew he came to see you. I didn't mention it to the investigators. I came straight over here to talk to you, hoping you would cooperate. I don't want to see you get into trouble."

"That's very noble," Troy said dismissively. "How come the other investigators didn't make the connection?"

"They don't know about you."

"But you do?"

Jack glowered. "They deal with traffic. I deal with crime." His expression softened. "I was a beat cop in 1993. When I made detective, I was assigned to partner with Ed Twomey. He told me about the rape and the outcome. For him, it was an object lesson in just how shitty police work can be. When Adan Jackson's name popped up a couple of months ago, I called Ed. He suggested that I find out what was going on with you. So, I checked you out."

Troy looked down and studied his hands, then he looked up. "That's a nice pitch, Jack. But I can't help you."

"Because?"

"I never found out what Beau was up to."

"What did he say?" the sergeant pushed.

"He said he needed my help and offered me money. Quite a bit of money. That sounded like a bad idea. I told him I didn't want to get involved and that he should forget about whatever he had in mind."

"He didn't tell you anything at all?"

"I wouldn't let him. I didn't want to know. I didn't want to have someone like you or your detectives coming around here harassing Marie and me."

"He walked in here and offered you a lot of money to help him with something. You said no on general principle, and he left. Is that the way it went down?"

"He didn't want to give up. I had to push him out the door."

"You have no idea what kind of help he was looking for?"

Troy shook his head.

Jack sat back to think about the situation. He crossed his arms and studied the ceiling. "Adan has three thugs working for him. He's probably in over his head. Maybe he and his brother decided to have it out with them. That adds up to serious trouble. So, Beau tries to hire you to even the odds."

"Makes sense," Troy said.

"Do you think he might have been planning a showdown with Adan's gang?'

Troy shrugged. "I don't know what he was thinking. I can tell you he was scared. I could smell it. He was desperate to get me on board."

Jack stood and offered his hand to Troy. "Thanks for taking the time to talk to me. If you want to talk or have a beer, let me know."

"I don't drink," Troy reminded him.

"Do you eat?" Jack asked. "We could go out for a pizza. All three of us."

"Jack, do you know Eve MacMahon?"

"Yes."

"Well?"

Jack rocked his head. "Our relationship is complicated."

"Could you give her a message?"

The sergeant nodded.

Troy said, "Tell her that I would like to review that article before she sends it out."

The sergeant laughed. "Does that mean she's out of the doghouse?"

Troy looked over at Marie and then turned back. "Yeah. She's out of the doghouse."

"She'll be happy to hear that," Jack said as he turned to leave.

66

Liz took a phone call just before six. "Hi, Jack."

The sergeant growled, "Where is Adan Jackson?"

"In his office. He's been there all day."

"Are you sure?"

"He drove in early this morning, and his car hasn't moved. I imagine he'll be leaving soon."

"Confirm that immediately."

"Hold on." She dialed the exec's direct line. After three rings, a woman picked up and answered, "America First Financial Services, Adan Jackson's office. May I help you?"

"Is Mr. Jackson available?"

"Who is this? Please." The woman sounded irritated

"Detective Liz Smith. May I speak with Mr. Jackson?"

"Not at the moment. I can take a message and have him get back to you."

"I need to speak to him as soon as possible. Is there some way I can contact him?"

"Is this about his brother? I already have a message. I have been trying to reach him."

"May I ask who gave you the message?"

"His mother. She called about an hour ago."

"I see. Would you have him contact me at this number as soon as you hear from him?"

"Certainly. May I ask what you want to talk to him about?"

"It's a police matter. I need to speak with Mr. Jackson."

"Concerning?"

"As I said, it's police business. Please have him call me as soon as possible." Liz hung up and went back to Jack. "He's flown the coop."

"You fucked up. Find that asshole now. And, Detective, assume he is armed."

"Yes, sir." But the line was dead before she finished. She called Bill and filled him in on the situation.

Her partner had followed Greg Jantzen to the Boundary Line Bar. He said, "Our guy just went into the bar. I guess I'll go in there and get some dinner."

"Any sign of Jackson?"

"Haven't seen him all day. I haven't seen much of anything. This guy just goes from one place to the next. He stops for a little while and then gets back in his car and moves on," Bill grumbled.

"He's playing you."

"I know. I've got three trackers. I'll stick them on his car before I go inside. One of them should survive the night."

Liz closed her eyes as she took a deep breath and forced it out through her lips. "I've got to find Jackson."

"Check his credit cards. He probably bought something somewhere."

"I've already done that."

After a long pause, Bill said, "Trackers are in place." He was breathing heavily. "I'll call Jack and let him know I'm coming in to give you a hand."

"What if he shows up there?"

"What if he doesn't?"

"Thanks."

* * *

Liz had the data and was piecing together a summary of Adan's day by the time Bill got back to his desk. "You remember that guy who pulled up to talk to Jantzen this morning."

"The guy in the Sonata?"

She handed him a photo on a sheet of printer paper. It was a blow-up showing the driver of the Sonata. "That's Peter Baeker, the alias Jackson uses when he's with Greg Jantzen."

Bill pressed his lips together and handed the picture back.

"I must have missed it because he was driving the Sonata instead of his Lincoln." She handed her partner another printout. It showed the front of the Sonata with the license plate clearly visible. "Abraham Jacobs rented that car at eleven this morning. Jacobs is the Jackson character who met with Eric Foster at the Fairfax on the fourteenth."

"Jackson must have rushed from the car rental to the meeting with Jantzen. Where'd he go next?"

67

Adan shed the ball cap and pillowcase as soon as he was past the surveillance cameras at the parking garage exit. He pulled down the sun visor and studied his face in the vanity mirror. He grinned. "Peter Baeker, you are one handsome devil."

He had snagged the latest thing in performance vehicles. The fire-engine red IROC-Z28 was a brand-new 2010 model that had rolled off the assembly line in early May. It was a beast with a 426 engine and a cockpit worthy of a fighter jet.

An LCD display hosted multiple screens that controlled everything. Adan was technically savvy enough to go beyond the 6-speed, stick-shift transmission and the built-in GPS. He had flipped through all the controls and made some adjustments by the time he was a few blocks from the hotel.

Adan programmed Jill Watson's address into the GPS. A screen displaying the route to her house popped up, and a woman's voice asked, "Use this route?"

"Yes."

The woman's voice began giving him turn-by-turn directions to a single-bedroom home in Glenn Dale, a quiet suburban enclave just outside of the Beltway. Adan liked the sensuous touch.

As he drove out of D.C. and into Maryland, he obsessed over the idea that this would be Peter Baeker's final act. *Exit stage right and never return. The perfect ending for a tragic life. It will be like the duel with Laertes that brings Hamlet's story to its climax. Tomorrow, I will have to die so I can be reincarnated and move on. Perfect.*

The GPS woman proclaimed, "You have arrived at your destination."

It was a single-story brick ranch with a flower bed along the front. A well-manicured lawn separated the building from the street. The drapes were drawn across the picture window, but lights were visible. Pete parked the Camaro in front of the house and went up the walkway to the front door.

Jill wore a big smile and little else when she answered the bell. Her pink tank top was loose and suggestive. Her denim shorts were in the hot pants league. When she turned to lead him into the house, he could see that the shorts had artful tears to show off her butt. Her slender, curvy legs were on full display. She was barefoot. *Not much to take off when we get down to business.*

"Can I get you something to drink?" she asked.

He pointed to a half-empty glass of white wine. "That looks good."

She sashayed into the kitchen to fill a wine glass from a large bottle of Woodmore Pinot Grigio. Peter meandered toward the kitchen, taking in the ambiance. Her living room felt warmer and more spacious than his. Maybe it was the woman's touch. A flowery fragrance dominated, but the rose scent of her perfume was hard to miss. The white walls and the dark brown carpet were provided by the landlord. She had added pink drapes over the picture window. The chairs and sofa had a soft gray cover. A cherrywood cabinet housing a set of fine china dishes occupied one corner of the room. A painting hanging on the wall opposite the sofa showed deer and birds relaxing in a mountain glen on a sunny day.

He stopped at the kitchen door to watch her pour the wine. She handed the glass to him and led him to the couch. They toasted Lady Luck and great chance encounters. Pete sank back into the sofa and put an arm around her shoulder. She slid closer and rested her head on his shoulder.

He stretched his legs and kicked off his loafers. "How long have you been working at the Patriots Club?"

"Almost two years."

He pulled her right hand to his lips for a kiss. "And how did you get to be so good with guns?"

"Believe it or not, I grew up in the same town as Annie Oakley. I always wanted to be her."

"Ah have to confess, Ah don't know much about her." Pete sipped his wine. "Ah guess if you grew up in the Wild West, you had to learn to shoot."

Jill's face scrunched up. "It was Ohio. Not 'the Wild West.'"

"Sorry. Ah was just under the impression she was a cowgirl."

Jill smiled and shook her head. "She became famous because she and her husband starred in Buffalo Bill's Wild West Show." She lifted herself up and gave him a peck on the cheek. "In your favor, she did make it into the Cowgirl Hall of Fame."

Pete brightened. "Thank you."

He leaned over and kissed her on the lips. Her mouth opened, inviting his tongue. They held the kiss for a long moment. He pulled back to gaze directly into her eyes as he pushed the tank top off her left shoulder. She slid her arm out of the strap, exposing her breast. He covered the nipple with his lips and suckled.

Jill sighed. She finished her wine and pulled his head down for a kiss. "Do you need a refresh?"

"Please."

When she returned, Pete stood, took the glasses, and set them on the coffee table. He pulled her in for another long, tongue-on-tongue kiss. Her hand slid down to stroke the bulge in his pants. His hand slid down her back and inside the waistband of her shorts. It was a tight squeeze. She opened the first button. He pushed down to her butt and pulled her clit against his cock. She moaned softly.

He pressed her body against his. Her arms wrapped around his torso and her head rested on his chest. They swayed to the rhythm of imagined music.

Pete unbuttoned Jill's shorts and pushed them off her butt. She wriggled free. As they dropped to the floor, she stepped out of them and away from him. He caught the neckline of her tank top. She let it slide over her head as she moved back. She grinned as she spread her arms. Only a pink thong with the words "EAT ME" printed in large letters above bright red lips remained. He laughed and pulled her in for another kiss. His hand went down to her butt and pulled her clit up against his rod. Her hand clamped on the back of his head as she pulled his cheek down to hers. She bit his neck.

They maneuvered onto the couch. Peter knelt beside her and ripped the pink thong away. Her fingers dug into his hair and squeezed as his tongue stroked her pussy. Her hands went to her face.

She shivered orgasmically. "Oh, God. Oh, wow."

He marveled at the woman's ecstasy. They grinned at each other as Jill sat catching her breath. She rolled onto the floor to kneel facing him. She slowly unbuttoned his shirt, kissing his chest and abdomen as she worked her way down. When she reached his belt, she pulled the shirttail out of his trousers and put her hands on his ribs. They slid up over his pecs and out across his shoulders, pushing his shirt aside. She continued down his arms. When she reached his wrists, she pulled his hands together behind his back. Leaning into him, she bit his neck. He took her trapezius into his teeth and pinched. Her nails dug into his skin.

Pete pulled free and got to his feet. She unbuckled his pants and pulled them to the floor. His cock stuck straight out like a rod. Jill pulled it into her mouth to suck him off.

He lifted her to the couch and climbed on top. As he penetrated her, he placed his left hand on her throat to create the experience of erotic asphyxiation. Jill grabbed his wrist with both hands and squeezed. Her body writhed while he screwed. They came in unison and collapsed into a heap on the couch.

When he had recovered, Pete pushed up into a kneeling position and nudged his partner's shoulder. Jill rolled over on her stomach. He massaged her shoulders and kissed her back while he climbed into position to fuck her from behind. His left hand encircled her throat and gradually tightened. He stopped thrusting and slid forward to sit on her hips. His right hand closed on her throat while his forearms pinned her shoulders.

By the time Jill realized what was happening, it was too late. She struggled fiercely for several minutes, kicking and bucking. It was futile. She couldn't dislodge the two-hundred-pound man riding her or pull free from his grip. Her body gave out.

Pete continued throttling his victim for a minute or two after the struggles ceased. When he was sure she must be dead, he got up. He pushed and poked in several places. No response. He went into her bathroom to piss and clean up.

He came back to the couch and checked again. Her body was soft and warm but unresponsive. Pete found the situation surreal. He knew she was dead, but he felt like she would get up in a second. He had a feeling that she would sit up and say something. Offer him another glass of wine and beg him to stay the rest of the night. He knew she was dead, but he could not grasp the reality.

Adan dressed, turned out the lights and locked the door. He walked to the Camaro and drove back to D.C.

* * *

Police cars with their lights flashing had converged on the hotel by the time Adan arrived. He drove another three blocks before he found a parking spot. At the front entrance to the hotel, he stopped to ask the doorman what was going on. "One of the guests went down to get something from his car, and it was gone."

"Any idea what happened?"

"He left the keys in the ignition. Somebody spotted it and drove off. The joker was wearing a Halloween costume."

"So, no idea whodunit?"

The doorman grimaced and shook his head. "Not a clue."

Adan smiled sympathetically, shook his head, and said, "That's too bad."

Liz spotted him on her computer screen as he strolled to his room, walked in, and shut the door. She wondered how long he had been out and where he had been.

68

Adan paced the hotel room in a rage. Nothing from Beau. No missed calls. No messages. *That asshole isn't going to call. He's lost his nerve. Probably took off.*

He stopped to study himself in a mirror. To wear a tie or not to wear. The expensive blue necktie draped around his neck had looked great yesterday, but not this morning. He needed a fresh shirt. The one he had on would have to do. He couldn't afford to go home for a change of clothes.

Adan had spent most of the night debating his options. He dropped off to sleep after convincing himself that he could lure Greg and his men into a trap. He would get them to kidnap the bitch detective and take her to the house on H Street, where the police would find them because of an anonymous tip. She would get away, but Greg would be taken care of. He was the more pressing problem.

The exec had overslept, and now he had to rush so he could take care of getting a new identity before meeting with Jantzen about plans for the kidnapping.

Adan held up the tie and looked at it. The left side of his face curled into a sneer. He shook his head. He scowled at the man in the mirror. "Focus. You have to take care of Greg and catch your plane to China." He glanced to his left before continuing. "That means you have to get to Georgetown, pick up your new ID, and set up a bank account."

He paused to check his phone one more time before leaving the room. Calls and text messages from his mother caught his attention for the first time. The last text had been sent twelve hours ago. It said Beau had been killed, and Adan needed to call home as soon as possible. He pulled up the news channel on the TV. According to the story that was airing an accident on 395 the previous afternoon had claimed the life of Beau Jackson, the son of a local financial consultant. "Damn it," Adan muttered fiercely.

After a few short, angry breaths, he turned off the TV and strode out of the room to face the day. His mother would have to wait.

69

Bill spotted Jackson in the corridor. "He's on the move. Do you want me to take him?"

Liz grabbed a towel to dry off and yelled back, "No. I'll catch up. You stick with Jantzen."

She had been showering after her shift on the Jackson watch. Now she threw on her clothes, grabbed her laptop, and sprinted down the stairs to the lobby. He was gone. She reached the garage just in time to see a Sonata pulling out onto the street. She called Bill from her car. "I just saw a Sonata taking off. What have you got?"

"He's heading west."

"Right. I've got him on my screen now. I'm on my way."

"I'll keep an eye on him. Give me a call if you have any trouble."

"Any sign of life from Jantzen?"

"Nothing yet."

"What if his car just sits there all day?"

"It won't," Bill assured her. "That's the only car he's got."

"But what if he takes the day off?"

"He never takes a day off." Bill stood and walked over to the window. He was wearing a hands-free cell phone device. He hated it, but it had some advantages. He began ticking off clues. "Jantzen and his friends went to Vermont for the first time in their lives. Jackson rented a car as Professor Jacobs and met with Jantzen. Then he rented a room at a hotel where he never stays." He wheeled and walked back to the computers. "They're planning something big, and they know we're watching."

Adan led the detective into Georgetown. She was a block back when he parked and got out to walk. She rolled past him as she searched for a parking spot. He entered The Art Shoppe, a small portrait gallery. She crossed the street to wait for him. She sent a photo of the store to her partner with the message: *Jackson's here. What's he shopping for?*

An hour later, her phone buzzed. It was Bill. "He's on the move again."

"He must have left by a back exit. Did you get anything on The Art Shoppe?"

"Not yet. Jantzen is on the move. I'm betting they meet at the Monocle again."

"Are you going to catch up with him?"

"You're following Jackson. I'll stay here and keep an eye on the situation."

"You're lazy."

"I'm conserving fuel. Reducing emissions and staying out of the heat and humidity."

"What am I doing?" Liz demanded.

"Staying off Jack's shit list."

Twenty minutes later, Adan pulled into the Monocle parking lot. Greg Jantzen was waiting for him. Liz found a spot a block away with a direct line of sight to the meeting, but that meant they could see her as well. She called Bill. "You were right."

"Of course. I have something. I've been searching financial databases. Jacobs put one hundred K down on a property in Northeast yesterday."

"You think that's important?"

"It's the scene of the crime." Bill bit his lip and nodded. "I'll stake my career on it. I'm going over there to check it out."

"What about Jantzen?"

"I'll track him on my laptop. He's not going anywhere without his car."

"You better update Jack first. And find out what Sanchez and Bailey are up to before you leave." That was an order. Liz enjoyed asserting her dominance. Bill was the senior partner only because he was a "he."

70

Rick Sanchez and his partner, Shane Bailey, were keeping Greg, Tony, and Mo under surveillance. The three perps were unusually active. They kept on the move and avoided contact except for brief meetings. Mo met with Greg. Later Tony met with Mo. The three were never in the same place at the same time. The detectives were forced to vary their assignments to give as much coverage as possible to three targets until they realized that Tony was working on something. Rick concentrated on him, while Shane did her best to keep an eye on the other two. She stuck with Adoyo after she learned that Bill was monitoring Jantzen.

Around noon on Wednesday, Andrews set up a four-way conference call to coordinate with Edwards, Sanchez, and Bailey. Jack backed his plan to monitor Jantzen's movements remotely while he set up surveillance of the house Adan had just purchased. Shane reported that Adoyo had a busy morning but was currently hanging out in a sports bar. DeLuca had spent the morning shopping for hardware and car parts. He touched base with Adoyo before driving to the old

Greyhound terminal. He was sitting in the passenger terminal playing chess on his computer.

* * *

Around two, Mo led Bailey to the house on H Street Northeast. A Sonata was parked in the driveway. Liz Smith was across the street standing in front of a house further up the block. Shane walked past Adan's house and crossed over to Liz. "Any idea what's going on?"

"Jackson got here over an hour ago. Jantzen showed up twenty minutes ago," Liz replied. "It looks like they are waiting for the other two so they can work out their next move."

Bailey shook her head. "DeLuca isn't coming. He's camping out at the bus terminal."

"Makes sense. They don't need him in the room. If Jackson was planning a double-cross, he's screwed."

"Do you think that's what he has in mind?"

"That might have been the plan." Liz shrugged. "He and his brother were working on something before Beau was killed. Adan probably has a gun, but it's not going to do him a lot of good now." She looked over at the house. "Any idea what they're up to?"

"DeLuca has been shopping. It looks like he's planning on doing some electrical work," Bailey said. "I don't suppose you bugged the place?"

Liz clenched her jaw and shook her head. "We just found out about it this morning. Bill rushed over to check it out, but Jackson got here first." She shrugged. "Think DeLuca's making a bomb?"

Bailey shook her head. "No. Rick would have given me a heads up if he saw any sign of explosives. Where's Bill?"

"Inside. We've hacked into Jackson's computer. We're watching the traffic."

Bailey turned to study the perp's place. She turned back to Liz. "Got any money?"

Liz pulled out her wallet. Shane produced a pack of gum and handed it to her in exchange for a twenty. She gave a thumbs-up and parted with a loud, "Awright, sistah. Stay safe."

Bailey walked to the end of the block, crossed, and made her way back to Jackson's place. She slithered around to the back, looking for a way inside. She found a broken window near the back door. The discussion between the three men was audible. She activated a cell phone app that amplified and recorded sounds and plugged in her earbuds to listen.

A deep, raspy voice growled, "No sweat. We can handle it."

Probably Jantzen.

A softer voice with a hint of a drawl. "She's a feisty bitch."

Definitely Jackson.

Greg sounded pissed. "We can take care of her. She'll be sleepin' in the trunk inside of a minute."

Long pause. "Ah want her finished in the basement."

Greg, still irritated. "We can handle it. I've got medication t' help her relax."

Adan, decisive. "Alright, bring her back here. Ah'll finish her in the basement."

Greg, threatening. "Where's the money? Nothing happens 'til we get paid."

"Ah told you, Ah can't pay until y'all deliver the goods."

"And I told you that you pay or I turn you over t' the cops for a long stay in the pen."

Adan condescending. "That's not how it works. Ah haven't actually done anything. As long as Ah haven't given you any money, no crime has been committed."

Greg, exulting. "Yeah. Well, you have given us money, and crimes have been committed. That adds up to more jail time than your pussy ass wants to deal with."

Adan, shocked. "You're contractors. Ah paid you for work to be done on this house."

Greg, "If things were to get outta hand right now, you could die here. A long, slow, painful death because nobody knows you're here, and nobody's gonna come lookin' for you."

Adan, "Ah'm not that stupid. My brother knows all about this. He also knows about the cop. If anything happens to me, he goes to the police."

Greg, "You shouldna said nothin' about the cop."

Adan, "Sorry. But your secret is only safe as long as Ah'm safe. Ah'll give you ten percent now and the rest when you deliver the goods."

Greg, "Fuck you. You'll give us the money now, or you won't make it outta here."

"Killing me doesn't help you because Ah have to be alive to transfer the money. Jail doesn't worry you, but a million-dollar payday does. It's ten percent or nothing."

A deep, melodic voice tentatively proposed, "Make it half now and half later. We can live with that, can't we?"

That must be Adoyo.

Greg, angrily. "Half now. In the next two minutes, before I change my mind."

Long pause. Adan, brightly. "Done."

Another pause. Greg, still seething. "Did he make the transaction? Do you see it?"

Pause. Greg, more calmly. "Did you take care of it?"

Pause. Greg, "Okay. We'll meet you here tonight."

Adan, "What time?"

Greg, "Just make sure you're here. We'll surprise you."

Laughter.

Bailey heard people on the move and put her phone away. One of them was coming toward the back. She slipped over to the house on the other side of the driveway. As she crossed over the alley, she spotted Mo walking back down the street. The back door opened.

The sound of the door behind her, sent the detective scurrying under the nearby porch. She scooted back into a niche formed by random piles of junk stuffed into the crawl space.

Greg stepped out on the porch of Adan's house and surveyed the area. He came down the steps and walked to the driveway. He looked around, checking hiding spots as if he thought someone had been spying on the meeting. Then he turned and walked away from Bailey's foxhole. He followed the alleyway between the backs of the houses until he reached the street.

71

Tony DeLuca started his day with a midmorning breakfast at the McDonald's in Union Station. From there, he drove into Maryland, where he picked up some supplies at an Ace Hardware and an AutoZone. Finally, he drove back to the old Greyhound Bus terminal on the boundary between Maryland and D.C.

The terminal building was very old and very large. It could handle two dozen buses at the busiest time of day. That translated to thousands of people with thousands of different plans passing through.

The terminal was a warehouse with accommodations for passengers. The main pedestrian entrance had four large doorways with two swinging doors each. A ticket counter with six windows was on the left as customers entered. Administrative offices were on the right. A cafeteria was at the far end of the building. There was a newsstand at the entrance to the cafeteria.

Temporary lockers lined the walls between the entrance and the administrative offices. Six rows of seats had been placed in front of the lockers. An additional five rows of seats had been placed between the ticketing area and the central aisle leading into the station. Twelve doors were situated directly across the room from the main entrance. These were gateways that gave access to the twenty-four bus bays. All the passengers and all the cargo arriving at the station or leaving for other destinations passed through them.

Passengers lined up at the gates when it was time for them to board a bus to their next destination. Arriving passengers entered the terminal through the doors. Porters carried luggage and other cargo to and from the buses through the doors. Traffic through the gates could be heavy. Most of the time, nothing was going through the doors. No one was lined up waiting to go out and board a bus. The drama was not great, but it could keep a person occupied when there was nothing better to do.

Detective Rick Sanchez walked into the terminal minutes behind Tony DeLuca. He wore a tank top that showed off his broad shoulders and muscular, brown arms, jeans, and a well-worn pair of Nikes. He had stopped shaving two days ago. The stubble made him look a little less clean-cut. He spotted his target at the end of the third row of seats in front of the lockers. The ex-con was opening up a laptop.

Rick was about to move into position when his phone rang. He was conferenced into a team meeting with Jack, Bill and Shane. The sergeant was checking status and coordinating the operation for the afternoon. Sanchez smiled and pretended to be joking around with a buddy. He noticed that his guy got a short phone call at the same time.

The detective continued to the cafeteria, where he picked up a sandwich and a cup of coffee. He bought a copy of the *Post* and some souvenirs at the newsstand. He walked back to the entrance, deposited his purchases in a locker, and found a seat two rows back and to the left of the perp. That gave him a view of Tony's laptop screen. The guy was playing chess.

Rick flipped through his paper while he sipped coffee and ate his sandwich.

Shortly before two, Tony received a second call. The conversation was animated. Sanchez picked up bits and pieces. Enough to convince the detective that his man was explaining why he couldn't come to a meeting. Tony plugged his earbuds into the audio jack on his phone and continued to listen. He put away his chess game and began playing solitaire.

Thirty minutes later, a pop-up on Tony's laptop interrupted the solitaire. It displayed a financial transaction. Sanchez didn't get all the details, but he caught enough. Someone had just deposited $750,000 into an account.

Tony immediately acknowledged the transaction and began moving the money to other accounts. He picked up his phone and said, "Yes. It's in there." He finished moving $250,000 into each of three accounts and reported, "It's all taken care of."

The ex-con nodded as if responding to something the other party said. He put his phone away, shut down the banking app, and closed his laptop. He fussed with his computer while checking out the other people sitting in the area. When he spotted the detective sitting behind him, he paused to study the man carefully.

Rick stayed busy with his newspaper and his coffee. After Tony had satisfied himself that he had not been spied on, he stretched out his legs and closed his eyes for a nap.

72

Liz rushed from her outpost as soon as she saw Mo leaving Jackson's house. She raced across the street to the driveway that Bailey had used to get to the back. She was almost too quick. Greg was still in the alleyway between the rows of houses when she paused to check that the coast was clear. As she rounded the back porch, Bailey greeted her with a big smile and a wave. "Good to see you, Detective."

"Likewise," Liz replied. "Adoyo is headed back. Jantzen took off in the other direction."

"Adoyo is probably going to catch a bus ride back to his car. No idea what Jantzen is up to."

"Do you want to catch up to him?"

"I should do that. Could you give me a ride?"

"I'll get my car." Liz took a couple of steps toward the street and then turned back. "Call Bill and tell him he'll have to keep an eye on Jackson."

Bailey made the call as she passed Adan's Sonata on her way to the street. Liz picked her up at the edge of the driveway.

They spotted Adoyo standing at a bus stop a few blocks away.

"He doesn't seem to be in any hurry," Liz observed.

"No hurry. They're planning to snatch a woman tonight and bring her back to Jackson's place to kill her," Bailey said. "Jackson is supposed to be there waiting."

"Cindy Foster?"

Bailey kept her eyes on Adoyo in the side mirror. "I don't think they mentioned a name. At least I didn't hear one. Foster sounds reasonable."

Liz pulled into the half-empty parking lot behind a pizza place. "You need to explain that, but we should get Jack on the line so he can hear it too."

The sergeant insisted on conferencing in the whole team. "When I got to the back of the house where they were meeting, I could hear voices, but I couldn't make out what they were saying," Bailey explained. "I was able to follow the conversation using an app called ListenIn."

"Bottom line," Edwards demanded.

"They're going to snatch a woman and kill her in the house tonight."

"Foster?"

"I didn't hear any names."

"Where's Adoyo?"

"Waiting for a bus to take him back to his car."

"What about Jantzen?"

Bill chimed in, "Looks like he's driving back downtown."

"You've got a tracker on his car?" Jack asked.

"Yes, sir."

"What about DeLuca?"

"He closed his eyes half an hour ago and hasn't moved," Sanchez said. "I'll call in if he leaves the bus terminal."

"Anything else, Bailey?" Jack rumbled.

"They argued over money. Jantzen wanted to be paid then and there. Jackson wanted to wait until the job was done. They compromised on half upfront."

"Jackson wired seven-hundred-fifty K to an offshore account," Bill said.

"I saw that on DeLuca's computer," Sanchez reported. "Then, he moved the money to three different accounts."

"So, we know that all three of them will be in on it," the sergeant said, "and we know it will be tonight. Best bet is that the Foster woman is the target, so we protect her. We watch them. They are going to come together for the attack. Bill, have you got eyes on the house and Jackson?"

"Yes, sir."

"And you're monitoring Jantzen's movements?"

"Yes, sir."

"Sanchez, you've got eyes on DeLuca?"

"Yes, sir."

"Liz, I want you to find Foster and protect her."

"What about Adoyo?" Bailey asked.

"Forget about him. He'll be with the other two when it goes down. You get back to the hospital and protect Eric Foster until I can get a guard posted."

Liz called back almost immediately to tell Jack that Cindy Foster was coming to the hospital to see her husband after she got off work. She would be escorted by Nickey Arnold.

"Meet them at the hospital. Tell Arnold you are taking over. Tell Foster you are placing her in protective custody for the next twenty-four hours."

73

An angular blonde hustling across the street toward the house had caught Adan Jackson's attention. She looked vaguely familiar. He walked over to the front window in time to watch her disappear into the space between his house and the one next door.

Minutes later, she came back out to the street and got into a car. She stopped at the edge of his driveway to pick up another woman before driving off. Adan came to the inevitable conclusion that the police knew about this place and had it under surveillance.

They must have seen Greg and Mo when they showed up for the meeting. They'll put them under surveillance if they haven't already. He returned to his seat to consider the situation. *That means the cops will be watching them when they grab the bitch. That means they'll catch Greg in the act and I won't have to call in a tip. She'll get away. I guess you can't win 'em all.*

Adan returned to the front window and looked for any sign of the cops. A few cars were parked along the curb, but no humans were visible. He shook his head.

I know you're there. I'll have to sneak out the back and use a cab to get over to the airport for my flight. He walked around the room, scratching his head. *If they know about this place, maybe they know the whole plan. The smart thing to do would be to keep the bitch at the hospital and use a cop as bait. When it gets a little darker, I'll go over and take care of her if she's still there.*

74

Detective Liz Smith was waiting in the lobby of Providence Hospital when Cindy Foster showed up, with Ellen Magee and Nickey Arnold on her flanks. She intercepted the trio on their way to the elevators, identified herself, and ordered them to follow her. When they reached a meeting room the police had commandeered, she had them take a seat.

The room was small. Four tables were set end-to-end in the center to form a square. Chairs had been placed along the outside perimeter. Cindy and her escort took seats near the door. Liz walked around to the other side and stood facing the three women.

Ellen demanded, "What's going on, Detective?"

"We have a credible death threat. Ms. Foster is the likely target."

The lawyer recoiled. She looked over at her friend, who was visibly shaken. She pushed for a clarification, "Someone has threatened to kill Cindy?"

The detective studied the women while she put her thoughts together. "We have a report that a gang plans to kidnap a woman and kill her tonight. We do not have a name. Ms. Foster seems to be the likely target because of the men involved."

Cindy blurted, "Troy."

"We have no reason to believe he is involved."

"Who is it?" Nickey pressed.

"Adan Jackson." Liz took a seat directly across from Cindy. She leaned forward, elbows and forearms on the table. "Mr. Jackson has been working with a gang of violent ex-cons for the last few weeks. Earlier this week, he put money down on a property in Northeast. A few hours ago, he met there with the others to discuss plans."

"And those plans include killing Ms. Foster?" Nickey asked.

"They plan to kidnap a woman and take her back to Jackson's place in Northeast," the detective insisted.

"How did you get this information?" Ellen asked suspiciously.

"That's confidential, but our source is reliable."

"What makes you think Cindy is the target?" Nickey asked.

"Two members of the gang match the description of the men who assaulted Mr. Foster."

"Why haven't they been arrested?"

"We don't have enough evidence. The eyewitness did not get a good look at the attackers. If our suspects are the men she described, they were wearing disguises."

Tears ran down Cindy's cheeks. She buried her head in her hands. Ellen put an arm around her and pulled her close.

"I'm very sorry about this, Ms. Foster," Liz said. "We have been working on this case, trying to get a resolution. We will make an arrest tonight. In the meantime, our top priority is to make sure you and your husband are safe." She leaned back. "We are putting a police guard outside his room, and we want you to spend the night in there with him."

Cindy raised her head and glared at the detective.

Ellen squeezed her friend's shoulder. "I'll stay with you."

Liz stood. "Come on. I'll escort you down to Mr. Foster's room."

"Do you mind if I just hang around here for a while?" Nickey asked.

Smith shook her head. "We will be using this room as our operations center."

"Is Jack going to join in?"

Liz glared at Nickey.

The PI grinned. "I need to speak to him. It's about this case."

Liz shrugged and started toward the door. "Stay out of the way."

As soon as she was alone, Nickey texted Eve: *Big story developing. Get over to Providence ASAP*

75

At 6:10 p.m., Tony left the bus station and walked to his car. He was the technical wiz in the group, and it was time to make another small but essential contribution to the job at hand. Greg was the boss and rightfully so. He had all the tools and attributes of a leader, but he was not a techie. Construction appealed to him. He was a craftsman by nature. The idea of using offshore accounts infuriated him. Tony changed his mind. The only reasonable way to handle the proceeds from a multimillion-dollar caper was to park them in offshore accounts.

Tony proceeded to set up three additional accounts that their mark knew nothing about and could not access. That put him in the position of money manager for the group. It was his idea to handle the financial transactions from a remote location while Greg did the negotiating.

The boss had maneuvered Baeker into paying millions for a hit on Nickey Arnold. She had provided the perfect setup as Cindy Foster's bodyguard. She picked the Foster woman up from work at 5:15 each day and drove her to Providence Hospital. At nine, she drove

Foster to an apartment in Northwest. Planning was simple. They knew where she would be a few minutes after nine. All they had to do was pick the spot. The critical element was a kill switch to disable her car when it was in position. That was Tony's job.

He cruised around the hospital parking lot until he found the dick's car. A backup was parked nearby. His first order of business was installing the remote kill switch. The second was disabling the other vehicle by slashing its tires. He knew his way around cars, and he knew kill switches. He completed both jobs in a matter of minutes.

The ex-con had no way of knowing that as soon as he disabled the alarm on Nickey Arnold's Lexus, she got a warning beep on her cell phone. The PI immediately pulled up an app that allowed her to monitor the feeds from dash cams on the cars.

Tony surveyed the parking lot for witnesses as he packed up his tools and trash. No one had bothered him while he was working, but that didn't mean he was safe. He continued looking around as he walked back to his ride. He did not see anyone until he reached the car. A woman, a real looker, got out of her car and walked toward the hospital entrance. But she didn't even glance in Tony's direction.

The witness who went unnoticed was a Hispanic man slouched in the driver's seat of a black Ford Focus parked thirty yards away. The ex-con did notice the Ford following him out of the parking lot. He watched it in his rearview mirror as it tailed him across 12th Street onto Allison. But it passed him without even slowing when he parked his car on 13th.

76

Jack showed up at 7:41 in a bad mood. Beneath a calm exterior, he was ready to explode. He took up a position at the back of the room. "Can I have two rows of tables facing in this direction?"

Three detectives and two guests jumped into action. The tables and chairs were reconfigured in a matter of minutes.

The sergeant surveyed the room. He paused to glare at Eve. "This is a police operation. We are dealing with armed and dangerous suspects. No civilians will be participating."

Eve blushed then grinned. She winked and blew him a kiss.

He turned to Liz. "Where is Ms. Foster?"

"She and her friend Ellen Magee are with her husband."

"And there is an officer stationed at the door to the room?"

"Yes, sir."

"Good. When we break up here, tell them that they should plan to stay the night. The protection detail is scheduled until noon tomorrow. Where is Adan?"

"He's at the house on H Street," Liz said. "Bill has him under surveillance."

"Contact Detective Andrews. Tell him to get some backup and arrest Mr. Jackson."

"On what charge?"

"We need something stronger than a public nuisance. Charge him with assault." The sergeant turned to Nickey. "I'll need you to file a complaint. You may have to testify in court." Turning back to Smith, he asked, "What about the Three Stooges?"

"Bill is tracking Jantzen's car. It appears to be parked a couple of blocks from the hospital. We let Adoyo go so Detective Bailey could join us. DeLuca showed up in the parking lot an hour ago and sabotaged Nickey's car. Then he drove off."

Sanchez said, "I followed Tony when he left the parking lot. He parked at the corner of Allison and 13th. They are probably planning to ambush us there."

"Why was Ms. Arnold's car targeted?" Jack demanded.

Liz and Bailey looked at Sanchez. He looked at them.

Nickey said, "Our routine is to pick up Cindy from work and bring her here to visit Eric. We leave here at nine. I drive Cindy to Ellen's condo for the night. I think you should assume they are expecting her to leave the hospital with me in my car."

"Is your car drivable?"

"I took it for a short spin around the parking lot. Liz and I checked it out. It looks like DeLuca installed a kill switch."

"You just walked out there and checked it?" Jack shook his head. "What if he had planted a bomb?"

Nickey grinned. "There wouldn't be much left to take back to Jackson's place."

"Alright. We'll have to use your car tonight," Jack said. "Detective Bailey, take your car and make sure DeLuca is still parked at the corner of 13th. See if you can spot any of the others."

The sergeant took a moment to look each of them in the eye. "We'll meet back here at 20:50 and pull out at 21:00. I'll be in the lead car. Detectives Smith and Bailey will be in Ms. Arnold's car, and Detective Sanchez will bring up the rear."

Nickey jumped up. "Jack, you are depending on the element of surprise. You need me at the wheel in my car."

"No civilians."

"I have to be the driver. These guys have probably been watching. They will know something is up if anybody else is in the driver's seat."

The sergeant's jaw tightened. He shook his head. "Not gonna happen."

"C'mon, Jack. I was an MP. I can take care of myself."

"But you are not a police officer. You can't be involved in making an arrest."

"You are going to be confronting three armed men on a public sidewalk. If a gunfight breaks out, you will be firing at people's homes. You need all the help you can get."

"There won't be a gunfight. I'll have them surrounded."

"Unless they get spooked when they see a cop driving my car," Nickey countered. She put her knuckles on the table and leaned toward the man. "You can't afford to have anybody else drive that car. It has to be me."

Jack glared at Nickey with his lips pressed into a thin line. "Okay, Ms. Arnold drives her car. Detective Smith rides shotgun. Ms. Arnold, you will stay in the car and let my detectives handle the police work. Is that clear?"

Nickey nodded and asked innocently, "Are you going to drive?"

The sergeant looked like he was ready to strangle her.

She continued, "The point is your car is one more variable in your plan, whatever that is. A driver could take care of it for you."

Jack studied her. "I'll ride with Detective Bailey."

"But you will still have to dispose of a car."

Jack rolled his eyes.

Nickey said, "Why don't you let Eve drive the lead car? Nobody is going to be shooting at it. She can drop you off and take care of the car while you're making the arrest."

"Any more bright ideas?" Jack looked them in the eye one by one. When no one responded to his challenge, he stalked out of the room.

Eve followed him. Fifteen minutes later, she returned with a quiet smile on her face. She winked at Nickey but said nothing.

77

Troy ran a workshop every other Thursday in a rented meeting room near his office. Sessions started at 7:30 and ran until 9:30. The room was generally cleared by ten.

Attendance varied from ten to thirty people. Twenty-one showed up on July 23, 2009. Troy stepped to the front of the room to open his meeting at the same time Jack began addressing his team. The ex-con took a moment to survey his audience. They were sitting five to a table. The tables were spread out to create separate small groups for the discussion part of the meeting.

The room was designed for business meetings. Gold velvet drapes over the windows, a gold shag rug, and comfy chairs with armrests gave it a classy feel. A coffee service with cookies and pastries was included in the cost of the room.

Most of the guests were attending their first work session. Troy had everyone stand and give a short introduction. As each person announced his or her name and stated what they wanted to get out of this meeting, Troy wrote up a list of topics he would cover.

He called for a break at eight so he could put up his agenda on a whiteboard for everyone to see.

During the break, Marie came over and patted him on the butt. "I'm going to have to pull out early."

Her partner turned to look at her. His eyebrows arched.

She said, "I have to go check on Eric."

"What's up?"

"I just have this feeling he needs me."

Troy took a deep breath and blew the air out through his lips. "I'll go with you if you want."

"These people came here to talk to you and get some encouragement."

"If you think this is important enough to go running over there on the spur of the moment, I think I should go with you."

She smiled and kissed him on the cheek. "Thank you, baby."

"I'll call them together and let them know a family emergency has come up."

Twenty minutes later, Troy and Marie were on their way to Providence Hospital.

78

Jack stopped by Eric Foster's room before setting his counterattack in motion. He was wearing jeans, a Redskins t-shirt, and an old pair of Nikes. A scrubby Nats ball cap sat on the back of his head with the brim angled up.

The guard at the door stood and blocked his path, "You can't go in there."

"I'm Sergeant Jack Edwards. I can go anywhere I want."

"I'll need to see some identification."

Jack pulled an ID badge from his hip pocket and slipped the chain over his head. He shoved the badge in the guard's face. "There."

The cop, a rookie, named Ted Cameron, turned bright red. "I'm sorry, Sergeant."

"Don't apologize. You did exactly what you're supposed to do. Nobody, not even the President of the United States, gets in there without proper identification." Jack slapped the man on his shoulder. "Now I have to give them a status update."

He stepped into the room to see how the inmates were doing. Eric was sitting up playing Gin Rummy with Cindy and Ellen. He looked terrified as the disheveled visitor approached his bed, but he couldn't speak because his mouth was clamped shut. The sergeant grinned, "I'm Jack Edwards. I just wanted to see how you were doing and give you an update."

Cindy eyed him warily. Ellen pivoted around to face him. She knew the name, but she had never met the man. Jack nodded. "I apologize for the inconvenience. I believe my detective explained the situation to you. We are getting ready to shut those guys down and make arrests." He looked directly at Cindy and said, "This should be over in an hour or two."

As the sergeant left the room, Cameron saluted and assured him that everything was under control.

79

Jack glided into the conference room at 8:48. He paused next to Bailey. "What did you see, Detective?"

Bailey hesitated as she studied the sergeant in his street clothes, then shook her head and rattled off, "Adoyo was stationed at the corner of 12th. Jantzen was in the middle of the block, and DeLuca was at the corner of 13th. Looks like they plan to stop Nickey's vehicle in the middle of the block and grab Cindy."

Jack nodded. He strode to the back of the room. "Campbell" was emblazoned across his shoulders. He turned and surveyed his team. "Detective Bailey, you're responsible for DeLuca. You and I will be in the lead car with Ms. MacMahon driving. We'll use her car. Detective Smith, you will be riding with Ms. Arnold in her car. Give us two blocks. We need to make it around the corner onto 13th before you reach the kill zone. Detective Sanchez, you bring up the rear, but stay at least a block behind the target car. Locate Adoyo as soon as possible and be ready to make the collar. Get into position but don't make any arrests until I move on Jantzen. Move out. We shove off at 21:00. Let's get this done."

* * *

The ride was surreal. Eve drove at a steady twenty-five miles per hour. Inside her white Toyota Camry, the cops were busy preparing for battle. Bailey, riding shotgun, ticked off the thugs as she spotted them. Jack was sprawled in the back seat, keeping a low profile.

After they passed Greg, Bailey turned around to ask the sergeant, "You're going to arrest him without your weapon?"

"I've got everything I need," Jack said. "I want to get in close and take him by surprise. I can't do that if I look like a cop."

She *tsk*ed.

"You've got a gun. Smith and Sanchez are armed." He grinned. Almost laughed. "Hell. Nickey Arnold has a gun, and she won't hesitate to use it." Then he scowled and rumbled, "Eve, are you carrying?"

She looked back at him. "Yes."

He shook his head. "Keep it in your purse. You're here to drive. That's it." He put a massive hand on her arm, squeezed, and gave a little tug. "Don't worry. These guys are pussies. They'll fold as soon as they see we've got them surrounded."

As they approached 13th, Eve signaled a left turn.

Jack spotted a driveway half-way up the block and ordered, "Pull in there." As soon as the car stopped, he hopped out and stuck his head in Eve's window. "Wait here."

He hustled to the back of the building and looked around the corner. He turned back and gave a thumbs-up before disappearing into the alley.

Bailey squeezed Eve's hand. "We're going to be fine." She stepped out of the car and walked rapidly back to Allison.

Eve pulled the Shield from her purse, loaded a full clip, and chambered a round. She returned the gun to its holster and hurried after Bailey.

80

Fifteen minutes after Cameron had assured Jack that everything was under control, it hit him. A giant hand grabbed his gut and squeezed. He was about to shit in his pants. He opened the door to Foster's room and hollered, "Emergency. Back in five."

The two women stopped playing cards, looked up at the panicked young man, shrugged, and went back to their game.

Minutes later, a visitor walked into Foster's room and stopped halfway between the door and the patient's bed. The movement caught Cindy Foster's attention. She looked up absently. It took a second to register who had entered the room. She jumped to her feet and stepped back, pushing her chair out of the way. "Adan! What are you doing here?"

He took a step toward the group. "Ah'm glad you're here, Cindy. Ah'm going on vacation, and Ah wanted to say goodbye before Ah took off."

Adan smiled broadly. He wore a navy-blue suit that looked like he had been wearing it for days. His right hand was shoved into the coat pocket.

Ellen pivoted out of her chair and turned to face the intruder. "What is this about?" she asked in a firm, quiet voice. "You shouldn't be here. If you are going on vacation, go now. Leave before Officer Cameron gets back."

"Hi, Ellen." Adan scowled. "Ah guess Ah'm going to have to say goodbye to you too." He pulled a Sig from his coat pocket.

"What's wrong with you? Are you crazy?" Cindy shrieked.

Adan glared at her. He snapped, "Don't say that." He relaxed. "This is all your fault," he scolded. "You shouldn't have sicced that bitch dick on me. Ah'm your friend. You could have just told me to stop."

Eric squirmed in panic. He was staring right into the barrel of Adan's pistol. He jammed his hands into the mattress and pushed back against the pillow that propped him up. Pneumatic sleeves clamped on his calves to stimulate circulation prevented him from moving more than a few inches. The bandage holding the top of his skull in place wrapped around his jaw, making it impossible for him to yell.

Another man stepped into the room. A woman was right behind him.

"Oh God. Troy." Cindy screamed, stumbled back, and fell into her chair.

Adan sneered. He wasn't going to fall for that stupid trick.

A low, throaty voice growled, "Let the birds be, mate. This is between you and me."

Adan roared, "Tom Jones."

He spun to get a look at his antagonist. As he did, Troy seized his forearm and guided the gun up to the ceiling. "It's over, Adan. Give me the gun."

Adan scoffed. "Let go and get over there with the rest of them."

"I can't do that," Troy said. "You need to surrender."

"Ah'm going to put you out of your misery," Adan snarled. He tried to bring the gun around to point at his assailant.

Troy held his arm firmly in place. "Adan, that woman behind you is ready to shoot you. Let me have the gun now."

Adan's head jerked around. Marie was pointing a Glock at the middle of his back.

"Go ahead. Kill me. Get it over with." His voice was angry but resigned.

The woman was solid as a rock. She didn't even blink.

"That's not going to happen, Adan," Troy taunted. "You're going to prison."

Adan stepped back and jerked with all the strength he could muster. But Troy held his arm with an iron grip, keeping the weapon pointed up at the ceiling.

"Give up, Adan," Troy snarled. "You're the one who is going to suffer if you don't let me have that gun." Troy held firm.

Adan looked over at Marie. "Go ahead, bitch. Shoot me."

She watched him impassively.

"Adan, we're in a hospital with top-notch emergency care facilities. You are not going to die." Troy jerked on the gun arm, forcing Adan to look him in the eye. "If she shoots you, they will take the bullet out and patch you up. You are going to jail." Troy stepped to his left and swung Adan's hand in one smooth arc, forcing his wrist back to his elbow. The gun hit the floor with a thud. A second jerk pulled the big man to his knees.

Officer Cameron charged into the room. "What's going on?"

"Assault with a deadly weapon," Marie said. "You need to take this man into custody."

81

Greg Jantzen was in a mood. He wanted this night to be over. Walking away was a real option. He already had $750 K in his off-shore account. But he stood to pick up another $250,000 after he pulled this off. He was not one to turn down that kind of money.

On the other hand, working with Peter Baeker was risky. *The guy takes too many chances and makes too many mistakes. The thing to do is grab the bitches and take them back to his place. Force him to turn over the money and then get rid of him.*

He'll say his brother will turn over the money when he gives the word. I'll say your brother was killed in an accident yesterday, Mr. Jackson.

He'll be ready to shit in his pants. I'll calm him down. Tell him I'm an honorable man who keeps his end of a bargain. All you have to do is transfer the money, and we'll get out of your life. I got tickets to fly out of the country as soon as I leave here. Yeah, that's what I'll tell him. I got tickets.

He'll give me the money because he wants to end this as bad as I do. Then we'll work that piece of shit over and tie him in a chair. We'll put bags over their heads—all three of them. Then we just walk away. Beautiful.

Greg spotted the Lexus crossing 12th Street. Mo was already walking over to join him. Tony saw it too. He was coming down the block to join them. The Lexus was ten feet away when the big man hit the button on his remote. Nickey's engine quit without warning.

Her car rolled to a stop in the middle of the street. The starter motor didn't respond when she turned the key. She looked over at the three men watching from the curb.

Greg smiled. He loved it when a job worked to perfection. *The bitch knows she's fucked, and there's nothin' she can do about it.* Greg took one step in her direction. Then he realized the woman riding shotgun was the cop from the bar.

He looked around for the rest of them. A Spic was twenty feet behind Mo, and a blond bitch was twenty feet on the other side. The cops had them surrounded.

82

Jack gave Bailey a thumbs-up and started down the alley. He could see the big man standing near the curb. The sergeant panicked and broke into a trot to get to the ambush in time. The Lexus rolled to a stop almost directly in front of Greg, but he didn't move immediately. Jack slowed to a walk and pulled a joint from his jeans.

The ex-con took one step and froze.

He sees the trap. Jack lit the joint and took a drag as he stepped out of the alley onto the sidewalk. He spotted Sanchez behind Mo and Bailey a few feet from Tony. He gave a hand sign for his detectives to stay back. Greg was just standing there. *Trying to come up with Plan B.*

The sergeant shuffled noisily toward the ex-con, who turned to appraise him.

When he got close, Greg growled, "Get lost, asshole. You ain't welcome here."

Jack kept shuffling closer until he was face-to-face with the ex-con. He took a last drag on his joint and dropped it on the sidewalk between their feet. He looked directly into the big man's eyes and blew smoke in his face. "Fuck you, asshole. You're in my house."

Greg recoiled in shock. That quickly turned to rage. But it took a second or two for him to go from shock to throwing a punch. Jack Edwards didn't need that second. Although he had studied self-defense at the police academy, he wasn't much of a martial artist. He was a boxer, and he was damned good. A natural. He could put enough power into a short blow from his hip to drop a man. His left hand drove into Greg's gut before the big man could decide on his next move.

The ex-con let out an explosive, "Oomph!" as his body folded from the force of the punch.

Without any break in his motion, Jack's left hand caught Greg's right wrist. Jack's right hand slammed into Greg's chest, rocking him back on his heels. The cop grabbed his opponent's shirt as he stepped across and drove a hip into the big man's mid-section. He jerked Greg forward, lifting him completely off the ground.

Continuing his sweeping turn, Jack threw Greg into Tony like a bag of garbage. As he came around to face Mo, Jack brought an expandable baton into play. The first blow smashed the thug's right wrist, knocking his gun to the ground. His right arm swept back, slashing Mo's face with the baton. Bones cracked loudly under the force of the blow.

The sergeant whirled around to deal with Tony. As he did so, he grabbed Mo and shoved him backward into the street. Tony was scrambling to get to his gun. Jack brought the baton crashing down on the back of his neck and kicked the gun out of the way.

Greg pushed himself to his feet and charged. Jack backpedaled. When the big man lunged to throw his arms around the sergeant, Jack stopped and stepped forward, driving his left fist into Greg's jaw.

Blood and teeth flew out onto the sidewalk. Greg collapsed in a heap.

Tony was on his knees, looking dazed. Jack stepped over and kicked him in the gut. "Are you the asshole who held a bag over my officer's head?"

Tony looked up and frantically shook his head.

Jack slapped him with the baton. "Who did it, asshole?"

"Him." Tony pointed at Mo. His hand was shaking. "It was Greg's idea."

The sergeant pushed the point of his baton into Tony's throat. "Are you going to be able to repeat that when the DA asks you in court?"

Tony nodded furiously.

Liz, Sanchez, and Bailey rushed forward to rescue the thugs from their boss. Liz got there first and pushed him back a few steps.

Jack surveyed the scene with a glazed angry expression. The righteous fury would not let go until Eve tugged on his arm. He looked into the worried eyes of his lover and relaxed.

"I'm okay." He brushed his right hand across her cheek. It was shaking. She covered it with her hand. The soft, warm touch brought a smile to his face. "It's just the adrenaline rush. I haven't done anything like that in a while."

Eve pulled his left hand to her lips. She kissed the torn, bloody knuckles.

"They'll heal," Jack said.

She grinned mischievously. "Your phone is vibrating."

He scowled at her but answered the phone. He listened. "I'll be there in a few minutes."

The sergeant turned to Liz. "Take care of this. I have to get back to the hospital. They've got Jackson in custody. It looks like he was planning to kill Eric and Cindy before skipping out of the country."

Jack pulled an evidence bag from his pocket and began picking up Greg's teeth.

Liz asked, "What are you doing?"

"Collecting evidence."

"I can do that."

He looked up at her. "This is to prove to Rhonda Johnson's family that I don't take their daughter's death lightly." He stuck the bag back in his pocket and straightened. "Let's go, Eve," he rumbled. "I need a lift."

ACKNOWLEDGEMENTS

I spent a year as a member of a group that visited with prisoners in a Berks County, Pennsylvania, jail when I was nineteen. On one occasion, I was allowed to go into a cell block to talk to one of my contacts. His cell was much like those shown on TV. It was an eight-by-eight-by-eight-cage with a bunk bed for two inmates and a sink and a toilet that seemed to be out of order. That visit was enough to convince me that I never wanted to go to jail for any reason. Staying one day, let alone years, in a situation like that was more than I cared to think about.

Demented started out as a story about a man who serves time for a serious crime and then faces life after prison. Incarceration for this character is much like prison for Andy Dufresne in *Shawshank Redemption*. He is trapped in a violent world with bizarre rules designed to dehumanize and break a man's spirit. He leaves jail to face a life of survival as a convicted felon and a violent sex offender.

The underlying crime that led to the events in *Demented* came from an episode of *Law and Order SVU*. Two college men rape a female classmate who had been making gang rape videos. One of the attackers is a rich kid. The one who is not rich admits his guilt, apologizes for his misdeeds, and is sent off to prison. Then he is dropped from the story. The rich kid is awaiting a resolution of his case at the end of the show. It looks like he will probably get away with his crime.

The porn star coed is kicked out of school for violating school policies designed to prevent violence against women. She goes back to making porn videos. Detective Benson goes to the dean of the college and berates her for mistreating the woman but doing nothing about the rich kid.

The young man who went to prison interested me. He is Troy Mondale in *Demented*. The rich kid becomes Adan Jackson. Cindy Smith Foster is the young woman. I added Adan's brother Beau because I liked having a third member of the gang. Lydia Bennett is a thinly disguised stand-in for Olivia Benson.

The final element of the story, the confluence of lives years after the fact, comes from an article that appeared in the *Washington Post* some time ago. A woman leaving the Senate Office Building runs into a man who got away with raping her and trying to kill her. He was entering the building because he was employed as an aide by one of the senators. In *Demented*. Cindy and her attackers find themselves thrown together years after the rape—sixteen years, to give Troy time to complete his prison sentence. Adan, Beau, and Cindy work for a big accounting and financial consulting firm with offices across the United States and around the globe. Cindy and Adan are both working in the D.C. office.

Several books helped me get a handle on prison life. *Earning Freedom* by Michael Santos was the most important. Santos had put together a small drug distribution company aimed at servicing the needs of white-collar customers in the Seattle area. Law enforcement charged him as a drug kingpin. He was sentenced to forty years but got out in twenty-five by focusing on good behavior. *Earning Freedom* is a memoir of his time in prison and his return to civil society. Santos is the founder and head of Prison Professors, which was the inspiration for Mondale Legal Consulting Services.

Inside, also by Michael Santos, is an earlier version of his prison memoir, written while he was still serving time. In this edition, Santos provides more details about the people he met in prison and talks about incidents that illuminate facets of prison life. The two books are complementary, but *Earning Freedom* was more helpful to me as a resource for *Demented.*

Lockdown on Rikers: Shocking Stories of Abuse and Injustice at New York's Notorious Jail describes the prison experience from a completely different perspective. The author, Mary Buser, started as an intern in the Mental Health Department at Rikers and worked her way up to chief assistant. She talks about trying to provide required counseling sessions despite staff shortages and about medicating men in solitary confinement to keep them from killing themselves. She is the one who wrote about men being imprisoned while waiting for a court hearing—not a trial, but a hearing to get a date for a trial—because they could not afford bail. She complained that many of these men plead guilty without a trial because they had no other way to end their imprisonment. Buser also pointed out that Rikers was used as a dumping ground for the mentally ill because there was nowhere else to put them.

Finally, *Derailed* by Mark Roseman is the memoir of a lawyer who went to prison for two years because he misappropriated funds entrusted to him as a settlement for his clients. His benign experience provided key details for Troy's imprisonment.

I owe a debt of gratitude to author Serenity Rose for her support from the first version of the story through the present. My sister, Kathy Benoit, read the second version and gave me a "thumbs-up" as well as some free editing. Kathy Loraw read, commented and edited out of the kindness of her heart. Mitchellville Writers Group read and commented on the initial outline, as well as the many chapters I gave them to review from time to time. My wife has read every chapter in every version. There is no way I can thank her enough for her support.

I also want to thank Donnielle Tyner, Tanya from The Book Gremlins, Randy Ladenheim-Gil and Jeni Chappelle for their work in critiquing and editing my novel.

Debbie O'Byrne provided the stunning cover art.